"I should have kissed you when I was thinking about it," Ry said.

Indi's jaw dropped open. The man had been... "You were thinking about kissing me?"

He nodded. Smirked. A sexy move that crinkled the corner of one eye. "Just now."

Indi forgot her question. Had she asked him something? The man wanted to kiss her? "Then why are you standing there staring at me?"

His smirk curled into an outright grin. And as he leaned forward, kiss forthcoming, the delicious aura of him surrounded Indi with a fresh, outdoorsy gush of man and might. Overwhelmed by his stature and the sudden glee that invaded her core, she could but remember to close her mouth as his lips touched hers and one of his hands slid across her back to firmly take her in hand.

Michele Hauf is a *USA TODAY* bestselling author who has been writing romance, action-adventure and fantasy stories for more than twenty years. France, musketeers, vampires and faeries usually feature in her stories. And if Michele followed the adage "write what you know," all her stories would have snow in them. Fortunately, she steps beyond her comfort zone and writes about countries and creatures she has never seen. Find her on Facebook, Twitter and at michelehauf.com.

Books by Michele Hauf

Harlequin Nocturne

Her Werewolf Hero
A Venetian Vampire
Taming the Hunter
The Witch's Quest
The Witch and the Werewolf
An American Witch in Paris
The Billionaire Werewolf's Princess

The Saint-Pierre Series

The Dark's Mistress
Ghost Wolf
Moonlight and Diamonds
The Vampire's Fall
Enchanted by the Wolf

In the Company of Vampires

Beautiful Danger
The Vampire Hunter
Beyond the Moon

Visit the Author Profile page
at Harlequin.com for more titles.

THE BILLIONAIRE WEREWOLF'S PRINCESS

MICHELE HAUF

Recycling programs
for this product may
not exist in your area.

ISBN-13: 978-1-335-62956-2

The Billionaire Werewolf's Princess

Copyright © 2018 by Michele Hauf

This edition published by arrangement with Harlequin Books S.A.

For questions and comments about the quality of this book, please contact us at CustomerService@Harlequin.com.

Printed in U.S.A.

www.Harlequin.com

Dear Reader,

This story started with a title. Here's some insider dirt on titles. Studies have been done and charts have been created that prove readers are attracted to titles with common keywords (it also makes it easier when searching online). So sometimes I'll hand in a book with a title that just doesn't quite work and I'm asked to turn in ideas for a new title. My goal this time was to use all the keywords. But you know, the fun thing was then creating a story to go along with that title, and I had the best time with this one! And here's another secret. The original all-keyword title was this: *The Billionaire Faery Werewolf's Changeling Princess*. I don't think that one would have fit on the cover.

Title aside, this story is about identity and knowing your true self. While writing this story, something remarkable happened. I learned (through one of those online DNA services) that I had a new cousin. Adopted at birth, she was seeking her birth parents, and her path crossed with mine. Hearing her story and watching her journey to discovery was really special, and I'm so glad she's now a part of my life.

Michele

To Marcy V. I'm so glad you persisted after that initial email to me.

Chapter 1

Paris

Indigo DuCharme's chin wobbled as she held up her head and bravely looked over the busy ballroom. She stood at the top of a stairway that curled down to the marble dance floor. Her heart pounded so loudly she couldn't focus on the waltz played by the orchestra. Her eyes threatened to tear up, but she blamed this on the brilliant glints from half a dozen chandeliers suspended above the dancers.

Clutching her pink tulle skirt with both hands, she toyed with the embroidered red poppies she'd added days ago. She'd also sewn a pocket in the skirt to keep her cell phone. She forced herself not to check her text messages again. For the sixth time. Or maybe the thirteenth time. Because...

He had jilted her.

The last text she'd read from him, ten minutes earlier, had the audacity to state: Sorry, hooked up with Melanie this evening. You and me? Sex was great. But never connected beyond the sheets, yeah?

Fingers curling into her palms, Indi winced as her perfectly manicured fingernails dug into her skin. Never connected? Beyond the sheets? She'd been dating Todd for over a month. They'd seen each other practically every day. She'd cooked for him. Shopped for him. Had sex with him and made sure he was a happy camper, meaning that she didn't always orgasm but he did. All week she'd been planning her dress and hair for tonight's date. The Summer Soiree charity ball was one of her favorites. And she looked…

…so pretty.

Indi had felt like a star when she arrived by limo two hours earlier. Todd always met her for dates; his work as a stock trader kept him at the office at all hours. Indi had glided out of the limo, her long, lush, poppy-red-and-pink tulle skirts floating about her legs. The beaded bodice hugged her like a dream and she had dusted her décolletage with fine glitter. Her blond hair was pulled up in a messy bun with tendrils framing her face. She wore a pink, cat-ears tiara, which she sold through her online business, Goddess Goodies. Her makeup was dramatic and sexy. Todd loved the smoky eye shadow and her dark matte red lipstick. Or so he'd said.

Had it all been a lie? Had she merely been a prolonged hookup? Who the hell was Melanie? And just how long could Indi hold off tears before she risked mascara running down her cheeks?

A waiter, wielding a tray of goblets shimmering with bubbles, appeared before her. "Champagne?"

Indi shook her head and forced a smile. She felt no mirth whatsoever. Reaching up to adjust the cat ears, she remembered how putting them on tonight had reminded her of the joy she'd felt as a kid. She'd worn cat ears for fun as a child, and then, after a few bad romances in high school, as a sort of confidence boost.

The cat ears had been the first of many luxury accessories she now offered at her online store. Goddess Goodies bought out-of-season and damaged designer gowns— sometimes they were donated directly from the designers. Indi refurbished them, and then rented them for the price of shipping and cleaning. As well, she sold some gowns outright for a pretty penny. Indi's business was designed to boost confidence and empower women, and to give the opportunity to those who might not be able to afford a pretty dress for prom or an important event. Goddess Goodies was treading toward its first million-dollar year. And that should make her feel on top of the world.

It was difficult to celebrate her feminine power when her goddess had just been trampled on by an asshole. Would her love life ever catch up to the success she was experiencing in her business life?

"Doubt it," she whispered, and sniffed back a tear.

Screw it. She grabbed a champagne goblet from another passing waiter's tray and tilted it back. It was number five, or six, that she'd consumed since realizing Todd had dumped her.

"One more," she muttered, and veered toward another waiter, her footsteps a bit unsure. "And then I'm going to blow this Popsicle stand."

"Indigo!"

Dread climbed Indi's neck at the sound of a familiar and falsely friendly voice. Sabrina Moreau, who hosted this ball, had never met a strand of pearls she didn't like, or, for that matter, an older married man. She tended to wear both as if battle prizes strung about her neck.

"Bree," Indi said, while sweeping another goblet of champagne off a passing tray. Her world wobbled, but she ignored the easy drunk that was riding her spine and up the back of her neck.

"That is the most gorgeous dress I've seen," Bree cooed. "One of your creations?"

"Of course. It's Gucci restyled. Mint green certainly is your color."

Bree blushed, which only emphasized how terrible the pale green did look on her artificially tanned skin. "Jean-Paul likes me in green. Where's your date? For as lovely as you look this evening, it can't be solo. You always have a handsome stunner on your arm."

"Todd is…" An asshole. And her heart split to even think that she'd thought she could love the guy. Had she thought that? No, not love. Certainly not so fast. But she'd invested a lot of time in him over the past month. "We broke up. And you know me, I'd never miss a ball, especially when I've got the dress."

"Oh, sweetie. That's so sad."

Tell her about it. Tightening her lips seemed to keep the tears at bay. Why had she stopped to talk to Bree? She needed to be out of here. Away from the too-happy glow of crystal chandeliers and laughing couples. Now. Someplace dark and quiet so she could lick her wounds.

"How old are you, Indi?"

Indi quirked an eyebrow at that delving question.

"Well, you know what I mean. We're not getting any younger, are we? Time to wrangle one and get him to put a ring on it. Am I right?" Bree rubbed Indi's forearm and patted her on the shoulder. "Do you want me to fix you up?"

"No." Because she was no longer in the market for rich assholes who liked to spend weekends on their yachts while working all hours and making business calls between kisses and—oh, yeah—between orgasms that never quite pleased her. "I'm good, Bree. Really."

Not really.

Where the hell was the exit?

"Well, if you need—"

Indi's tolerance level dropped out the bottom of her Swarovski crystal strappy heels. She turned and fled from Bree's prying questions, suspecting she might look like Cinderella fleeing the ball. It was near midnight. But she couldn't wear the false smile anymore.

And tears had started to spill without volition.

Aiming down the hallway toward the front doors, she suddenly stopped and spun, thinking an escape out the back would be much easier. The paparazzi always lurked out front. And while she was no A-list celebrity, she didn't want to risk photobombing any shots with her distraught tear-streaked mug. She could walk down the street and hail a cab.

Weaving through the coat-check area and then down a darkened hallway, she passed a few waiters who informed her she wasn't authorized to be in this area of the building. Flipping them off, Indi mumbled something about not feeling well and needing to be away from the crowd. Finally, escape loomed ahead.

Pushing the back doors open, she wandered through what must be the loading area. Filing around a parked truck that smelled of diesel fuel, she clutched her skirt so it wouldn't skim the ground. She'd spent last Saturday afternoon adding the red chiffon poppies to this dress to give color and interest to what had been a crop of beaded green leaves growing up from the hem.

Finally making the cobblestone street, she looked both ways. La rue Joséphine was to the left; that's where all the cabs would be parked. Yet the promise of bright streetlights and neon revealing her tears to all made her turn to the right.

She'd walk a bit. Even if her heels were much too high for a comfortable stroll and the uneven cobblestones made walking with some decorum a joke. She inhaled deeply, as she thought it would help, but instead, the sudden influx of stale air only increased her tears. And she started to sob. The champagne made her head swim.

Who was she kidding? She was drunk. Which was probably why she hadn't toppled over yet. The drunkeness was counterbalancing the wobbly-heels-to-ground ratio. Ha!

She wandered by a homeless man sitting on a piece of cardboard. He cast her a wide-eyed look.

"What?" she said testily. "This is Paris. Haven't you ever seen a woman in a ball gown wandering the streets in the middle of the night?"

She just needed to find a quiet place to break down and bawl. Loud and long. To let the goddess who had been standing at the top of the steps feeling so pretty and special exude the pain of such a sharp and cruel rejection. And then she'd find her way home to curl in on herself.

At the very least, Todd could have texted her *before* she'd left for the soiree tonight. The bastard!

"Melanie," she muttered, and wandered forward. The woman sounded high-maintenance. And like she'd go down on a man on the first date.

What was wrong with her? She was a nice person. Reasonably pretty. Not too big and not too thin. She had always agreed to whatever Todd wanted to do. She ate at the restaurants he'd chosen, and she even wore the tight red dress that pushed up her tits to her throat when he'd asked her to. What had she done wrong?

"Wasn't I good enough for him?"

Tears spilled down her cheeks. Indi pushed forward,

wandering mindlessly, then turned down another, narrower street. She knew this neighborhood from girls' nights out with her BFF. Maybe?

Pausing, she thrust out her arms to balance as her heel wobbled in a crack between cobblestones. Where in Paris was she?

"Who cares?"

Unable to fight the call to release her hurt, Indi released her tears, loudly.

Ryland James stood in the center of a dark, quiet street in FaeryTown. The sword he held in his right hand curved like a scimitar, and was bespelled to kill faeries. He'd found it in a tree years ago, guarded by a dryad, and had claimed it as his own. Of late, Sidhe Slayer was the whispered title he'd been hearing about himself.

He didn't need a label. Someone had to stop the collectors who snuck in at midnight from Faery through this, a thin place insinuating FaeryTown. It was smack-dab in the middle of the eighteenth arrondissement of Paris. The collectors arrived in pairs and, if they could get past him, would seek the first human they could find and assume control of that person's body, then steal a human baby and take it back to Faery.

Not on his guard.

Checking his watch, he noted four minutes until midnight. FaeryTown was normally bustling this late at night, but when Ry walked onto the scene the residents scattered, shuffling behind doors and peering out windows to witness the slaughter.

Lifting his chin, he sniffed the air. His werewolf senses were attuned and he picked up the usual odors of faery presence and very little from humans. FaeryTown overlay this part of Paris. Humans could walk through and would never know faeries occupied the same space only on a different dimension. Humans hadn't the ability to see faeries, such as he did.

The sudden sound of a human voice—crying—alerted Ry. He swung about to spy a woman in a fancy pink gown wandering along the brick wall that fronted a human-owned bakery, yet the faeries, in their altered dimension, used it as a dust den that lured in vampires addicted to their ichor. Hair pulled up and looking like a princess, the woman choked out tears and sobs. He noted the sparkly ears on her head. And the streaks of mascara running down her cheeks.

Why was he seeing her now? When he focused on the FaeryTown layer of this area, he saw only the sidhe and their ilk. Any humans present slipped away into the background. She was so vivid. Almost as if she treaded FaeryTown herself. But she wasn't faery. Even though her gorgeous breasts sparkled above the pink fabric. That wasn't faery dust, just glitter that women loved to dust all over themselves. No, she smelled human—coppery and tinged with the earthy presence of skin and bone and yet also a delicious overlayer of perfume and soft woman.

Ry shook his head. He shouted at her. "Hey! Get out of here! You can't be here right now."

She dismissed his worry with a swinging gesture of her hand and plopped down to sit on the curb. Her skirts fluffed around her, the hem edged with dirt, and…she was missing a shoe.

She should not be able to see him.

She sniffed loudly, then muttered, "Can you call me a cab? I seem to have gotten lost. My phone is here—" she patted her fluffy skirt "—somewhere…"

"I don't have time for that." Two minutes until midnight. Gripping the enchanted sword firmly, Ry swung it behind him, pointing toward the main street that edged the border of FaeryTown. "Get out of this area. It's not safe. I'll call you a cab later."

"He dumped me!" she announced.

Ry winced at the woman's utter lack of recognition for the imminent danger. There was no way she could be in FaeryTown unless she also had the sight or had somehow gained admittance. Humans couldn't simply enter FaeryTown unless they could see it. And it appeared that she was merely wandering the streets...

Why was this gorgeous princess wandering about alone?

"Listen, Princess Pussycat," he hissed. "Bad things are going to happen. Right now. So run!"

As he spoke the final word, the fabric between Faery and the mortal realm glimmered. The gray night sky above a two-story building tore and shimmered along the edges of that tear.

Ry swore. The woman on the curb still sobbed, her head caught against her open palms. He felt a moment of compassion for her. What asshole would be so cruel to such a pretty woman?

But really? Things were about to get rough.

Swinging his sword arm, Ry prepared as the first of the collectors entered this realm. The creature's body was long and wispy, barely holding the form of a human. It was black, so black it was like peering into a void in the shape of the creature. And yet it sparkled with so much faery dust it was as though that void formed a black hole speckled with stardust.

Not about to become enchanted by the sight, Ry swung toward the approaching collector. It floated nearer, and when it spied him, it stretched its maw wide to reveal a piranha row of vicious teeth.

"What the hell is that?" the woman called.

"I don't know how you can see this, but you need to listen to me and run!"

"I lost my shoe."

"Mademoiselle! I'm serious!" He swung the sword but missed the collector.

It soared high, the wispy tail of its form spilling black, oily fog over Ry's head. He swept the substance aside to keep an eye on the creature. Out the corner of his eye he again saw the fabric between realms glimmer. Always, they arrived in pairs.

"This is crazy," the woman said. She stood and wobbled. Drunk? Had to be. "I need a cab. I can't find my pocket. My skirts are tangled… Hey, that thing is swooping toward you!"

Ry averted his attention from the crazy lush sight of the most gorgeous woman he'd ever seen to the sparkling black void that aimed for his throat. Its curved, sharp talons wrapped about his throat. Gagging, Ry stumbled backward. Slipping his sword arm back and thrusting the tip up, he managed to stab the thing, but not in the substantial main body, instead only in the wispy tail. It released him and, with a twist of its misty shape, soared toward its approaching partner.

"That way!" Ry pointed down the street. "Go!"

"What are those things? And why are you so angry with me? Can a girl get a break?" She now stood in the street not ten feet from him. "I have only ever tried to please people. And what do I get? Dumped at the ball. Todd is such an asshole."

"Fuck Todd!" Ry said hastily.

"Right?"

One of the collectors took note of the woman. She wouldn't have time to get to the street and out of FaeryTown.

Ry raced for her, grabbed her by the arm and shoved her

between the dust den and another brick wall. She screamed and landed on her hands and knees, which he regretted, but only so long as it took for him to turn and dodge the lunging collector.

Now he was angry. And the twinge of a shift crawled across his scalp. His werewolf did not like these nasty things from Faery. Ry's upper body, of its own volition, shifted. T-shirt tearing at the seams, his shoulders grew wider and his head assumed wolf shape.

Growling, Ry marched toward the collector and led it back to the center of the street. He swung his sword repeatedly. When it shot upward into the sky, hovering above him, Ry positioned himself below, waiting. In his peripheral vision he could see the other collector approaching the alley where he'd shoved the woman.

The creature above him dropped like a rock. He thrust up the sword, and it pierced the collector's heart. Ichor spilled over Ry's fur and wolf-shaped head and down his arms and paws. Without a death scream, the thing dissipated into black faery dust.

But the next sound sent a chill up his spine. The scream was not that of annoyance, drunkenness or a jilted woman. It was of fear—and pain.

The collector slashed a razor talon across the woman's décolletage. She fainted. And the thing turned to gnash its teeth at Ry as he approached. Sword thrusting as he ran, Ry caught the creature as it lunged toward him. More black dust and the eerie, quiet dissipation of the collector in the air before him.

On the ground was a scatter of pink fabric. A sparkly rhinestone shoe peeked out from the fluff. The woman's chest bled where the collector had scratched her.

Shaking off his werewolf with a seamless shift back to human shape, Ry bent over her. "Damn it, how did you manage this?" He touched two fingers to the side of her neck. The collectors' bite was deadly to humans, but he wasn't sure about their talons. The things were literally bags of floating poison.

He felt a heartbeat, but it pulsed and then slowed. Quickly.

Instinctually, he knew. "She's going to die."

And that did not sit well with him. This was his beat. He was responsible for any and all who got in the way of his efforts to keep the collectors off the streets. And she was an innocent. Just like those he was trying to protect.

Lifting her into his arms, Ry rushed down the street, deeper into FaeryTown. He knew no more collectors would arrive tonight. There were never more than two nightly.

"Sorry to make your night worse, Princess," he said as he turned, heading toward the faery healer he had once or twice used for his own injuries. "We're going to have to talk about how you were able to breach FaeryTown."

She moaned in his arms and muttered something about Todd not deserving her.

"Todd's a jerk," he said. "Any man should be proud and honored to have your company."

Unless she was a pill. Hell, even the pretty ones could be tough to deal with. But damn, she smelled great. Sweet and soft, like something he wanted to taste.

Giving his head a shake to chase away that random thought, Ry kicked the door to the faery healer's home. This was not a situation he wanted to be in right now. Standing on Hestia's doorstep? She wasn't going to be happy.

"To the devil with you!" a voice hollered from behind the door.

To be expected. They had a history.

But the woman in his arms would soon be history if he

didn't hurry. Ry kicked the door again, and the chains on the other side broke, the door slamming inside against the wall. He rushed across the threshold and down the tight, narrow hallway to the healing room where Hestia helped so many of her afflicted species. He laid the woman on the bed of leaves and vines that immediately coiled and twisted to embrace her arms and one exposed shoeless foot.

Ry turned to the fuming faery behind him. Her skin tone was a shade of cotton-candy pink, which she accented with a green slip of a dress. She was tiny, compared to his hulking height, and yet her annoyance hit him like a punch to the gut. If violet eyes could ever burn with the flames of hatred, hers did.

"I know, I don't deserve your help after the last time," he began. "Please, Hestia, she's an innocent. Got caught between me and a collector. See that scratch on her collarbone?"

The healer bent to inspect the woman. She then licked the wound with a snake-long tongue. Shaking her head, she announced, "She will die."

"No. You can heal her. I know you can. Do this, and I promise I'll never ask for another healing from you again."

Hestia looked him up and down. Lately, with his battles against the collectors, he took on a lot of injuries that challenged his innate ability to quickly heal. And she knew it. And the last time they'd spoken? She had nearly died to save him from a fatal wound. And she might have thought he cared for her more than he really had. It had been a fling. Apparently, though, she had thought differently.

"You willing to pay for this?" she asked. "Lots of mortal realm euros?"

Money meant nothing to him. And he had far too much of it. She could ask for untold riches and it would be like handing over a few bills to her.

"One million," she said.

He nodded eagerly. "I'll send a courier with the cash as soon as the banks open tomorrow."

She eyed him cautiously. For as much as she hated him—and had every right to—she had to know he was good on his word. But she tilted her head and asked, "What does this one mean to you?"

"Her? I hadn't met her until five minutes ago. I don't want an innocent to die because she got in my way."

The healer nodded, then pointed over his shoulder. "Very well. Go stand out in the hallway. It will take some time."

Chapter 2

The beautiful man with impossible muscles—he wore an oddly tattered shirt that revealed oh, so many tight, bulging muscles—held a sword and fought weird black creatures that flew in the air about him. In the middle of Paris.

And as Indi was lying there on the ground, watching with her mouth hanging open, she thought, for a moment, the tall, handsome man…changed. When he looked at her, his head was shaped like a wolf's.

The eerie image made Indi scream, and she pushed herself up abruptly. And hit her head on something above her. Dropping her cheek back onto the hardwood floor, she groaned.

That had been a weirdly detailed dream. Very real. Almost as if she could smell the strange black creatures' ozone scent and hear the man's sexy voice as he had bent over her. Prodding her. Asking if she was okay.

Eyelids flashing open, Indi darted her gaze about the

room. She was lying on the floor? Not a familiar floor, either. She didn't have hardwood in her home. And...what had she hit her head on?

Rolling to her side, she realized she still wore the ball gown. The beaded leaves on the bodice crunched as her body turned on the wood floor. Above her stretched a flat piece of wood, supported by a table leg...

"Why am I lying under a table? Oh..."

It hurt her brain to talk. Had someone taken it out, rolled it across the ground like a *pétanque* ball, then shoved it back in through her ear? Mercy, what a bender. Champagne hangovers were the worst!

But this didn't look like her friend Janet's floor. And Janet had moved to New York two months ago.

Where was she? And how had she gotten here?

"When I got up this morning I couldn't figure why you were under the table," a male voice suddenly said.

A pair of bare feet, with a slouch of blue jeans hanging over them, stopped but a foot from her face. Indi placed both palms on the floor before her and craned her head up as far as she could manage, but her neck ached, so her line of sight only stretched as far as his crotch. Not a terrible sight to wake up to. Just...unexpected.

She dropped and rolled to her back.

"You insisted on crawling under there after I deposited you on the couch last night," he said. He bent to display two mugs. "Coffee?"

Heartbeat suddenly racing, Indi inhaled deeply a few times to calm her panic. But really, she *should* be panicking. "Where am I? Who are you? I, uh..."

"My name's Ryland James. I don't know your name. You were buttered when I found you last night."

Buttered? Hell yes, she'd been so drunk.

"When you found me? What the hell? What did you...?"

She winced. No, she was still dressed. Which didn't mean much. If the man had had his way with her while she was inebriated…

"You stumbled onto a strange scene," he said, sitting on the black leather sofa and setting one coffee cup on the floor near her shoulder. "I wanted to bring you home, make sure you were safe, but I didn't know where you lived. And…after a bunch of wild-and-craziness you passed out. For the night."

She closed her eyes and slapped a palm to her chest. Wild and crazy? Seriously? She'd let that bastard Todd get to her that much? And now she was lying on the floor in a strange man's home.

The coffee smelled deceptively good. But from experience, she knew if she drank any she'd get sick. Hangovers were never kind to her.

She spoke her fears. "I need to get out of here."

"I can drive you home if you'll give me your address."

"I don't think I should do that. I can hail a cab."

"Suit yourself. I'm not going to hurt you. I just wanted to make sure you were okay after…"

Indi skimmed her fingers over her chest and throat. Something hurt. She winced at the slight pain and felt the rough line of skin along her collarbone. Had she been cut?

"It should heal more quickly than you expect," the man, Ryland, said. "I tried to get you out of there, but you were, well…"

Buttered.

"Sorry. Some guy broke up with you?"

She'd told him that? What had happened last night?

"He dumped me at the ball. And I was feeling so pretty." She sniffed, feeling all the emotions well in her gut again. Oh, she couldn't do the ugly cry in front of this handsome stranger!

Turning and crawling out from under the table, she managed to bump the coffee cup and topple it. It soaked into her skirt.

"I'm so sorry."

"Don't worry about it."

A strong hand helped her to stand by grabbing her upper arm. And when she swayed near his chest, Indi smelled fresh, outdoorsy aftershave on him. Or maybe it was his innate scent. Like wild captured yet never tamed. The man was handsome. Long dark hair, trimmed mustache and a beard that was short and hinted at the dark hairs that might grow on his chest. And so many muscles in the biceps she clung to.

Indi had never been one to let opportunity pass, but…

She also wasn't stupid.

"Thank you for, uh…" She wandered to the door, tugging up her wet skirt and realizing a long piece of it dragged behind. The outer tulle layer had torn, and the hem was blackened with dirt. One of the chiffon poppies dangled from a thread.

"Oh, God, you must think I'm the worst case. I was… upset. And yes, he broke my heart. I have this tendency to get attached, too—" What was she doing? She didn't need to detail her pitiful emotional failings to a stranger. "I needed a good cry and…"

She turned, thinking Ryland looked like the man she'd seen in her dreams. He had been. She'd never forget such a handsome face. And those brown eyes pierced her with intensity. "Last night." Peering intently at him, she asked, "Did you change?"

"Did I, uh, what?" He set the mug on the table and approached her.

Indi backed up until her shoulders hit the door. She slumped. Her head was spinning and she predicted the hangover would play revenge on her soon. And she did not want the guy to witness that.

"Change," she muttered, though she wasn't sure why she'd asked him that. How could a person change? Yet she had seen something odd last night. Maybe? "Were there flying creatures?"

He bent before her, and long brown hair spilled over his chest and the T-shirt that he wore inside out to expose the seams. Earth-brown eyes studied her for a pitiful moment. "I think you might still be a little drunk, Princess Pussycat."

"Princess..." She reached for the top of her head and felt the cat ears sitting up there, but at a tilt. "I'm not drunk. Not anymore. And my name is..."

She should leave. Right now. Before things got weird.

Indi turned and grabbed the doorknob, hoping the door wasn't locked and that he didn't have plans to toss her in a dirt pit in his basement. It opened. She exhaled and dashed across the threshold.

"I hope you feel better!" he called after her. "And I hope the guy who did that to you gets his just. No woman deserves to be treated so poorly."

Indi paused at the top of a stairway that led down to the building's entry. She lifted her skirts and imagined she must look a nightmare to him. A kind man who had only wanted to ensure that she was safe last night.

"My name's Indigo," she said, then took the stairs, hands firmly clutching both railings for support.

By some strange luck that she was not accustomed to, a cab was parked curbside. Indi climbed into the back seat, gave the driver her address in the eighth arrondissement, then flopped down, hugging the seat as if it were a life raft. Shoving her hand in her skirt pocket, she was relieved her phone was still in there. She checked her texts. There were none.

Had she expected to hear from Todd after his night with Melanie?

Oh, that she could even think of him again. Stupid, stupid, stupid!

She needed to talk to Janet. To spill all the details of her horrible, terrible, no-good very humiliating night. She'd call her when she got home.

Ten minutes later, the cabbie offered to help her to the front door, but Indi said she'd manage. She paid him with a scan of the credit card app on her phone and then meandered up to the house.

Her head wasn't quite so spinny now, but her limbs felt heavy. As if she'd run a marathon. Exhaustion hit her hard as she opened the front door and wandered inside. She could only think to lie down. Right. Now.

She eyed the alpaca rug before the white velvet couch and stepped down into the sunken living room. Dropping the phone on the couch, and then falling to her knees, Indi collapsed onto her stomach on the soft, inviting rug. She curled her fingers into the fur and closed her eyes.

And then she fell asleep.

For a very long time.

Ry strolled into the small office he kept in the fourth ar-rondissement. His secretary, Kristine, blew him the usual good-morning kiss and handed him a full and steaming mug of coffee.

"How'd hunting go last night?" she asked while focus-ing on a spreadsheet she had opened on the laptop before her. Her long purple nails clattered on the keys.

"It was…" Ry sipped the coffee and winced. He could

never get her to add even a smidge of cream to the wicked black concoction she brewed. "Different."

That got her attention. Turning on the swivel chair and crossing her legs, she dangled a very large pink vinyl high heel and eyed him through a flutter of thick false lashes. She didn't need to speak. He could hear her thoughts plainly.

"A human woman stepped onto the scene while I was slashing through collectors."

"Oh, *mon cher*. That is not acceptable. How did that happen? I thought FaeryTown wasn't something we humans could even access."

"Exactly. Not unless you're wearing an ointment to see the sidhe. I'm not sure how she saw me or the collectors, but she did, and…" He sipped again. He probably shouldn't tell Kristine everything. But then, she was a confidante, and he trusted her with the information about his nature. "She was scratched by one of them. Would have died had I not rushed her to a healer. By the way, I need to send Hestia a million-euro check."

Kristine sighed. "Really? The old girlfriend? I'll take care of that."

"She was not a girlfriend. More a—"

Kristine put up a palm. "Nope. Don't want you to mansplain that one to me. So, what happened after that big adventure?"

"I took her home with me, and she spent the night on the floor under the coffee table."

"Ryland Alastair James."

He winced at the admonishing tone. "I put her on the couch, but she wouldn't stay there. She was drunk and… the healer drugged her with some wacky faery stuff. I'm surprised she could even stand to run away from me this morning."

"You let her run away? Without making sure she got home safe? Who are you?"

He sighed heavily. Kristine knew him well. Normally he would never allow a woman to run off like that without seeing to her safety. But she had been freaked by him. And he'd not been given an opportunity to explain the cut on her chest, which might have been a good thing, all things considered.

"She'll be fine," he said. "And both collectors are dead. No babies stolen last night."

Kristine crossed her arms, and her dangling foot increased in bobbing speed.

"I don't know her last name, so it's not like I can look her up and check in on her. She was dressed fancy and I think she's probably well-off."

"Doesn't mean she made it home safely."

"I accept your admonishment, and confess I'm worried about her, too. But there's nothing I can do now."

"Can't you track her down with your sniffer? Didn't you once tell me you werewolves can smell a peppermint candy five miles away?"

"She wasn't wearing peppermint. She smelled like champagne and roses." And not just any kind of rose perfume. She'd smelled like fresh-from-the-garden roses.

"Was she pretty?"

"Does that matter?"

"No, but she's going to stay in your brain until you know what became of her after she fled your place. Fled! Seriously, Ry, what did you do to her?"

"I offered her coffee."

Kristine chuckled and turned back to her work. "Only you can manage to simultaneously slay weird faery marauders and hook up with a pretty young thang."

"We didn't hook up. I set her on the couch and…in the morning I found her under my coffee table."

Kristine raised an eyebrow in judgment.

"And that's the end of this conversation. Did you compile research on the Severo Foundation?"

"I did. And I've a report for you. I'll print it up and bring it into your office in two twitches. This is a good one, *cher*. You'll want to donate to them."

"Thanks, Kristine. Give me ten minutes before you come in. I need to—"

"Think about the poor sweet thang that fled your place this morning?" She winked at him. "You have some weird problems."

Ry entered his office and closed the door behind him, thinking Kristine was right on. But oddly, the human interference last night had been the weirdest. Not the faeries.

Only a desk, a chair and a couch decorated his tiny office space. The far wall opposite the door was completely window, and no cabinets blocked the view of the nearby Seine River. He didn't do the fancy. Much as his multibillion-dollar philanthropic foundation could afford it. He wasn't into the bling or showing off his riches. It wasn't him. And while he could put on a suit and blend in with the wealthy at the snap of a finger, he preferred the casual look and lifestyle.

Yet he did do the expensive watch. He liked to know the time to the exact second. And right now it was eleven fifteen, on the nose.

He sat on the leather sofa and stretched his arms along the back of it. Clouds were rolling in, and rain was in the forecast, yet the color of the sky was wildly vivid.

"Indigo," he muttered.

Interesting name for a woman. She'd been more of a

soft pink last night, mixed with a few streaks of jet-black mascara. Poor thing.

Kristine was right. He should have followed her out of his building this morning. But he'd watched from his loft and seen the waiting cab. She'd beelined into it and it had pulled away. She'd made it home safe.

What hell of a hangover would she have? If not from the alcohol, but from the mysterious concoction of herbs and who-knew-what Hestia had given her?

"Should have gotten her last name," he said with a regretful twinge that he felt in his heart. "She was pretty."

And she had seen too much. That wasn't good. He needed to keep his secret, and the secret of FaeryTown, from the human public. And if she had seen him in those few moments when his rage caused him to partially shift, then he needed to make sure she thought it was just an effect of the alcohol. Not the truth.

Because his truth always managed to fuck things up.

Indi lifted her head from the alpaca rug. It was dark. Really dark. She was lying on the floor in her living room for reasons that escaped her...

"Ah, really?"

She dropped her head and realized she must have slept the entire day. Twenty-four hours had passed since Todd dumped her last night. And what had happened after that had been even more remarkable. She'd watched a handsome man with P90X abs and biceps kill weird sparkly creatures with a sword. And then she'd woken up under his coffee table.

"This is definitely one for the diary," she muttered as she sat up. "Oh, my aching bones, have I become an old lady?"

She pressed a hand to her back and winced as she

stretched. Either she was growing old quickly or sleeping on the floor was no longer something she could do and recover from with ease. Her college days had often found her sleeping on the floor, or a table, or even in a big box once.

"Shouldn't have sucked down all that champagne."

With some groans and grunts, she managed to stand. Inspecting her tattered and dirty gown made her moan. "It was so pretty. *I* was pretty. Asshole."

Grabbing her phone from the couch, she intended to call Janet, but…

"It's ten at night?"

Now she stomped toward the curving marble staircase and her second-floor bedroom. She didn't bother to turn on the lights. Passing through the bedroom, she clutched the cat ears still clinging to her head and tossed them onto the king-size bed. Tripping a few more times on her torn hem, she made it into the bathroom and flicked on the lights as she stopped before the wide vanity mirror specially lighted for putting on makeup.

Indi chirped out an abbreviated scream. Then she slapped both palms over her mouth. Staring back at her from the mirror was a bedraggled bit of tattered lace and smeared makeup. Her mascara had streaked down her cheeks, but—perhaps when she'd been passed out on the floor—most of it had rubbed off. Had that happened before or after she was at the handsome stranger's place?

"He saw me looking like this? Oh, Indi, you really know how to impress a guy, don't you?"

Her hair was half out of the messy bun. One jut of hair managed to stick straight out on the left side. "What hurricane did I walk through?" She pulled out a leaf from her hair. "Where did this— Oh, I want to die! I just…"

She slammed her hands to the vanity and shook her head. But instead of tears, laughter burst out. Lung-tugging, gut-clenching laughter. Dropping and settling onto the soft pom-pom rug in front of the tub, Indi laughed until her ribs ached.

"Lowest point in my life? Last night," she muttered. "Lesson learned? Lay off the champagne. Never date a guy whose most important accessories are his cell phone and day-planner app. And…" She sighed and wiggled her toes through the tear in the pink tulle. "Always thank the handsome stranger who rescues you from the idiocy of yourself." And from a strange creature she thought might have been trying to eat her. "Did I thank him? I don't think I did. Ryland James? And he never did answer my question."

She had seen things while shivering in the alley last night. More than a few weird things. And he had most definitely changed into…something different. It hadn't been the alcohol. Couldn't have been.

"Who are you kidding, Indi? Of course it was the champagne. People don't change shapes."

She touched her chest where she had rubbed over a cut earlier this morning at her rescuer's place. Her skin felt smooth now.

Indi stood and studied her collarbone in the mirror. The skin did not show a cut or mark of any kind. And if she had been hurt, shouldn't there be, at the very least, a faint or red mark?

Was it possible she'd imagined it all?

"Anything is possible," she said to the tawdry princess in the mirror.

He'd called her Princess Pussycat. And his eyes had smiled before his mouth had.

Indi smiled. A weak, pitiful and bedraggled smile, but it was the best she could manage. It would be a crime not to see that man again. And she really did need to thank him. At least some man had been concerned about her last night.

More important, she wanted to ask him questions. To make sure she wasn't going crazy and hadn't started to imagine strange creatures walking the streets of Paris.

"Tomorrow," she said to the disaster in the mirror. "Now a shower, and a bath, and maybe another shower after that."

Chapter 3

The next day

"The proposal is very well done." Ry laid the file folder on Kristine's desk. He'd been in the office all day making phone calls and was ready to kick back with a beer and some sports TV.

"The Severo Foundation is amazing." Kristine brought up the website on her laptop. "Started by Stephan Severo decades ago to buy up forested land in Minnesota to protect the natural wolf population."

"And I do appreciate that it's also helping the Save the Wolf Foundation. His son wants to take the project international."

"Yes. Pilot Severo continued to support the project after his father died," Kristine said. "I dug a little deeper with my research. Most isn't in the proposal. Pilot is not werewolf. His mother, Belladonna Severo, is a vampire and his father was werewolf. Pilot was born straight human. I kind of relate to him." Kristine tapped her highly lacquered red lips in thought. "He was born into a body that was so different from what others must have expected of him. And can you imagine the parents' disappointment when their son was not a werewolf or vampire, but rather merely human?"

"I can," Ry said.

His thoughts flickered back to that day he'd first discovered he was different. Not quite the werewolf he'd always believed he was. And then his mother had confirmed it, and his entire world had been tipped off its axis. The time had been seventeen minutes and twenty-one seconds past three in the afternoon. Not a good time. Not something a seventeen-year-old man should have to experience.

"Get me a phone meeting set up with Pilot Severo," he said. "I want to send him funds and would also like to be a part of the international project, if possible."

"Perfect." Kristine typed as they conversed. Multitasking, as usual. Something Ry appreciated but could never manage himself. "It's morning in the States. I'll give them a ring in another hour."

"You don't have to stay late, Kristine."

"You know I don't mind. And I want to finalize the donations for the upcoming charity ball. You know the full moon is this weekend? You heading out to your castle?"

"I, uh…" Ry winced as he considered that this full moon would be different from the previous one. He had a new commitment that wouldn't allow him to leave the city. To escape from the possibility of being seen in his shifted form. "I don't think I can."

"You can't stay in the city. Not unless you hook up with that new girl fast. And by *fast* I mean in the three days before the weekend. Don't you need to have sex before the full moon to keep the werewolf at bay? You up for that challenge?"

"Always." He cast her a charming smirk. "But I don't think I'll see her again. She ran out on me so quickly. I do have some solutions available."

"Uh-huh. But even if you do find a woman to have sex with the day before and after the full moon, there's still the night of the full one, *mon cher*. Don't you need to wolf out no matter what?"

"That I do."

"Maybe FaeryTown can go one night without you."

"If I miss one night of patrol, then a baby could be stolen from his or her crib, never to be seen again. Do you think that's fair for me to put my needs before one so innocent?"

"But you'll wolf out during the full moon. *In Paris.*"

"That's something I'm going to have to deal with. I don't see any other option, Kristine. Text me the appointment after you've talked with Severo. I'll see you tomorrow afternoon."

He left the office in the wake of an unenthusiastic "sure" from his secretary. He knew she was right. She knew she was right. A werewolf shouldn't risk staying in a populated city on the night he was called by the moon to shift to his half-man/half-wolf shape. And while he wasn't a wild and crazy beast intent on destroying or maiming humans in that shape, he didn't need to be seen loping about the Parisian streets with tail wagging and tongue lolling. That was inviting trouble for him and every other werewolf who needed to remain a myth to all humans.

Yet if he went to his private property in the countryside, as he did every night of the full moon, then FaeryTown would be left unguarded for the collectors to come through.

As he strode down the sidewalk and angled for his

parked Alfa Romeo, Ry wished the choice was easier. But then, nothing good ever came easily.

Indi slept until three o'clock the next afternoon. She decided to mark it off as the worst night of her life. Getting dumped, being chased by a creature and then being sort-of kidnapped by a man she didn't know.

But it was the memory of that mystery man that compelled her this afternoon. Pouring herself a cup of coffee, then dousing it with creamer, she curled up on the couch, wrapped a light summer blanket about her bare shoulders and pulled the laptop up to browse online.

"Ryland James," she said as she typed in his name.

Not expecting to find anything more than a Facebook page, she was surprised when the first page of Google spilled down a whole list of hits. And the image bar featured some paparazzi shots of the man wearing either a tux or a well-tailored business suit, and in all of them he was either facing away from the camera or had his hand up to block his face.

She clicked on the first entry posted by a dishy entertainment channel. A photo showing Ryland James leaving what looked like a nightclub with a hand blocking his face was captioned Parisian Billionaire Camera-Shy.

"Billionaire?" she whispered. "What have you stumbled onto, Indi?"

She scanned the article and it mentioned that Ryland James was a philanthropist who gave away billions but was noted as media-shy, and while he was occasionally seen with a date, no woman could ever be pinned to him as a long-term relationship. He was always the talk of the party when he arrived, and socialites listed him as their BILF— B standing for *billionaire*—on their social media pages.

"I was rescued by a billionaire?" She couldn't help the

incredulous tone. But at the same time… "Why have I never heard of him before?"

She was a socialite. She participated in all social media and liked to know who was who and what they were doing with whom and for how long. Of course, she'd never followed the philanthropy hashtag before. As a trust-fund baby, she'd grown up, admittedly, with a silver spoon in her mouth. But now that she was on her own, she was perfectly happy to create her own riches. And was doing a great job at it.

And yet.

"Why would a billionaire be out in the middle of the night wielding a sword and chasing weird monsters?"

Because that was what she'd witnessed. Much as she didn't want anyone to hear her say it out loud, she had seen exactly that. Monsters. Big, black, sparkly monsters that had sort of faded out in a long wispy tail of darkness. And a tall, muscled, handsome man who had swung a sword like a Viking marauder.

"And I woke up under his coffee table. If only I had known he was rich, I would have stayed for breakfast. Ha!"

No, she wasn't the gold-digging type. Generally, a man's checkbook did not influence his attractiveness. And hadn't she given up on rich, self-involved men because of the extremely humiliating dumpage from Todd?

"For sure. No more rich businessmen."

Scanning through a few articles on him, she didn't learn much more, other than that he had been wooed by major modeling agencies and had refused contracts from all of them. Was known for driving a black Alfa Romeo down the Champs-Élysées at top speed. And could be rude to reporters when they pushed him for information. A rumor that he'd once dated Lady Gaga could not be confirmed. However, according to a tabloid, they had been in the same

New York concert hall on the same night and both had left in the same limo.

Teasing her tongue along her upper lip, Indi double-clicked on the one photo that showed his face. The man was so freaking gorgeous. He wore his long dark brown hair loose, yet in other pictures it was pulled back behind his head. Always, the shirts he wore strained across strapping biceps and pecs. And the mustache and trimmed beard framed some seriously kissable lips.

"Billionaire or not, I most certainly need to thank him. And ask him the burning questions. Today. I do remember where he lives."

Now to figure out what to wear when thanking a man for saving her life, while also wanting to enhance her assets without looking desperate. But she had just been dumped. She really should go into mourning for a bit.

"He's not worth it," she muttered, dismissing Todd with the breezy apathy she should have had the other night. But if she hadn't been so distraught she would never have had a few too many drinks and wandered the streets, *and* she would never have run into Monsieur Sexy Billionaire.

"Not chasing after another rich man," she said, confirming her drunken decision to forgo them. "But I do need some answers."

Grabbing her half-empty coffee mug and heading down the hall to her bedroom, Indi tore off her robe and entered her closet to stand naked, perusing the possibilities. She owned a lot of clothes, and she wouldn't apologize for the extravagance. Shopping was in her blood. Her closet had always been bigger than her bedroom since she could remember, even from when she was a toddler. Dressing up made her happy, just as wearing cat ears gave her confidence. Besides, her job required she seek out vintage, and off-season, designer clothing. If she happened on the perfect item of clothing for herself, she would never deny that want.

She touched the red dress. "Too aggressive." And it was the one Todd had always asked her to wear. "Never going to wear that dress again." It was Betsey Johnson. She'd gotten it off the rack during a discards sale. "I'll make a few adjustments to it, then sell it on the site." She pulled out the pink lace number. "Too summer-wedding." A white pantsuit with navy pinstripes was what she called her power suit. "Too businessy."

The blue sundress with a fitted bodice and full skirt would look great with some rhinestone heels.

"Or some stop-him-dead-in-his-tracks gladiator sandals."

Decided, Indi went about getting on her A-game.

An hour later, she stood before the door to Ryland James's apartment. At least, she hoped it was his place. When she'd fled the other morning, she was pretty sure she'd walked down four flights of stairs. This was the only apartment on the fourth floor.

She knocked and someone called out from the other side of the door to "hold on."

Primping, she quickly pushed up the girls. A lather of her pistachio-almond moisturizer over her décolletage, and some soft heather eye shadow along with pale lips, had given her a summery look. She liked to wear her hair pulled up, and today she'd gone with a bouncy ponytail high at the back of her head, with long strands teased out to frame her face.

Why she was nervous was beyond her. It wasn't as though she intended to throw herself at the man. She was getting over a breakup. And she didn't do rebound guys. That was crazy waiting to happen. But she did have good reason to return to his place today. And that reason was what made her anxious.

The door opened to reveal a man a good foot taller than her, wearing loose jeans that hung low on his hips to reveal gorgeous cut muscles that veed toward his crotch. He wore no shirt, so she followed those ridges upward, over abs of steel and pecs that might have been formed from stone. Indi finally met the man's piercing brown gaze. His smile beamed.

And she lost all means of rational communication.

The prettiest pair of blue eyes gazed up at him. Blue? Maybe more like blue violet. They emulated jewels, for sure. For a few seconds Ry forgot his name. Not that he needed to know his name. A guy should remember a thing like that. But…ah, hell, what was going on in his brain?

"Princess," he said. "Minus the pussycat ears. I didn't expect to see you again."

"Oh." She looked aside.

He immediately picked up on her sullen expression. "But I'm happy to. I just wasn't sure you'd remember, uh…things."

She shrugged and offered him a straight smile. "I remember more than I probably want to. And I remembered where you live. I hope you don't mind that I stopped by. I wanted to talk to you, and I didn't have a phone number, so…"

"I'm glad you stopped by. Come in. I was warming up some nachos in the oven. You hungry?"

"I, uh…maybe? If I'm interrupting your meal—"

"Not at all. I left work early today and felt like bumming around home, catching up on some reading for business projects. Come in." He grabbed his T-shirt from the back of a chair and pulled it on. "Have a seat on the sofa. Uh, unless you prefer under the coffee table?"

She gaped at him, then shook her head and nodded a grinning acknowledgment to the dig.

Ry took in her gorgeous pale skin, which was exposed from shoulder to neck to cleavage, and then her pretty knees and down to those very sexy sandals that wrapped thin leather straps up to her knees. Up along the soft blue dress. Her breasts rose from the low-cut top in a sensual yet not-too-blatant invitation. And he couldn't stop looking at her mouth, pursed and the palest pink. And were those lashes for real? So thick and black and...

She paused and looked over the coffee table. Offering him a smirking grin, she sat on the sofa. "I can't believe I slept under your table."

"Me, either. Couldn't have been too comfy. You look like you're feeling one hundred percent better," he said as he wandered into the kitchen to peek into the oven. Another ten minutes and the cheese would be melted. "How are you feeling?"

She turned and looked over the back of the sofa. "Good. Not quite a hundred percent. Still a bit tired. I guess I went on a crazy bender. Slept on my floor when I got home, too. Apparently, when drunk, I'm a floor sleeper."

"Does that happen often?"

"The drunk?" Her laugh was soft but she waved off the levity with a gesture. "Not usually. But champagne goes straight to my head. I shouldn't have had that fifth goblet."

Ry whistled and wandered over to sit on the arm of the couch. "Believe it or not, wine is my bête noire. I can't handle the vino."

"Really? A big guy like you? It must take quite a few bottles to get you wasted."

"Try one glass. I'm not sure what it is, but it lays me flat. And I can drink vodka and whiskey like it's juice. Weird."

He didn't normally reveal himself so boldly like that, but he'd sensed her need for reassurance. The woman had lain under his coffee table all night.

"You must have thought I was a case," she said. "And when I got a look at what I looked like when I got home? I can't believe you didn't think I was a homeless person."

"Wearing a designer gown and diamonds? The homeless are never so stylish."

She laughed. "Yeah, I guess. But they weren't diamonds. I never go for the splash when rhinestones will do." She leaned an elbow on the back of the sofa and pulled up a knee, catching it with a palm. "I needed to come see you because I don't think I ever thanked you. You were so kind to make sure I didn't lie abandoned in some dark alleyway. I can't imagine what would have happened to me if you'd walked away. So, thank you."

"You're welcome. I'm not much for leaving a helpless woman in a dangerous situation. I hope you weren't too freaked to wake here in the morning."

"I was, but that's to be expected. And speaking of dangerous situations, I do have questions."

This was the part Ry should have foreseen, but still it had snuck up on him. Questions. Always questions. And they were never easy to answer. "Like what?"

The oven timer went off and, thankful for a moment of respite, he rushed over to pull out the nachos. He'd made a whole pan of chips with jalapeños, tomatoes, onions, shredded chicken, black beans and heaps of cheese. His favorite comfort food. A guy could never find good nachos in Paris.

"You have to share these with me," he called over his

shoulder, and was surprised when she answered from close by.

Indigo leaned over the pan of steaming nachos and inhaled. "That smells heavenly. Last time I had something like this was when I visited a girlfriend in the States. You can't find good nachos in Paris."

"Exactly. I use pickled jalapeños on them. That's the secret recipe."

She rubbed her palms together. "Dish me up!"

Could he get so lucky that she'd forget she'd come here with questions? With hope, maybe she would.

Chapter 4

It had been a while since Ry enjoyed the company of a woman so much. And since he'd felt so comfortable with one. Usually his dates were high-maintenance, slipping into the bathroom every half hour to check their makeup, texting or doing God knew what on their ever-present cell phones. He had yet to see Indigo glance at her phone.

They both sat on the sofa, facing the slanted windows that lined the east side of his flat from the floor, where they rose vertically about six feet up the wall, then angled at forty-five degrees to the top of the high ceiling.

Indi's hand rested on her stomach and she'd slouched down and declared, "You've ruined me for any other kind of nachos. I am your servant for life. Pay me with melty cheese and those fabulous pickled jalapeños."

"I have never seen such a pretty, petite woman put down the cheese and chips with such gusto. I promise to call you next time I have a nacho craving."

She met his fist with her own. And Ry tilted his head against the back of the sofa and slouched down as well. He'd had a couple of beers in the fridge, and the now empty bottles sat on the coffee table. An evening sharing brews and junk food with a pretty woman? This was a hell of a lot easier than doing the fancy-restaurant thing and then trying to figure out if he should suggest a museum or a boring concert. And how to read a woman regarding whether she was on board for sex or if she was the sort who had a three-date minimum or even longer.

But he reminded himself this wasn't a date. The woman had been dumped by her boyfriend. And Ry did not do the rebound-guy thing. No way. He didn't need that kind of baggage to sort through.

He wasn't sure what was going on besides that he was warming to Indi fast and hoped they could get to know each other better. As more than friends, if that appealed to her. It did to him. When she decided to start dating again, he wanted to be tops on her list of potential dates.

Indi suddenly sat upright, turned to face him and asked, "Now about what I really came here for."

Ah, hell. The fun couldn't have lasted forever. Ry sat up and set the empty plate on the table, then prepared to face the tough questions.

"This is going to sound strange," she began, "but…why do I feel as if I was drugged the other night?"

Because she had been. "You did say champagne goes straight to your head."

"True, but I've been on a champagne bender once before. This was different. The aftereffects have been exhausting. I've slept like Sleeping Beauty minus the beauty part. I didn't even get up until three today. It's like I'm fighting to come back from an illness, or something. And I still don't feel right. Tired and achy. Usually after a bender

I puke, pass out, then wake with a headache. But a few hours later, I'm good to go. You didn't… I mean, I don't think you would. You seem like a nice man. But… I have to ask."

He picked up on where she was headed. "I did not roofie you, Indi."

"Oh. Right. I mean, it's never happened to me before, so I wouldn't know what to expect. I'm sorry, but I had to ask."

"Understandable. Let me see if I can help you to sort out things."

Ry shoved a hand over his hair, then pulled it back and held his hand at the back of his head. How to explain this to her without going into so much detail she'd develop even more questions… Could he trust her with the details? She already knew some things, so he'd only get caught if he tried to twist them into something they had not been.

"And while you're at it, what were those black things?" she asked. "I saw them. They were…creatures. Totally black and creepy and yet weirdly sparkly."

Ry blew out his breath and dropped his hair. No way around this one. And lying never felt right to his soul. He'd have to give her the truth. Some of it. She seemed smart and capable of handling such information. And if not, she could run away from him again, and he wouldn't go after her. She'd just think she'd met a totally whacked guy with a weird way of looking at the world.

"You were drugged," he said. "Or rather, you were treated with a complex healing process that involved herbs and some…" He couldn't say *faery magic*. No human was that open-minded. "And I'm sure that was what has you feeling so blown now."

"Herbs? What the hell?" She pressed her palm over the base of her throat. Today there were no signs she'd even been injured by the collector. "I remember something about getting cut. Maybe from the creature's claws? Then you picked me up and carried me… And then I draw a blank. Ryland, please. I know this is crazy, but I need to fill in the blanks so I don't think I'm going nuts."

"You're not nuts. At least, as far as I know. I don't know you well." He winked, but she didn't return the playful vibe.

Right. She was worried, and he had no right to keep her in the dark.

"There was a creature," he confessed. "Two of them. I was there to slay them. Which I did. Because if I had not stopped them they would have entered the mortal realm fully and done some terrible things."

Indigo thrust up a palm between them. But she didn't speak.

Ry felt compelled to clasp her hand and give it a reassuring squeeze, then he set it on her leg. "This is going to be tough to hear, but you have to keep an open mind. Okay?"

She nodded. Winced. Closed her eyes tightly. Then opened one eye and nodded again.

"First," Ry said, "I need to know if you've been in that area of the eighteenth before. At night?"

"A lot of times. I used to party there with friends a few years ago. Janet and I did the Club Rouge for her going-away party this spring. Why?"

"No reason. Well, yes, there is a reason. That particular section of Paris is a strange place. Actually, it's called a thin place. Two worlds overlap."

She didn't react, but her attention grew fierce. He was jumping deep, but something about the woman made him feel as if she wouldn't be satisfied with anything but that dive, so Ry continued. "Do you know about faeries?"

"You mean like the little twinkly ones I see in my garden?"

He bent to level their gazes. "You see faeries?"

She shrugged. "Not all the time, but I have. And just that you're asking about it means that I don't have to say to you 'don't think I'm weird.'"

"I don't think you're weird. You've seen actual faeries before?"

"I guess so. Out of the corner of my eye. I believe in faeries. Just like I'm sure all the other mythical creatures exist in the world. Not that I've seen anything but a few faeries. I've have never run in to a vampire, but until something is disproven, I keep an open mind."

Ry's exhale released a lot of tension. "Good. Because those black sparkly creatures were from Faery."

"Really?" Her response was so enthusiastic Ry leaned away from her. Would it have been easier if she'd laughed at his fantastical suggestion and walked out on him? Much less to explain that way. "But those creatures were big. The same size as you. Can faeries be all sizes and shapes?"

He nodded. "Basically. They are a species, and within the species are hundreds, probably thousands of breeds."

"Cool."

So far, so good. Time to hold his breath and do the free dive to the deepest depths.

"That part of Paris you were in last night is called Faery-Town," Ry said. "It's where the realm of Faery overlaps the mortal realm. It's always been there. Humans aren't aware of it. They walk through never knowing that faeries are all around them, living, existing, doing drugs."

"Drugs?"

"Rather, the faeries sell their dust to—" Er, she probably didn't need to know about vampires and their addiction to faery dust right now. "Anyway, I saw you sitting on the curb, and you could *see* me."

"I did see you." Her eyebrows narrowed. She was starting to think too much.

Ry jumped in for the save. "At that moment, I realized I shouldn't have been able to see you, so I figured that you had somehow breached the fabric between the two realms and were actually in FaeryTown. And since you say you've seen faeries in your garden, then maybe you have the sight."

"Is that an ability to see faeries?"

"Yes. I have it. And that's what allows me to enter FaeryTown and to interact with its inhabitants."

"Which is why you were there with a big sword and hell gleaming in your eyes?"

"You did see those black things flying above me."

"I did. Not nice?"

"The nastiest of the not nice. I can't allow them to enter the mortal realm, so I go there every night to slay them."

"Every night?"

"At midnight. One or two collectors come through from Faery."

"Collectors? That's what you call the black sparkly things?"

"Yes. And while you don't need to know everything, just know that it would be a very bad situation if one got through to this realm. Meaning, they pierced the borders of FaeryTown and completely entered the human realm."

"Uh-huh." She rapped her fingers on her leg a few times, then tilted her head at him. Her big blue eyes were so deeply colored they were almost violet. Faeries had violet eyes. But she wasn't faery. He'd sense her faery nature if she was. And she had bled the other night. Red blood. Faery blood was clear and sparkly.

"So you're like Batman, then?"

"Batman?" Ry crimped his eyebrows. "I just fell off this conversational thread."

"Well, I, uh—" she tapped a finger against her lip and squinted one eye shut "—kind of sort of…googled you."

"To be expected."

"I know you're a famous billionaire philanthropist. That's totally Bruce Wayne. And then you fight the bad guys at night?" She shrugged. "Batman."

"I, uh, would never call myself that, but whatever works for you." Probably more like wolfman, but he was trying to avoid that branch of conversation right now.

"So…" Indigo placed her hand over her throat again. "One of those things, a collector, scratched me. I think?"

"Yes. And they are deadly to humans. By the time I got to your side, your breathing was shallow. You were going to die."

She gaped at him.

"I carried you to a faery healer and she saved your life. She owed me one. Well, not exactly, but I wasn't going to take a no from her because of our history."

"Your history?"

"It's not important. Hestia agreed to heal you. I didn't watch, but it took about twenty minutes. And whatever she gave you—the herbs or faery magic she worked on you—must be what's making you so tired and feeling as if you've been hit by a truck."

"That was how I felt yesterday. Only a small car this evening. So a real live faery healed me? Kept me from dying?"

He nodded.

"And then you carried me here to take care of me?"

"I wouldn't call letting you crawl under a table taking care of you."

"I was probably delirious."

"Close."

"Okay, so faeries exist and they are doing some bad things in Paris, and you go out nightly with your sword to make sure it doesn't happen."

"I try my best."

"What are these collectors doing? Killing people?"

"No, uh…" He winced.

"Ryland." She touched his leg and it sent such a shock of intense desire through him that he sucked in a breath. But now was no time to kiss her. Even if the compulsion was screaming for just that right now. "You seem like a smart man. Doing good for others by giving away your money. Avoiding the celebrity because that's not you. I did creep on you online. Don't hold that against me. Anyway, you don't seem like a man prone to flights of fancy."

"I never take to fanciful flight."

Her smile was so cute, curling the corners of her lips like a heart. "I think I can believe everything you've told me. I want to, anyway. It's the best explanation for my worst night ever. But you have to tell me everything. Please?"

"I don't know what else there is to say. As for what I've told you, I would normally never tell things like this to anyone. Well, I tell Kristine."

"A girlfriend?"

"No, my secretary. She knows me inside and out. And she knows that this realm is populated by more than merely humans."

"You keep saying *human* like it's something you're not." She dipped her head to meet his gaze. "Are you a faery?"

"I thought you wanted to hear about the collectors."

"I do, but… Okay. Tell me."

He hadn't dodged that one and knew the bullet would

ricochet around to hit its target soon enough. Stalling for time had never been his thing. He always liked to come right out with it. Unless it related to revealing his true nature.

"Collectors have only recently been infiltrating this realm," he said. "I know because I got curious after a news reports about stolen infants."

"I remember that a few weeks ago. Such an awful thing. Something like three newborn babies taken from their cribs."

"Right. Do you know about how faeries take human infants from their beds and replace them with changelings?"

"I've only read about such a thing in faery tales. That's something that really happens?"

"It does. Or it did. It's been almost thirty years since any major baby thefts have occurred and changelings were left behind. Related to Faery, that is. But it's started again. Only this time, the faeries have decided not to leave a changeling in the human baby's place. They just take the baby and run."

"What do they want the babies for?" She pressed fingers to her lips. "Oh, my god, do they eat them?"

"No. Faeries have a thing for half-breeds. Unless its half demon. That's a long story. But suffice, they raise the humans in Faery and when they are grown, breed them with their own. It's not like a breeding farm. Some are treated as family. But it's how things have always been done."

"That's fucked."

"Gotta agree with that assessment."

"It sounds like human trafficking."

"When you put it that way, it is similar."

"You're protecting innocent babies. That's so honorable."

"I try. I've gone out every night for the past two weeks.

Each night I slay one or two collectors. They often come in pairs, sometimes just the one."

Ry stood and paced to the windows that looked out over the city. Twilight was creeping up and the streetlights below fought with the remaining daylight. The sky was a hazy azure-and-gray violet. Behind him, he heard Indigo shift on the sofa.

"You don't have to buy everything I've told you," he said over his shoulder. "But it's the truth. And..." He turned to face her. "You can't tell anyone about this."

"Who would believe me? I've got enough problems without adding crazy faery lady to the list. And I do believe you. Can I just say it's kind of cool to know you? I mean, you really are Batman."

"Call me what you want. But I'm not a superhero. All I want is to stop innocent families from having their precious children stolen."

"I wish there was a way I could help you. I'm glad you trusted me to tell me."

She walked up beside him, and when he sensed she was looking up at him Ryland met her gaze. The outside light gleamed in her eyes and gave her skin a soft matte texture that looked finer than the most expensive silk. He wanted to kiss her. He should kiss her.

"One last question," she said. "And this one is the most important."

"Shoot."

"When I was hiding out in the alley, watching you battle the collectors with your sword, I saw something."

"Like what?"

"I saw you change. Briefly. Your whole body bulked up and your face... Ry, what are you?"

Chapter 5

"I should have kissed you when I was thinking about it," Ry said.

Indi's jaw dropped open. The man had been… "You were thinking about kissing me?"

He nodded. Smirked. A sexy move that crinkled the corner of one eye. "Just now."

Indi forgot her question. Had she asked him something? The man wanted to kiss her? "Then why are you standing there staring at me?"

His smirk curled to an outright grin. And as he leaned forward, kiss forthcoming, the delicious aura of him surrounded Indi with a fresh, outdoorsy gush of man and might. Overwhelmed by his stature and the sudden glee that invaded her core, she could but remember to close her mouth as his lips touched hers and one of his hands slid across her back to firmly take her in hand.

This was a slow and focused seduction of her senses

that lifted Indi onto her tiptoes to taste his lips, his teeth, his tongue. He clutched her tighter and deepened the kiss. The move made her feel safe and owned, yet also alive and sensual. The man knew how to hold a woman.

Gliding her hand up his chest, she slipped her fingers through the ends of his long hair and clutched at it, inadvertently pulling him closer to her, into her, if possible.

She sighed against his mouth as he tilted his head to change their angle. And when his other hand slid down her hip and over her ass, Indi couldn't resist lifting a leg to hook at his hip. And then the other leg. He held her there, wrapped about him, sinking into his taste, his smell, the hardness of his body and the gentle control of holding her.

Something perfect about this moment. But she wasn't going to analyze right now. Now was for pressing her breasts against his chest. Her nipples hardened and the man who held her groaned into their kiss. It sent an erotic hum through Indi's system. She rocked her hips forward, wanting the sensations to travel deep, and knew she was growing wet. Just from a kiss. A stunning, all-consuming kiss.

All of a sudden, Ry broke their connection and said, "Whew!"

Indi realized she'd actually jumped into his arms and decided that had been a bit forward, so she disengaged from him. With reluctance. Tugging at her ponytail and stretching her gaze along the floor, she couldn't prevent a giddy grin.

"I think I forgot my name," she confessed. And then when she looked up into his eyes, and he delivered her a waggle of eyebrows, she lost it and broke into a giggle. "Seriously, that was some kind of powerful kiss."

"I could give you another one. Unless that one was too much to handle?"

"Oh, I can handle a lot. Bring it."

Ry's smile collided with hers. And with a giggle, Indi again jumped up to fit her legs about his waist. He reached around and cupped her derriere, all while diving deep into her.

Had she come here to make out with the man? It hadn't been her intent. She'd had questions. That had been answered. Most of them. Yet the flexing of his pecs and abs against her torso enticed her to abandon her previous worries and simply fall into the moment.

Hot and firm, his mouth. And he knew exactly how to kiss her. She clung to his wide biceps as he opened her mouth in a deep, lush takeover. He wanted to be inside her? Yes, yes, and oh, baby, yes, please.

"You are some kind of delicious, Princess Pussycat."

"I like when you call me that. But it reminds me of my tattered dress that will never get clean. How could you have thought me a princess when I must have looked like—"

The next kiss was immediate and urgent. And it felt like the admonishment it had been meant to be. She'd been going down the route of complaining and putting herself down, and Ry stopped her. Bless him.

Clutching at his hair behind his neck, she curled it around her fingers and felt her toes curl within the strappy gladiator sandals. Had a kiss ever been so sensual? Targeted to her very core? Every part of her reacted to every part of him. And if she could get any closer to him she would, but she was already clinging to him for all the sweet, hot contact he would give her.

When they finally parted, she lingered in his arms this time, enjoying the feel of his warm chest against her torso and she hugged him. She wrapped her fingers about each of his biceps. So strong. Then she remembered how he'd wielded the sword as if a Viking warrior.

And those creatures. *Collectors.* From Faery.

Indi slid down from the embrace and tugged at her skirt. "You're very sneaky," she said.

One of Ry's eyebrows lifted in question.

"That was a well-timed kiss. And the follow-up kisses distracted me from the question I asked you. But I can't forget. What I saw that night is seared into my brain."

She gave one of his biceps a squeeze, feeling the strength in his pulsing reaction. She felt sure many men who worked out were as solid and pumped as him. But did they wander about a place where faeries and humans overlapped carrying big swords? And did they…change?

"What are you, Ryland?"

He stepped back from her, swooping a hand over his hair, a devastatingly sexy move that spilled the brown locks over an ear and forward against his neck and under his jaw. Indi's fingers wiggled, anticipating another glide through that delicious darkness.

And yet he looked down at her with an expression she couldn't figure. Challenge? Or an intense anxiety that he tried to bolster with silence?

"Are you a faery, too?" she prompted, unwilling to ignore her curiosity. "Because, you know, I am on board with all the faery stuff. Apparently."

He was the last example of what she'd expect a faery should look like. But then, those black sparkly things had never been in her mental catalog of what should and shouldn't be a faery. The few she'd thought to see in the backyard garden had been no higher than her index finger and had looked human and had sported glittery wings.

He exhaled heavily, one of those disapproving sighs that could go either way. Resignation or acceptance.

Indi dared to meet his gaze again, and this time he nodded and shoved his hands in his front pockets. Walking to the windows, he stood there for a while. The streetlights beamed and, while the sky was yet light, the moon was nearly full. It hung above the distant spire of the Eiffel Tower. A pretty picture. Made even more intriguing by the silhouette of the handsome yet seemingly troubled man standing before her.

"Ryland?"

"Just Ry, okay?" he said softly. "That's what all my friends call me."

She was relieved he had added her to his friends list. But after that kiss, and the following one, and then the next one, she had been hoping for something a little more than merely being friends.

"The things I told you," he said, still facing the window, "about FaeryTown and what I've been doing, have to be kept in strictest confidence."

"Of course. Like I've said, no one would believe me anyway."

"I'm not sure why I told you. Well, I had to. You were there. And for some reason beyond my ken you could see Faery. And, of course, if you believe in faeries, then you should understand there's a whole lot of other sorts out there that are best believed as only myth."

"Like vampires and witches?"

He nodded and turned to her. "Does that freak you out?"

Indi gestured calmly with splayed hands. "Do I look freaked?"

Now he narrowed his gaze at her, and there was that growing smirk again. "You don't. But maybe you'll go home and have a real good think about everything we've discussed and then the freak will pounce on you."

She shrugged. "Possible. But I'd like to fall on the side of me being a smart woman who can rationalize and decide for herself what is real and what is not. Show me a faery? I believe. Tell me vampires exist? Next time some guy flashes fangs at me, I'm going to guess it would be wise to run. Not sure what to do if I ever meet a witch, though."

"You wouldn't know it if you had met a witch. Or a vampire, for that matter. Unless he flashes his fangs at you. And then? How would you know if he's real or one of those poseurs that dances in the clubs and has a weird fetish?"

"Exactly. The world is filled with oddities. But what about mermaids?" she asked suddenly as her thoughts drifted. "Do they exist? Oh, please, tell me they do, because I so want to see one of those someday."

"They do, but you'd never want to meet one. They're vicious."

"Seriously? Have you met one? How do you know about all these creatures, Ry? If you're not a faery...?"

"I'm part faery," he said suddenly. And before Indi could ask for clarification, he added, "But mostly werewolf."

Chapter 6

He should not have stopped kissing her. Because then *the* question had been asked.

Ry had a thing about the first kiss. A man could tell a lot about a woman from that kiss. Awkward and graceless? There was always room for improvement. Sloppy and aggressive? Nerves could be the culprit, or just an overzealousness with which he didn't want to deal. Firm and accepting, yet also the woman jumped into his arms and wraps herself about him like she was made to fit his body?

Mercy.

His heart was still thumping from that incredible contact. And he wished his erection would chill. Because there were more important matters. Like his confession about being part faery, part werewolf to a perfectly human woman. He never did that. And on the one occasion he had told all? He'd known her for months, and her name was Kristine, and he trusted her implicitly with his secret because she knew all too well that secrets could be painful.

He'd known Indigo for less than forty-eight hours. Didn't know her last name. Wasn't even sure she believed in faeries or if she was playing along with him until she could laugh at his stories later. Who was this incredibly compelling woman who had loosened his lips so much that he'd laid it all out there like that?

That was it, wasn't it? That kiss of hers had loosened him up.

And now?

He wanted more from this woman. And for some reason, his better judgment had abandoned ship and decided he needed to tell all.

"Werewolf?" she said. Her voice was soft and awe-filled. Or was that fear? She stared up at him, hands clasped together below her chin. It looked like wonder in her gaze, but he could be wrong. Could be disgust. "And faery?"

With a heavy sigh, Ry knew he wouldn't be able to push her out the door and send her on her merry way now. The deep dive had occurred. Now to surface without sustaining too much damage.

"Sit down," he said.

She sat immediately. Eagerness lifted her chin, and yes, that was weird awe in her beaming gaze. "That's what I saw," she said. "I thought you changed to something like a wolf. Your head and shoulders and chest…they were—"

"I didn't realize it happened. In the moment, my anger and the fury at trying to destroy the collector overwhelmed and I briefly shifted. You shouldn't have had to see that."

"Why? It didn't scare me. I mean, from what I recall. Still kinda fuzzy from that whole adventure. And sore." She pressed a hand to her back and arched it forward. "I wonder if I could talk to that faery healer. Ask her what she did to me, and how long it's going to take to feel better?"

"Give it a few more days. You went through a lot the other night. And I'm sure I shoved you less than gently to get you out of the way."

"You were trying to protect me."

"A lot of good that did. You almost died, Indigo."

"There is that. I have no memory of a near-death experience, though. But let's talk about you. Come sit by me. Tell me about being a werewolf. And a faery! Please?"

In for the dive, Ry sat next to Indi and pressed his palms together before him as he summoned the strength and downright calm to put himself out there. He didn't have to tell her all. He would never do that. Because he didn't know her. But she knew too much. Enough that leaving her hanging would only push her away from him, and could likely result in her telling others his secret.

For once, Ry wished he had a vampire's skill of persuasion. They could change a human's mind, convince them they'd never been bitten. Or that they had never seen a werewolf shift halfway while battling vicious critters from Faery.

"Okay, here goes," he said.

She wiggled expectantly and leaned forward.

"I was born werewolf. My mother was a werewolf, and my father…" This part he didn't need to go into detail. "It's a twisty thing. My father was a faery, but my mother was married to the pack leader. She had an affair. Leave it at that. So I'm half-and-half, but I have more werewolf tendencies than faery. I don't have wings," he said quickly as she opened her mouth to speak.

"Oh." Her shoulders dropped. "I was going to ask about that. Do you have a tail?"

Her fascination disturbed him on a level he couldn't quite measure. Such a question made him angry, and a little humiliated. But why he felt that way went back to being ousted from the pack because he was part faery. Too many bad memories.

"I don't have a tail. In my *were* shape. *Were* means man. Werewolf means half man, half wolf. Like you saw the other night. Though I didn't shift completely. If so, my clothes would have split and fallen off and…you would have known for certain you'd seen a werewolf."

"Your clothes fall off? Is it like an Incredible Hulk thing?"

"Incredible…?" Ry couldn't help a chuckle. "What's with you and the superheroes?"

She shrugged. "I like comic-book heroes. Anything wrong with that?"

"Nothing at all. Not like the Hulk. When I shift to werewolf my body grows a little taller, more muscular and hairy, and my head takes on wolf shape, as do my legs and feet and hands. I'm mostly man but a lot of wolf."

"And you're naked?"

"Uh, yes?"

"Sorry, I like to have all the details. Helps me to picture it better. And then you run around naked in the city?"

"I never shift to werewolf in the city. Not completely, anyway. It would be foolish and asking for trouble. We of the paranormal ilk know the only way we can survive in the mortal realm is to keep our truths hidden."

"Wow, I suppose so. That's got to be tough. Trying to survive in a world that doesn't believe in you. And if they did, they'd think you're a monster. You're not a monster, are you?"

"Do I look like a monster?"

"Not now you don't." But she wasn't completely on board with believing otherwise, he suspected.

"I'm not a monster, Indi." He clasped her hand and rubbed the back of it along his cheek. She smelled so good.

And he didn't scent fear in her. Interesting. "I am a man first and foremost, who happens to have a proclivity for nature and running about as a wolf, especially on the night of the full moon. I also shift to wolf shape, which is exactly the creature you know as a wolf."

"Four legs and a howl?"

He nodded.

"That's so interesting. Do you have wolf friends?"

Despite the odd and uncomfortable questions, at the very least, Ry could be thankful she was open and not screaming right now. "Wolf friends? You mean who I run about with in the forest?"

She nodded.

"Yes. And no. Most werewolves live in packs. I haven't been in one for a while." Not by choice, either. "When I shift I do it alone. I own some property a couple hours out of Paris that is wooded and has a lot of acreage. If I encounter another of my species while shifted, we might have a tussle or just avoid each other. We're protective of our property."

"Alpha?"

"Yes, but I'm considered a lone wolf after leaving my pack."

"Why did you leave?"

"That's not something I want to get in to right now." He pulled up her hand again and this time kissed the knuckles. "Any more questions?"

"Well, tons! I mean, how does the whole faery thing work in? If you don't have wings? You can't fly?"

"Can't fly. Don't have the desire to fly. I have a faery sigil on my hip that allows me some weak faery magic and the sight that I've already explained to you. And I do dust when I come."

"You what?"

Ry smirked. That was always an interesting one to explain. And it only happened with a forceful orgasm. Something he tried to avoid when with women. Otherwise, how to explain the sudden glitter explosion? The jacking off when he got home thing was getting stale, though.

"When faeries have sex," he explained, "they put out dust when they orgasm. I, uh, do that."

Indi's jaw dropped open, so he pushed it closed and then she caught his hand with hers, thumbing the side of his hand as she stared at it.

"A werewolf," she said in that awe-filled voice. "Who would have thought? You're not even Batman, you're Wolfman."

"I don't like that term. Just call me Ry."

"Ry. Ryland James. The billionaire werewolf who fights crime. What compelled you, a werewolf, to fight the bad faeries?"

"As I've explained, they are stealing human children. Isn't that reason enough to want to stand up and make it stop?"

"You're amazing. So selfless. And your philanthropy. You're quite the package, Ry."

And his own package was starting to harden again. She hadn't dropped his hand, and each time she stroked her thumb over his skin he grew a little harder. He'd love to kiss her until she begged him to strip her bare and have sex with her on the sofa. But she might like that. And he was in a weird place. A little freaked that he'd spilled all to her.

Could he trust his instincts right now?

"You probably need to give what I've told you a good think," he mused.

Pulling out of her grasp, he tapped her lips and pondered another kiss. That was the easy way out. Now was no time to press the easy button.

"I need to repeat how important it is to keep this information about me quiet," he said. "If the paparazzi and tabloids ever got wind of this—"

"Oh, never. I promise." She made an *X*-ing motion over her chest. "I swear to you. I won't tell."

He could almost believe her. "The photographers for those trashy rags have their ways. They find out I have a new friend? They'll go after you."

"Why?"

"Those bastards are always trying to dig up something on me. Can't accept that I don't do interviews and that there is nothing to tell. Except that there is a lot to tell. Which is why I avoid the press like the plague."

"And that only makes them go after you all the more?"

"Exactly. I'd rather battle hundreds of collectors than face down one hungry tabloid reporter. They're ruthless."

"I've seen that. I myself am a socialite." She beamed, but it wasn't one of those entitled poses, but was rather sweet actually. "I attend a lot of balls and social events. I've never been in the spotlight like a celebrity, but I do understand. You can trust me, Ry. We don't know each other that well, but we've been through something together. And… I want to know you better."

"I'd like to get to know you better. Can we go out on a date? Something official? I mean, if you can handle dating someone who isn't human."

"I'd love that. And you seem very human to me. How about this weekend?"

He winced. "Can't. Full moon."

"Oh." Her shoulders slumped, but then she perked up. "Oh? So you and the full moon…?"

"I have to shift on the night of the full moon. Which is going to be an issue this month. I've only been slaying the collectors for a couple weeks. This weekend will present a challenge. I normally leave for my cabin on the night before the full moon. There I have the freedom to shift without worry of being caught out. But I can't leave Paris this weekend. I have to be in FaeryTown at midnight to stop the collectors."

"But if you shift to werewolf in FaeryTown, will humans see you? You said they couldn't see FaeryTown, so…" She offered a hopeful shrug.

Ry hadn't considered that. *Could* he shift in FaeryTown? Of course, he wouldn't be seen by humans. But he risked the chance of his werewolf leaving FaeryTown for regular Paris. And would that wild part of him be satisfied with a romp about the city? No trees or fields? No long stretches of human-free acreage to let loose and howl in?

He'd have to figure this out within the next few days.

"It's something to consider. Can we make the date for next week? Sunday maybe? Because the day before and after it's full I also…have needs."

"Like what?"

The days before and after the full moon? He also wanted to shift, but that compulsion could be squelched with sex. A lot of it. How to work that out this weekend? "Another one of those things you don't need to know about."

"You certainly are a man of mystery. But I'm glad you felt comfortable enough to share some of those secrets with me. You can trust me, Ry. Sunday?"

"Later in the day, after I've returned to Paris."

"Maybe we could do a late-afternoon picnic?"

"Sounds like a plan." He grabbed his cell phone from the coffee table and handed it to her. "Enter your info for me so I can call you. I don't even know your last name."

"I'm Indigo DuCharme."

"Of course. A princess wouldn't have any other but a

romantic name. We'll figure things out Sunday morning when I give you a call."

"I can't wait. In the meantime, I'm going home to—"

"Google werewolves?"

She bowed her head, because he'd hit it right on the nose. "Maybe." Indi typed in her name and phone number, then also put in her address.

"What you read online will only be fiction," Ry explained, feeling the need to do so. "Although some writers do get a few things right. Just take it all with a huge chunk of salt, okay?"

"Deal. I imagine it may be weird for you to have someone asking you questions about yourself, but I'm going to warn you that I may have many more questions on Sunday."

"It is weird, but I'm not feeling so nervous about this as I was when you initially asked me. Maybe we both need a few days to let this sink in. If by Sunday you're not on board with me, then I'll understand." He took the phone from her.

"Sounds like a plan."

Indi stood. He'd just given her an opportunity to leave. And while he wanted her to stay for a few more kisses, Ry guessed her brain was humming with so much new, strange and curious information that she would need to be away from him for awhile, take it in and give it a good think.

She thrust out her hand for him to shake. Really? They'd gone beyond that silly gesture.

Ry pulled her in and bent to kiss her. The woman's body melded to his as if fitting into a mold. And as his hard-on gave him away, Ry delved deeper into the kiss to grasp her sweetness just in case he might never see her again. Parting from her happened with a sigh from them both.

"Sunday is so far away," she said, walking to the door.

"It's going to be a long week. Thanks, Ry, for being honest."

"Thank you for not freaking out. But if you freak later, you can call me and we'll cancel plans."

"No canceling. And besides, my BFF is always on call for my freak-outs."

"No telling the BFF about me."

"Right. I can tell her I met a handsome man, though. She'd never forgive me if I kept that one to myself."

Another kiss sent her on her way. And Ry waited in the doorway, listening as her footsteps sounded down the stairs.

What had he just done? Revealing himself to a woman he barely knew? Something was wrong with him.

"Or maybe it's finally right."

Chapter 7

Days later

After slaying the two collectors in FaeryTown, Ry hopped in the Alfa Romeo and headed out of Paris. For reasons that were innate, the full moon always seemed to pull hardest at him around midnight. The witching hour? More like the wolfing hour. Even though, rationally, he knew the moon would hit its peak fullness around 2:00 a.m. this month. Other months it could be fullest during the day, but no matter, his werewolf waited until midnight to clamor for release.

But he could hold it back with the knowledge that soon he'd let out his werewolf and it would be free to run. The drive to the cabin was one of the prettiest trips when he managed it during the day. His night vision was excellent, and as he neared his property, he spied groups of deer in the ditches and the paralleling forest.

Ry pulled up the long curving gravel drive to his place and left the car out front. He'd considered having a garage built to protect the Alfa, but he wasn't so hung up on material possessions, and while he kept it maintained, he wasn't owned by the upkeep of it.

He unlocked the front door and tossed his duffel bag to the floor. It was cool and quiet inside. He didn't bother to close the door because he immediately began to strip and toss aside his clothes.

Nothing felt better than a four-legged lope through the forest. And it was rare he got farther than the front doorway when he came here for two or three days of quiet and relaxation.

Shifting was immediate. His limbs loosened and shortened and coalesced to that of a gray wolf, which, when standing next to a natural wolf, would be perhaps six or eight inches taller and longer, but not much bigger.

Strutting out into the night, the wolf loped around the fieldstone walls and then raced toward the grassy field spotted with wildflowers. When he reached the forest, he let out a long and rangy howl that was answered by another natural wolf many miles off. He would ignore the howl. It was merely a property marker, not an invitation.

Charging through the forest, the night crisp against his fur, the wolf reached the small clearing that was lit like a stage with cool white moonlight.

And as the beast soared into the wild grasses and, briefly, all four limbs were off the ground, again the shift overtook Ry and his body lengthened. His legs grew and tight, furred muscles wrapped about his burly chest. He landed on legs similar to a man's, yet his feet were powerful paws with claws that could dig into the ground for propulsion, or kick and kill with a slice of those sharp weapons.

Head growing and yet remaining in wolf shape, Ry stood tall. He thrust back his shoulders and arms, and lifted his chest. His lungs deflated as he let out a howl that mastered the night and laid claim to his territory.

And with a sniff of the air and a tilt of its ear, the werewolf tracked a nearby fox. He took off toward the small creature, the invigorating rush of adrenaline, and the release after a month in human form, quickening his strides.

The website had been updated. The bills were paid. And the new product samples had been delivered an hour earlier. Indi looked over the many assorted boxes that she'd received from companies vying to be featured by Goddess Goodies' new self-care line. While she'd thus far stuck with adding a few hair accessories and one pretty moonstone necklace to the website, Janet had suggested she branch out to a few more female-centric items. Books on self-care. Healthy teas. Crystals. And…why not a vibrator? Self-pleasure was a big part of being a happy, gorgeous goddess. So Indi had agreed to at least consider the vibrators.

And the research could prove interesting, if not also satisfying.

Chuckling at what her job description required, Indi stood up from the boxes she'd unpacked and stretched. She'd been working all morning. Her office was the front living area at the side of the house. It was walled on the curved side with windows and sat up two short steps from the main sunken living room. A dressmaker's dummy, currently wearing vintage Alexander McQueen, was her main project. While she employed a staff in a small warehouse, and they managed the bulk of the sewing and online orders, she did choose a few gowns to revamp because she loved the process of redesigning what had been a gorgeous piece to begin with, and she was an excellent seamstress. Home economics had been a favorite course in high school, and she'd taken fashion, textiles and business in college.

It was Saturday and the sun was high in the sky. She tried to keep her weekends free and not work too much. And she did have fresh peaches in the fridge...

Stripping away her clothes, Indi walked away from work and into the weekend.

Later, she floated on an inflatable lounge chair in the pool behind her home, eyes closed and one hand clasped about a peach sangria. No swimsuit. Nudity was her thing. Her shrubs were tall enough that she didn't worry about nosy neighbors.

Indi wondered what Ry was up to. She'd told him she had intended to give the news about his nature a good think. But she'd been so busy the past few days she hadn't taken a moment to look up *werewolf* online.

The man was a werewolf.

Half werewolf. And half faery.

And why was she not überfreaked about that? Shouldn't she be worried that he was mentally disturbed and that to date him could put her in a dangerous situation with a psychopath? It was a stretch to go there with a man who had only been kind to her, but she had to consider the psychopath possibility. The world had gotten less kind and more strange. And that was just the humans.

Yet at the same time, she had seen those black sparkly faeries. Collectors, he'd called them. And she had witnessed Ry partially shift. His entire head had changed to a wolf's head. Despite being drunk that night, she would never doubt her instincts, which confirmed everything he'd told her was true.

Now to decide where she stood with all this information. Could she date a werewolf? Because he'd intimated he'd wanted to get to know her better. What was different about him than any other man?

"Besides that he can change into a wolf," she muttered. The sun beamed across her skin, glistening in the water droplets. "I wonder if he has sex with other wolves. As a wolf? Would he have sex with me as a wolf?"

Because those were the squicky questions that needed answers.

But she was rushing far ahead of herself. First things first. Ryland James was an amazingly sexy man that she wanted to date. And their first date was already on the calendar. He was also, seemingly, very kind, philanthropic and concerned for others. The man was keeping babies safe from abduction. It didn't get any more honorable than that. He really was a superhero.

And didn't all the superheroes have a dark and secret affliction that made them different from the rest? Something that would challenge anyone to love them and welcome them into their life?

Like being a man who was also a wolf?

He hadn't said anything about his dating history. He didn't look like a man who had trouble finding dates. Certainly, he could not be desperate. Indi reasoned he probably didn't need to reveal what he was to a girlfriend. If he left Paris to shift only during the full moon? Would be easy enough to keep his secret safe.

And yet he'd shared that secret with her. She wanted to honor that trust. And she would.

A weird twinge at her back folded Indi in the water. Toppling off the inflatable chair, she clutched at her back, unable to reach up as high as where the pain was while trying to keep the sangria up in the air. Spitting out water, she kicked her way to the edge of the pool and propped an elbow on the edge.

What was up with the sudden shot of pain up and down her spine? It had zapped her and yet faded as quickly as it had come upon her.

"I really need to talk to that healer."

The exhaustion was gone, but now that she thought about it, she'd winced at a stretch of pain in her back this morning when she reached for a dress in her closet. She'd never had the flu, so she didn't know what a body ache should feel like. But this was not normal. She was an active young woman, not a creaky geriatric.

"Something weird happened that night in FaeryTown. And I need to know what that was."

Ry had called the healer Hestia. Indi had no recall about being in her presence or witnessing what she had done to her. And Ry had acted defensive about her when Indi prodded for more information. Did the man have something going on with the healer?

With a wince at the snapping tug in her spine, she pulled herself up and sat at the pool's edge. Her phone rang and she leaned over to grab it. "It's him." Had he changed his mind about their date?

Had she?

She pressed a hand to her chest to still her frantic heartbeats. No, it was all good. So far, anyway. She could go on a date with a werewolf. Talk about an adventure.

"Ry, good to hear from you. You still at your cabin?"

"Yes. It's not really a cabin, it's more a… Just thought I'd give you a call, see what you were up to. I hope that's okay."

That was encouraging. The man had been thinking of her.

"As a means to honor my no-working-on-weekends rule, I'm floating in the pool, getting some sun."

"You have a pool?"

"Yes, I do live in the eighth."

"Fancy neighborhood. Then you're doing well with your goddess thing, eh?"

"Not too shabby. It's a lot of work, but I love it. And I have a small but awesome bunch of employees. Later I get to do some field testing for a new product I may introduce with the next site update."

"Puppy ears?"

She laughed. "No. It's not an accessory."

"What is it?"

Should she tell him? She had felt as if they'd crossed the more-than-friends barrier with those fabulous kisses.

"Indi?"

"It's vibrators," she said as casually as she could manage. A trace of her finger across the water's surface tracked the glint of sun. "A lot of them. A dozen different companies want me to consider their product to sell on our site."

"Seriously? And you have to— I suppose product testing is important. Wow. I'm glad I called you. This is the most interesting conversation I've had in a while."

"Seriously? Because I think our conversation at your place the other night took the cake."

"For you, yes. For me? Vibrators are extremely interesting."

She laughed. "Chick toys interest you? I'm liking you more and more, Monsieur James. Are you returning to Paris soon?"

"Probably tonight. I drove out to the cabin last night after I slayed the collectors. I'll see how I feel about shifting after that. What I really need to do is stop slaying and figure out the source. Who is sending them in the first place."

"Otherwise you could end up slaying them forever with

no end in sight. Makes sense. How could you find out something like that?"

"I'll have to talk to my brother."

"Brother?"

"Half brother. I have…hundreds of half siblings."

"Seriously?"

"My faery dad is a manslut. That's about the only way to put it. But I only know a few. Never, one of my half brothers, makes his home in Paris. I'm stopping by his place on the way in tonight. You mentioned you wanted to do a picnic tomorrow? What should I bring?"

"Nothing. Let me make all the food. Maybe you could bring wine. No, wait. You and wine don't mix. Bring beer."

"I can do that. Can I pick the place?"

"Yes, surprise me."

"What time should I pick you up?"

"How about a midday siesta? Around four?"

"I've got your address. I'll see you tomorrow afternoon."

"In the meantime, I have a lot of research to do."

"And now I'm going to have some sweet dreams thinking about you and your research. Thank you, Indi."

The phone clicked off and she smiled to herself. The man would dream about her jilling off? She could dig it.

It was a Saturday night. The Moulin Rouge and the Pigalle area featured assorted strip clubs, and the sex shops weren't far away, either. People were out partying, drinking, making general merriment…and even not-so-general merriment.

Wishing he was holding a drink instead of flexing his fingers in readying them to wield an enchanted weapon, Ry stood in FaeryLand, sword sheathed at his back and shaking out his hands at his sides. He shook because it was the night following the full moon and his werewolf was jonesing for release like a drug addict hungered for the needle. And the only way to subdue that jittery need was to shift. Or to have sex until he was sated.

But he wasn't having sex with a pretty blond woman who liked to wear cat ears and could eat as many nachos as he could at one sitting. No, he was waiting for some creepy, sparkly creature to come charging for him, talons flashing in the moonlight, intent on taking out the werewolf who stood between it and human babies.

Something wrong with that scenario.

Beside him stood Never, the half faery and half vampire who had been sired by the same faery Ry had. Never stood as tall as Ry but was lanky and dark. He did not spare the guy-liner. Ry was sure the man had to blow-dry his hair to get it to stand up all spiky on the top like that. Add in the black shredded jeans, boots and chains and spikes all over his clothing? Ry thought he looked like a goth reject from *The Rocky Horror Picture Show*.

"Doesn't it hurt to sit?" Ry had noticed the spikes that formed a spade on his brother's ass pocket.

"Depends on who I'm sitting on," Never said drily.

He wasn't a big talker. At least, he and Ry hadn't quite found their groove yet. They didn't go out of their way to spend time with each other. And that was only because Ry sensed the man liked to be alone.

He'd met him years ago, here in FaeryTown, when Never strolled up to him and insisted Ry smelled familiar. And then he'd mentioned their father's name and they'd had a drink and hadn't actually hugged and promised to call each other every weekend, but they had become as amiable as two weirdos could be.

"I seriously have not noticed anything out of the ordinary over the past few weeks," Never said. "'Course, my current chick lives across the river in the fifth." Moonlight gleamed in his violet eyes. Eyes that sported red pupils. "I've never seen what you call a collector. And I do spend a lot of time in FaeryTown."

Ry checked his wristwatch. "In three minutes you'll be a believer. Pay attention. I need to know where they're coming from and, most important, who is sending them. I can't keep up this slaying for much longer."

"What's wrong if a few human babies go missing?"

"Really?" He cast Never a look of disdain.

His brother shrugged. "They're so noisy and smelly."

"Remind yourself to always use condoms, all right, bro?"

"What's a condom?" Never chuckled and nodded. "You think I want to take after our dad? By-blows spread all over the world *and* in two realms? For all we know we've got siblings in Daemonia, too. Make that three realms!"

"I do know one of The Wicked is related to us. So it is possible." The Wicked were half demon and half faery. Faeries hated demons, and the half-breeds were ostracized to a strange and distant part of Faery. Most escaped to the mortal realm for freedom from such oppression. "Think she married a werewolf, actually."

"Right, that's Beatrice," Never said. "I've met her. She rocks. You want me to introduce you to her?"

Ry hadn't any burning desire to gain siblings, but he wouldn't push them away, either. "Too busy at the moment. Check with me in a few months. Here one comes."

They watched as the fabric between Faery and the mortal realm undulated, sparkled and spit out a collector.

"Wow," Never said. "Now, that's working the glam Goth look."

Chapter 8

Indi loved the Luxembourg Garden. It had once been Marie de' Medici's private garden on the south side of the royal palace, which still stood. Now the lush emerald grounds were neatly manicured and populated with statues, trees, groomed hedges and flowers. The metal chairs around the octagonal pond were occupied by parents watching their children play with the rentable model boats. Photographers wandered with their attention on their cameras, and lovers held hands and giggled and embraced.

Ry had led her away from the crowd, down an aisle of horse chestnut trees and to a secluded spot. The grass was off-limits for sitting, so Ry spread out the blanket she'd packed on the bench and helped her set out the food. Egg-salad sandwiches with spicy pickle relish, cut veggies and the requisite soft cheese with a long chewy baguette. And a growler of craft beer that Ry said was his favorite. Except he'd forgotten to bring along glasses, so they took turns drinking from the awkward growler. But it was all good.

The sun was high. The birds chirped. And not too many tourists wandered by their spot under the shade of the tree canopy.

Having consumed six of the eight sandwich halves Indi had brought along, Ry now laid back, head resting on Indi's lap. He closed his eyes. His long body stretched the length of the bench, and his biker boots, which were loosely laced at the tops, propped against the iron armrest. His T-shirt had ridden up to reveal a notch of chiseled abs. And his hair, pulled into a neat queue, splayed to one side across a shoulder.

Finishing off the last carrot stick, Indi toed the picnic basket closer and rested her sandaled feet on the wicker edge. Ry reached up to stroke his fingers over her hair, which she'd combed back into a ponytail again today, sans cat ears. The tickle of his touch behind her ear felt great and she quickly went from fun and chatty to hot and horny.

But she wasn't one for public displays of affection. Not the intense kind she imagined happening with this hot specimen of man. It involved kisses melting into tongue lashing over skin and body parts. And, oh, so many gasping moans.

"How did it go at your cabin?" she asked him to divert her lusty thoughts.

"As usual. But with the added driving back and forth. Saw my brother Never last night. He's going to look into things for me. He hasn't a clue who might be sending the collectors into this realm, but he spends a lot of time in FaeryTown. If anyone there knows anything, he'll be able to root it out."

"You live such a fascinating life."

"I'm not Batman, Indi."

"I know. But it must be interesting, probably difficult, straddling two worlds at once. Not to mention the added fact that you are a minor celebrity who is always being hounded by the paparazzi."

"Only during special events. Which I'm attempting to do less of lately. No time what with the midnight watches."

"I love a good event." She stroked her fingers down his cheek and teased them through his trimmed beard. "The ball gowns and diamonds. The glitter and the high heels."

"Sounds like it doesn't matter what the event is, so long as you get to dress up."

"I have been attending balls since I was five or six. My parents were always going to one or another. I begged my mom to take me along. I could live in a ball gown."

"Is that so? Then today's ensemble is definitely dressing down for you."

She wore another sundress, fitted green seersucker with thin straps and deep cleavage. As deep as size 34-Bs could manage.

"Not as far dressed down as I would like," she said. "It's either a ball gown or nothing at all for me."

His gaze found hers in an upside-down smirk. "Are you a nudist?"

"That I am. Give me skin or give me ruffles and rhinestones. I do enjoy being a girl."

"I also enjoy that you're a girl." He rolled to his side, facing her stomach, and slid his wide palm up her torso, not quite reaching her breast. "I had a dream about you last night."

"Did it involve vibrators?"

He laughed unexpectedly. "Maybe?"

"I hope it was more satisfying for you than my night was. I spent it going over some SKU numbers the factory screwed up."

"Then definitely more satisfying. We guys do tend to think about sex." He winked at her. "A lot."

"Sex is never terrible to think about." And that they were talking about it wasn't bad, either. It was a bit daring, considering how short a time they had known each other. So…why not push it? Once again, Indi's curiosity raced to the fore. "I know this may be forward, but tell me about werewolves and sex?"

"That is rushing things."

"You're not interested in me?"

"I'm very interested in you, Indi. But as a man and a woman."

"That's good to know. But still, I couldn't find any information on Google…"

"All right, all right, I'll give you the basics. Werewolf sex. It's like two humans going at it when I'm in were shape."

"Were shape is your man form, like you are now."

"Yes. I'm all male right now."

"You most certainly are," she said in breathy agreement. The man chuckled.

"But it can be different?" Indi prompted.

"If I was dating a female werewolf, we might go at it in our shifted forms."

"Do you know a female werewolf?"

"Not well enough to have sex with her. I have a friend from my former pack. But she's engaged. And I've only ever thought of her as a buddy. Besides, it's been years since we've talked."

"Do you want to have sex that way?"

He shrugged. "When I'm in werewolf shape I think as a man and as a wolf, so things are different to experience. And I don't always recall, when I'm back in this form, the things I did when in another shape. So, yes, it's something I would do because it comes naturally to me. It is what I am. But I spend most of my time as a man, so I do most things as a man and that is great, too."

"Have you ever had sex with a human woman while in werewolf shape?"

"I haven't. But I could."

"Would you want to?"

He quirked an eyebrow. "Not sure. The opportunity hasn't presented itself. And the question would be more would *she* want to? Does that freak you out?"

"The opportunity hasn't presented itself, so I guess not."

"Do you always ask your dates about how they prefer sex *before* you've had sex with them?"

"Sometimes. I am a curious chick. But now that you ask, it does seem like a good thing to communicate beforehand. I mean, most people tend to stumble through the act. Why not go into it informed and educated?"

"Like learning that the woman you are dating likes to research vibrators?"

"Exactly." And he'd just said they were dating. Score! "Maybe I'll let you help with the research sometime."

He sat up abruptly and scooted over to sit close to her. "I'm in."

And together they laughed and collected their things and repacked the basket.

Ry checked his watch. "It's six fifty-seven."

"It's early. Want to head to my place for a swim?" Indi offered as they strolled down the tree-lined alley toward the main pond in the park.

"I don't have swim trunks," Ry said.

"Somehow I don't think I'll mind that missing item one bit."

"Fine, but if I'm going in the buff, then you have to as well."

"I did confess to being a nudist." She winked at him.

"Skinny-dipping it is!"

Out behind Indi's home the fieldstone patio stretched around a kidney-shaped pool. She dropped a couple of fluffy white towels she'd retrieved from the bathroom on the double lounge chair with the canopy over it, then joined Ry as he stared off toward the maple copse that marked the back of the lot.

"You have a lot of land for midtown Paris," he said.

"It's one of the larger lots in the city. It's been in my family for generations. We can trace ownership of this land back to the seventeenth century and some royal vicomte from King Louis XIV's court."

"Impressive."

"You didn't happen to know him, did you? Louis XIV?" He cast her a strange look.

"I thought werewolves were immortal. Like vampires?"

"We can live three, four, sometimes five hundred years. But I'm only twenty-nine. Sorry to disappoint."

"I'm not disappointed. What about faeries?"

"Life span? A long freaking time." He wandered to the pool's edge and tugged off his T-shirt. At the sight of his wide, muscled back Indi caught her lower lip with her teeth. He turned a look over his shoulder at her. "We going to do this?"

The waggle of his eyebrows was all the invite Indi needed. She unzipped the back of her dress and stepped up beside him. "I'll have you know," she said, "if I see you in the buff I will probably want to have my way with you."

"Challenge accepted."

He unzipped his jeans and dropped trou so quickly, Indi paused with her dress halfway down and managed to step back in time as the tremendous splash from his cannonball into the pool soaked her feet and calves.

Tossing her dress aside, she dove into the pool and surfaced ten feet away from the man who treaded water with a shit-eating grin on his face. She lunged forward into a front crawl and swam toward the deepest end. When she reached the edge she turned to find him floating on his back, spitting up water like a fountain.

"This is heated!" he called.

"Of course it is. Otherwise my skin would goose-pimple and my tits would turn to rocks."

"Sounds painful." He lifted a hand from his floating position and made a rubbing motion with his thumb and forefinger. "Why don't you swim over here and let me make sure that doesn't happen?"

The sexy tease had begun, and Indi was all for it. She swam over to Ry and dove to swim under him and come up on the other side. When she surfaced, he pulled her to him to kiss.

They floated, but if she stretched she could just touch the bottom of the pool with her big toe. She didn't need the support, as Ry's arms held her against him. And with that security, she bent her legs and wrapped them about his hips. It was a position she seemed to naturally go into when kissing him. Seeking haven and finding it with ease.

He shifted to float on his back, which broke the kiss, but he didn't let her go. Lying on top of him, she laid her head against his neck and closed her eyes to take in every hard and slick bit of him that supported every wanting, wet bit of her.

His hand slid down her ass and cupped it. His erection nudged her thigh. It was a sizable asset that put her product research to shame.

"Let's move to the shallow end," he said. With a swish of his hands, Ry directed them around and he sailed them both across the pool. "Your tits against me are making things so hard."

"I noticed. Can you swim when you are a wolf?"

"Very well, but not in deep waters. Wolves weren't designed for that kind of movement. But I'm doing pretty well right now, aren't I?"

His shoulders hit the lowest step of four and he sat up and pulled her onto his lap. Indi straddled him. The water sloshed at their shoulders and made her breasts buoyant, lifting the tops of them above water.

Ry bowed and kissed each one. Then he gently cupped them both and kissed her beneath the water, sucking in a nipple. She rose onto her knees, lifting her breasts out of the water, and the man spread one arm across her back, holding her to him as he devoured her.

The hot, sucking tease shimmied through her system and coiled in her core and lower to her groin. Indi arched her back, showing him how much she liked what he was doing. She clutched at his wet hair and tilted back her head.

"Indi, your breasts are perfect."

"A little small," she said before she could catch herself. Goddesses did not put themselves down.

"Nope. I like this size. Made for my mouth. Mmm…" He nipped her gently, and one of his wide hands squeezed her derriere. "They're so hard. You're not cold out of the water?"

"Against you? I feel like I'm pressed against an inferno. And it is so good." She bowed and kissed him deeply, clasping his jaw with both hands as she swung out her legs to float behind her. "Let's do this," she said. "I want you, Ry."

"I've wanted you since the moment you looked up at me from under my coffee table."

"Really? Not before that, when I was drunk and apparently dying?"

"I was too worried about you then. Now? You're fine. And I do mean fine."

Swimming her out a little ways, so she could still feel the bottom, Ry held her securely and kissed her deeply.

His free hand slipped between her legs. With a sensual hiss, Indi reacted to him finding her clit. She squeezed his arm, digging in her nails.

"That okay?"

"Oh, yes. You don't have any trouble without a map, do you? Oh… That. Right. There."

He performed a slow circling rhythm. It moved in a tight counterclockwise motion that was first firm and then a little gentler, and then back to the firm command. Her body shuddered at the instant-orgasm move.

Indi leaned in and kissed Ry's shoulder as his motions brought her to an edge she didn't want to grip, and couldn't, for she was surrounded by water and man. And when he tilted his head to breathe against her neck, moving his lips to kiss up under her jaw, and his finger hit the right spot, she came in a shout of release and joy.

Wrapping herself about him and shivering with the incredible muscle-clenching excitement of the orgasm, Indi kissed his forehead because that was where her mouth landed. His fingers nudged at her breast. A tweak of her nipple stirred the orgasm to a second wave, and that made her clutch him all the tighter. And then she released her muscles, letting him go and slipping into the water.

It was only when he caught her across the back and pulled her to him that she remembered it was probably a good idea not to drown.

"You come like the proud, sexy woman you are."

"That was…a surprise. Especially for, you know, a new lover. You focused right in on the task." She shivered and sighed, sliding her hand down his abs. Her fingers landed on his cock. Mercy, she could feel its power in her grasp. "My turn to get you off."

He hissed as she pistoned her hand about his length. "You've got a nice firm grip. Oh, Indi…"

He floated backward to notch his shoulders and head against the pool edge. She kissed him, long and deep, teasing him to dance with her tongue, while jacking him faster and faster.

"I probably shouldn't come in your pool," he said through a tight jaw.

"That's what the chemicals are for. Come on, lover. Let go." She lashed her tongue under his chin and felt his shiver. "For me?"

The man closed his eyes and let out a moan as his hips bucked and she held his erection firmly. He swore and bucked harder. And she noticed the surface of the water before him glittered in the setting sunlight. He'd said something about faery dust when he came. Wow. He really was part faery.

Ry pulled himself up to sit at the edge and then with one arm swung up Indi to sit beside him. She caught her balance against his thigh, then noticed the purple mark on his hip.

"What's that?"

"That's the faery in me," he said, and stood, offering her his hand to help her stand.

Once upright, she bent to study the marking, which looked like a violet design drawn by a tattoo artist before the actual ink was administered. "It's sort of like a mandala."

"It's supposed be the source of my faery magic, but… eh, it's just a mark. I've never experienced any real magic with it. It might be what makes my blood sparkle, and well…" He glanced over the water. "I did mention faeries put out dust when they come."

"My pool has never looked prettier. I love glitter, you know that. I want more. We need to do it again." She grabbed his hand and tugged him over to the chaise longue. "Hurry, before we dry off!"

She dove onto the chaise and Ry crawled on top of her,

dripping hair splattering her chest and throat. "Water's not the best lube."

"No, but it makes your skin slick and I want to lick you." She pushed him to the side and, with another nudge, he surrendered to lie on his back. "Where should I start?" She looked him up and down.

The man's cock was already hard again, and she couldn't not look at it, again, and again, and…

"Right here." She bowed and licked the bold red head of his erection. The heavy shaft bobbed, so she held it firmly and squeezed at the base.

Ry's groan was a mixture of surprise and satisfaction. He gripped her by the wet hair and eased his hand along her neck as she took him in her mouth and brought him to another, trembling, shouting orgasm. This time the sparkle misted into the air in the wake of his ejaculation. Faint, but it glittered on his skin and her fingers.

"Cool."

Ry kissed her nose and grabbed his watch. "You girls and your love for glitter. I've gotta say, this is much easier than trying to come up with an excuse like maybe the glitter came from the woman's makeup. Or else having sex in the dark."

"I can't imagine."

"It's an issue, that's for sure." He checked his watch. "Ah, hell. I have to get going. It's almost eleven thirty. Mind if I use your bathroom before I leave?"

"It's upstairs and through my bedroom. You'll see it. Will you grab an extra towel and bring it down? I want to wrap up my hair."

"Be right back." He kissed her, then wandered inside the house.

Indi stood and stretched her luxuriously aching muscles. This had been a perfect date. Could a girl get a hallelujah?

"Oh."

Too soon to celebrate. She caught her hand at her back, wincing at the stinging pain that focused in her spine, but high up, too high to reach. Not like the usual aches and pains she would expect if she'd lifted something wrong or had maybe gyrated too much while in the pool having sex with a hunky werewolf.

Ry returned and placed a towel over her head. He bent to look into her eyes. "You still feeling some pain? Is that from the other night?"

She nodded. "I don't know what it is, but it sneaks up on me, and it seems to be getting stronger. I wonder if I sprained something when I stumbled in the alleyway."

"Possible. I'll look for the healer tonight and ask her what's up. Maybe she can enlighten me to what she used on you and if it has any side effects." He bent and pulled up his jeans. "By the way, that is a hell of a lot of vibrators you have in your bedroom."

Indi giggled and fluffed the towel over her hair. "That it is."

"If I wasn't in such a hurry I'd help you with your research."

"There's always tomorrow."

"Sign me up?"

"Consider yourself recruited. Do you work tomorrow?"

"Yes, I go in to the office every weekday. Kristine has a new list of potential recipients that I want to go through and call for interviews."

"Who are your recipients?"

"Mostly paranormal-related causes. Though the one I'm excited about buys land to protect natural wolves. They want to start an international office."

"Sounds right up your alley. I'll be out and about tomorrow running errands. Is it all right if I stop by your office with lunch?"

"That'd be thoughtful of you. Would you mind bringing along something for Kristine, as well? I'll foot the bill."

"I can do that. My phone is inside on the kitchen counter. Leave your office address in the contacts and I'll see you then."

He pulled on his shirt, then flipped his wet hair over a shoulder. Kissing her, the man growled. "It's tough walking away from you."

"That'll give you more incentive to walk back to me."

"I like the sound of that. Thanks for today. I like spending time with you. And having sex with you."

"Ditto. See you tomorrow, lover boy. Can I call you lover wolf? It sounds sexy."

He waggled his hand before him. "Whatever makes you happy?"

"I'll think about it. Good luck stopping the big bad sparklies tonight. Be careful!" she called as he wandered into her house.

Wrapping the towel around her body and tucking it in front, Indi collected the wet towels and dropped them in the hamper that connected to the laundry room.

She wasn't sure she had the energy or desire to do any research tonight. She was a woman sated. Who was dating a werewolf. How strange was that? Was she prepared for this? Could she do this?

Up until a few days ago, her life had been exquisitely normal. Ball gowns and tiaras? Check. Wolf fur and big, deadly swords?

"Check," she whispered, and then smiled. "Bring on the not normal. I'm in for the ride."

Chapter 9

Indi gave her name to the doorman at the business building overlooking the Seine. He said she was "on the list,"
so he let her walk through to the elevator bay. It wasn't a
swanky building, was rather run-down, but it might have
been glorious in its 1920s heyday, judging by the aging
azure-and-maroon art deco tilework on the walls.

Once in the elevator, she thought that this getting
dumped thing was not so bad after all. Look at the rebound man she'd scored!

"Not a rebound guy," she whispered. "Please don't let
him be a rebound. That never ends well. He's the new guy.
The new wolf," she muttered as the doors opened and she
walked out onto the third floor.

There were four office doors to choose from, and three
of them had brass plaques that detailed more than a few
last names or a product name. She chose the door without
the plaque and walked in.

A woman behind the desk looked up from the laptop. She was certainly…oh. Indi was briefly taken aback by her stature and broad shoulders as she stood and offered a wide hand to shake.

"You must be Indigo DuCharme. The cat ears are gorgeous, and don't get me started on your shoes. *Très magnifique!*" she cooed in a deep voice. "Ry said you might stop in today. I'm Kristine."

"Nice to meet you, Kristine. Ry mentions you often."

"He'd better. I do keep his life on course, and you'll never find a faster typist than me, sweetie. Even with these luscious nails." She fluttered her, indeed, glossy and lushly violet nails for Indi to see.

"Is Ry in?"

"He's in his office. You bring him lunch?"

"Yes." Indi held up the take-out bag. "And for you, too. Do you like crepes? I picked up some with everything on them and salads for sides."

"That was so sweet of you, Indigo. Thank you."

She set out the boxed lunch for Kristine on her desk, then gestured she was going in to see Ry.

Ry met her at the door to his office, opened it and invited her in. "Smells like cheese and ham."

"And mushrooms and basil and lots of other stuff. I told the chef to toss everything in them."

"I'm hungry." He closed the door and then tugged her by her free hand to stand in his embrace. The kiss was masterful, and delving, and she was glad she'd not snuck any of the spinach before coming here. "You taste better than lunch."

"Well, if you're not hungry anymore, I can eat them both."

"Not so fast." He grabbed the lunch bag and gestured for her to sit on the couch. "So you met Kristine."

"I did."

Ry sat next to her and Indi leaned in close and whispered, "You do know your secretary is a man, right?"

He chuckled and handed her a box and a plastic fork. "Kristine is a woman. She just hasn't transitioned yet. Won't take my money to pay for the surgery. Stubborn. And I love her like a sister. Not even like a half-blood sister, either. She and I are tight."

Endeared by his acceptance and love for the woman, Indi felt awful she'd called her a man. She had difficulty knowing how to label some people, but knew the label wasn't so important as simply accepting them as human beings. But when it came to humans…

"Don't tell her I said that," she said, opening the box. "I feel terrible."

"You shouldn't. It's natural to not understand people who aren't like you."

"You mean like understanding you?"

"I think we get along pretty well, even for our differences."

They clicked forks and both dug in to the steaming crepes. "We do indeed. But tell me this. Is Kristine…paranormal?"

"Nope, as human as you are. Paranormals live in the city, but we're not everywhere. At least, not we wolves. Most of us tend toward the country."

"Then why do you live in the city?"

"It's the furthest thing from what I had, and…" He frowned.

Indi suspected some bad memories were struggling in his brain.

"It works for me right now."

"It's good to be close to all the action, I guess. How did it go last night?"

"Only one collector came through. Stabbed it right through the heart. Er, if they have hearts. Not sure about that one. But the thing disappeared in a silent scream and a cloud of sparkling dust."

"Can they speak? Maybe you could capture one and question it?"

"I've considered that. But I don't think they can speak or make vocal utterances. They do have a mouth. I've seen the rows of teeth and felt them on my skin, but still haven't heard a peep from them."

"Curious. But your half brother is looking into finding who controls them? That must be the person who wants the babies. It's so strange."

"Strange is normal in Faery. So are malevolence, violence and tricksters. Faery is not a place for the weak. My faery father has asked me to go there and—"

Indi paused with a forkload of crepe before her mouth, waiting for him to elaborate, but Ry instead set down his fork and opened the door. "Kristine, would you mind bringing in something for us to drink?"

"Sure, boss, be right in."

Indi waited silently for the transaction to occur. Kristine winked at her when she handed Ry two bottles of water, then closed the door behind her.

He sat down again and handed her a bottle, then resumed eating.

"Uh…" She twisted off the bottle cap. "And?"

"And?" he asked, looking to her with question.

"You were saying something about your father wanting you to go to Faery."

Ry sighed. She was learning that he did that a lot, usually when he didn't want to tell her something. What more could the man possibly have to tell that could shock her?

"That slipped out. I don't talk about my father much. I don't like to."

"Fair enough. But Faery is out for you?"

"Definitely. It's not my home." He tilted back half the bottle of water. "It was nice of you to bring lunch. And I'm sorry because I looked for the healer last night, to ask her about how you've been feeling, and wasn't able to find her. Tonight, I promise I will camp out on her doorstep until she talks to me. You feel any better today?"

"In general, I feel fine. No longer exhausted. But I keep experiencing weird twinges of pain right between my shoulder blades and lower. It has to be a pulled muscle."

"Probably. But I'll ask. If she'll talk to me."

"What does that mean?"

"Hestia and I had some issues a few years back. She doesn't like me very much."

"But she was nice enough to save a dying human woman when you asked. Unless." Indi looked to him. "Were you two dating?"

"What? No. Maybe. No. It was just…" He dropped his fork onto the foam box and then wobbled his hand before him. "A few nights. She was in love with the idea of making it something more. I was not."

"And I take it she never got over it?"

Ry shrugged. "Apparently not. You women are a tough bunch to figure out most of the time."

"It is in our nature to be contrary. But if she doesn't like you, maybe she did something to me?"

"I can't imagine she would be so vindictive. She has no reason to harm you. And like you said, it's probably pulled muscles. How often do you do something so physical as dodging collectors?"

"Never. But I am a swimmer. I'm not out of shape."

"You don't have to tell me that. I've seen your shape. It's sexy."

He kissed her cheek, and warmth flushed Indi's cheeks. "You can take a gander at my shape any time you like. As for the aches and pains, they'll go away." She stood and looked for a wastebasket to toss her box in.

"You can leave the garbage and Kristine will take care of it," he offered. "You going to eat that salad?"

"No, you can have it." She sat on the comfy office chair behind his desk. The far wall was all windows, and boasted a view of the Seine, and just down the river loomed the Notre Dame Cathedral. "This is a small office. You certainly don't go in for bold and flashy, do you?"

"Why spend the money I hate on stupid things?"

"You hate your money?"

He tilted his head back against the wall and set the salad aside. "More delving questions from the sexy swimmer in the cat ears."

"I am sexy." She tapped the black velvet ears she wore today; they went with the black velvet trim on her pink sundress. "And the ears are my thing."

"They are. I like them."

"So, the money," she prompted, knowing she was pushing it with her nosy questions.

Ry leaned forward to prop his elbows on his knees and clasped his hands between them. "My faery father wants me to move to Faery. I refuse. I like the mortal realm. It's all I've ever known. He tried to bribe me right after I left the pack. I didn't know at the time, when he plucked a couple leaves off a maple tree and handed them to me, that would change my life forever."

"Leaves?"

"Faeries can enchant things. They've a talent manipulating human objects. Those leaves turned to thousand-dollar bills in my hand. My first compulsion was to toss them, but I'm not stupid. And I wasn't bringing in much cash at the time, being on my own and trying to make a living. So I invested the cash. Within months it grew to millions. Billions within a few years."

"How is that possible?"

"It's the enchantment. The damn investment keeps multiplying. And I can't give it away fast enough."

"Wow. I wish I had your problems."

"It's not money I want. It came from a person from whom I don't care to take charity. So I give it all away as fast as I can."

"Doesn't it ever change back to leaves?"

"It would if my father died. Then all his magic would die with him. And he's been around for more than many centuries. Not sure about faery years. He's old, but I don't expect him to start pushing daisies anytime soon, despite his suggestions otherwise. If you ask him, he's on his last leg. I doubt that very much. He's a pompous bit of wing and sparkle."

"You and your father don't get along. Can I ask why?"

"Not today."

She sighed and caught her chin in her hand. "Fine. I can deal. I'm thinking learning about the paranormal should be taken in small chunks and not tossed at me all at once."

"I imagine it would be like an alien learning about earth. There's so much to learn, Indi. Don't worry about it. I'm just glad you can accept."

"Like I said. Show me proof." She leaned her elbows onto the desk, but before her a stack of papers lured her eye. It was the gold engraving and soft violet paper that caught her attention. She tilted her head to read it. "You're going to the Hermès ball in two nights?"

"No. I hate those things."

"I thought you said you go to them to schmooze."

"I do, but the photographers…and with the midnight slaying calls. I try to avoid them as much as possible."

"I get that, but this one's for raising awareness for endangered species. Like wolves?" She winked at him, feeling the giddy stir that always accompanied the planning and anticipation for a fancy event. "There's got to be some of your people at an event like that. Why don't you go? The charity seems like something that would be right up your alley."

"It is. And I should learn more..." With a sigh, he offered, "I don't have a date."

She cast him a gaping stinky-eye look.

Ry laughed. "But it's in two nights."

"You think I can't put together a ball gown and makeup in forty-eight hours? Ry, my natural habitat is a ballroom. I breathe tulle and eat rhinestones like candy. Oh, please, take me with you. I know we've only started this thing between the two of us, but—"

"But what?" His eyes glinted with a tease that reminded her of their dip in the pool. And then afterward, sprawled on the chaise longue. Had it not meant as much to him as it had to her?

"Well," she began cautiously, "if you took me along, you wouldn't have to introduce me as your girlfriend."

"What would you be? My female friend? The chick who begged to come along?"

She nodded eagerly, knowing she seemed desperate, but also sensing he was stringing her along. They *were* dating.

Ry flipped his hair over a shoulder and winked at her. "Your natural habitat, eh?"

"I've been gliding across a ballroom floor since I was a little girl."

"That's right. It's either the big fancy or nothing at all for you. And I've seen you in both scenarios. Know which one I like best?"

"You can have both options because I love nothing better than, after the big fancy, to strip it all away."

"You don't need to tempt me with such promises. You had me at those big pleading blue eyes. All right, then. It's a date."

"Yes!" She clapped her hands in glee.

Ry narrowed his gaze on her. "Why do I suspect you're less excited about going with me and more excited about the fancy dress-up?"

"Because it's true! I love to dress up and be a princess." She spun around the side of the desk and approached him.

"A Princess Pussycat. Promise you'll wear the kitty ears?"

Bending over him, Indi leaned in and whispered in his ear, "If you promise to make me purr after we've danced all night."

"Oh, that I can do." Tapping his forefinger on her lips, he added, "But we'll have to pull a Cinderella."

"What do you mean?"

"Me and my midnight FaeryTown date."

"Oh, right. But after Batman fights the bad guys he goes home to someone, right?"

"I believe that's Alfred."

"Then I'll be your Alfred tomorrow after the ball."

"I'd much prefer Catwoman purring in my bed, waiting for my return."

"Meow."

Indi straddled his legs and kissed him, running her fingers through his loose hair and snuggling her breasts against his chest. He hugged her closer and deepened the kiss until all she knew was the taste and fire of him coiling within her.

Had she in mind to give up on rich, self-possessed men? She had. And she had done so. Ry was the furthest thing from self-possessed. And she felt his wide and giving heart every time she was near him.

"Yay! It's a black-and-white ball. I have the perfect dress. And the shoes. Oh, wait. I think that pair is broken. I have to go home and figure this out."

"You do that. I've a lot of phone calls to make this afternoon. It might be a long day that stretches into tomorrow."

"I'm good. Much as I'd love to spend more time with you, I have a ball gown to create."

"Can we meet up on the night of the event? What time does the ball start?"

"Seven. But one must never arrive exactly at the starting time. Fashionably late is de rigueur."

"Then I'll pick you up at seven."

The next night

"Three down…" Ry checked his watch. "In four minutes, seventeen seconds. A new time."

He sheathed his sword behind his back and jumped over the pile of dissipated collectors. The ash had fallen like soot and sparkled. He had the stuff in his hair and on his shoulders and arms.

Shaking briskly, he got rid of most of what had fallen on him.

He eyed the direction in which the healer lived. Hestia would talk to him. If he approached her with his heart in his hands. Women. That one, in particular, knew how to hold a grudge. He'd not told Indi all the sordid details. That he and Never had been on a binge one evening right here in FaeryTown and Ry had tried a drink called Devil's Spit. He'd never been so wasted in his life. Or horny.

He'd laid eyes on Hestia and sweet-talked her right into her bed. For three days straight. That was how long it had taken for the loopy space-out effects of that bizarre drink to wear off. He'd woken on the fourth morning, Hestia gazing at him adoringly and calling him her one true love.

And Ry had run from that bed as quickly as possible. He'd not been in a place for a true love, or even a girl-friend. But that hadn't kept him from returning to her for healing a time or two. He'd not noticed her adoring looks or possessive hand clasps until that third time, when he crawled to her doorstep after a violent fight with another lone wolf who had been attempting to claim FaeryTown as his own—it belonged to no wolf—and had left him with a blade stuck through his lung. Hestia had given him her vita that night, and had nearly died in the process. She'd saved him.

But that still hadn't made him want to call her his girl-friend. She had seen it another way, and had raged at him, calling him a tease and saying that he had been stringing her along.

"Women," he muttered.

Now as he reluctantly walked toward Hestia's place, Never called out to him from the open door of a faery club that vibrated with weird harp and electronic tones. Ry nodded acknowledgment but kept on walking. Never would follow.

And he did. He might be funny-looking, but the guy was predictable.

"How's tricks?" Ry asked as he slowed his strides and they wandered side by side. A blue-skinned faery flut-tered past them wearing a sandwich board that advertised "Bliss'shrooms direct from Faery." The contraband mush-rooms were probably fake, but the Sidhe Cortege made a pretty penny extorting the weak. "You do any sleuthing?"

"I did," Never said. "Riske wants to talk to you."

"Is that so?" He'd just been thinking of the Sidhe Cortege.

Riske was the ringleader of the Mafia-like organization that worked the mortal realm. "Tell him to come talk to me. My office is in the fourth."

"You know he's le Grande Sidhe, right? Big man on campus. The grand poohbah."

"I thought he was the leader of the Sidhe Cortege."

"Exactly. I've worked a few jobs for him. Thug stuff."

Ry cast a gaze down his half brother's lean form. Faeries were strong as fuck. He certainly wouldn't stand against Never's strength. Not for long. As well, he was an excellent marksman with any weapon he could get his hands on.

"He's fair, but brutal," Never continued. "Me asking him questions for you? That put up his hackles."

"Does he know who is behind sending the collectors to this realm?"

"He wouldn't say. Wants to discuss it with you face-to-face."

"Then I guess I'll have a talk with the big faery on campus. I got a gig tomorrow night, though. When does he want to do it?"

"Tomorrow night."

Ry's smirked. Wasn't that always the way it went? "I'll be in FaeryTown at midnight again," he said. "I can talk with him after that."

"I'll let him know. And, uh, no bringing along any humans."

"Wouldn't dream of it. You see Hestia anywhere?"

"I think she's down at the jazz club. You don't want to go in there tonight."

"And why is that?"

"Her girlfriend is hanging all over her. She's a witch."

An involuntary shiver skittered down Ry's spine. "Witches creep me out."

"That they do. You want to head to that new nightclub down the street? I'll match you in dust shots."

His brother had a hunger for faery ichor, as opposed to blood, and he drank it like water. Indi had texted him a "good night" earlier as she'd made it an early evening after a long day of work.

"Sounds like a plan." Ry would order the dust-free vodka shots.

Chapter 10

Indi answered her ringing phone. Her heart dropped when she saw it was a call from Ry. It was six thirty and she was dressed up and ready for the ball—

She wouldn't think the worst. That way lay madness. "Hey, Ry. What's up?"

"I'm going to have to meet you at the ball. Kristine has an emergency and she needs me to pick her up. I'm headed toward the eleventh right now."

The ball was at the Grand Palais in the eighth. If he had to pick up his secretary, he'd never make it to her place by seven.

"I see." Indi clutched the back of the chair. Tears bubbled at the corners of her eyes. This could not happen a second time in such close proximity to the previous disastrous jilting. It. Could. Not.

"Indi, you there?"

She nodded.

"Listen, I'm not ditching you tonight. Promise. I would never do that. And I feel terrible that I can't pick you up, so I've sent a limo for you. It's on the way right now. If I could change things, I would, but Kristine…"

"Of course. She's like your sister. You sure things will work out? If you don't think you can make it…"

"I'll be there. I've got the tux on and I intend to dance with you all night under that amazing glass ceiling at the palace. Now, don't let those tears fall."

She quickly swiped at a tear that loosened from the corner of her eye.

"I know this is freaky news for you," he said. "I'm not that insensitive. I'm shooting for getting to the palace around seven-thirty. Will you wait for me on the *escalier d'honneur* leading into the ballroom?"

She nodded again.

"You're going to have to verbalize, Indi."

"Sorry. I… Sure." Her hand shook as she smoothed it down the gown's sleek black taffeta bodice. "I'll be there."

"And so will I. Promise. Now go check for the limo. It's probably already arrived."

She glanced out the front window. Sure enough, a black limo rolled up to the curb.

Again, Indi nodded. Why was she finding it so hard to speak? It wasn't as if Ry was going to pull a Todd on her.

Maybe. How well did she really know the guy?

"Ah, hell, maybe I can find someone else to drive Kristine."

"No!" Indi blurted, finding her courage. "It's fine, Ry. And if something happens that keeps you from attending the ball—"

"Nothing will. Swear to it. See you in a bit. Okay?"

"Yes. See you there."

She clicked off and almost dropped the phone her hands

shook so much. Pressing a palm to her heart, she leaned over and breathed deeply.

It couldn't happen to her again. It simply must not.

Ry glanced over at Kristine, who sat on the passenger seat. Head bowed and mascara streaked, she gazed out the window.

A couple of assholes had decided to tease the chick who wasn't their idea of what a woman should be. They'd pushed her around on the Métro and she'd rushed out of the subway car but had caught her elbow in the automatic doors. A bruise had darkened her skin.

This had happened once before, and she'd told him about it after the fact. He'd made her promise, if it ever happened again, to call him immediately. It had only taken him fifteen minutes to get to the subway stop. Good thing he'd been ready to go, all dressed up.

He turned the car down Kristine's street in the fifth arrondissement. She lived in a cozy top-floor flat owned by an elderly couple who were always inviting her to join them for breakfast. Ry was glad she lived in a good, safe neighborhood. But assholes would never go away. And she was, to most, different. He could relate to her in a vague way. Both of them appeared to be something they were not. But he'd never try to compare himself to her, and her troubles.

He pulled the Alfa to a stop and leaned across the shift to stroke a finger along her cheek. She offered him a weak smile. "They were idiots. You know that, right?"

"I do know that. I feel more terrible that you were on your way to pick up your girl. I forgot all about the ball. I never would have called—"

"I'm glad you called. I'm always here for you, Kristine. Always."

"You're my guy, Ry. The big brother I never had."

"You know it."

"You'd better get going."

He grabbed her by the wrist to stop her quick escape. "Not until I know you're not going to head up there and wolf down that hidden supply of vanilla mochi I know you keep in the freezer."

She laughed at that one. "You know me too well. And I am so lucky to have a friend like you, Ryland James. I hope this new girl realizes that, too."

"We're not serious. Just having some fun."

"You'd better adjust your fun meter. I saw the way she looked at you. That woman is head over heels for the wolf in the billionaire's clothing."

"I don't think she's attracted to my money. She's a trust-fund baby. Has her own fortune."

"Good to know. And that does explain her excellent taste in footwear. Those togs she had on the other day were not cheap. Let me go. I don't want you to stand her up."

"I'll get there in time. I've got a good fifteen minutes yet. Nothing will keep me from showing up to dance with the Princess Pussycat."

"You know that sounds like a drag-queen name."

"It does?"

Kristine shook her head. "Just teasing." She leaned in and kissed his cheek. "Love you, *cher*."

"Love you back. No mochi!"

"Just one?"

He tilted a concerned look at her.

"Oh, you're right. A girl can't eat just one. I'll watch reruns of *Braquo* instead. You know I love to moon over Jean-Hugues Anglade."

"That I do. See you at the office, Kristine."

Ry waited until she was inside the building foyer before pulling away. The ball was on the right bank just off the

Champs-Élysées. He could get there in twenty minutes if the traffic cooperated.

He turned the corner. Behind him, a work truck screeched its brakes as it turned and pulled up close enough to touch bumpers. Ahead, flashing red lights alerted him there had been an accident. Three cars before him were all stopped. He scanned for a way out, but he was in the middle of a block.

"Shit."

Laying on the horn wasn't going to help the situation, but he did it anyway. The woman in the car ahead of him flipped him off. And behind him the trucker's horn blasted the neighborhood.

Pulling out and making a sharp turn—he only had to back up and forward once with the sleek sports car—Ry drove in the opposite lane about four car lengths before the police vehicle pulled out from the right and flashed its lights at him.

Shaking his head, Ry shifted into Park and decided he'd deserved that one. The police officer approached and took down his name and information from his license, then scanned inside the car.

"Monsieur, I'll ask you to please step out of the vehicle."

About to protest, and unsure why such a request had been issued, Ry figured it best to comply. If only to move things along. He got out, hands held up before him. The officer then scanned inside his car again.

"Is there a problem, Officer?"

"Yes, Monsieur James, there is. Can you tell me the reason for the weapon you have hanging on the back interior wall of your vehicle?"

Ah, hell. He'd forgotten the three-foot-long battle sword he used to slay collectors from Faery come to steal human babies. He'd put hooks on the back wall to keep it close and for easy access. Once again, he wished he had the powers of persuasion that vampires possessed. They could whisper or touch humans and make them forget their names, let alone seeing a deadly weapon in the back seat of an Alfa Romeo.

And in his next thought, he wondered what Batman would do in a situation like this one.

Chapter 11

"Do not hyperventilate," Indi whispered as she stood at the top of the stairs looking down over the bustling ballroom. Hundreds of couples dressed in black and white and dazzling with diamonds, silver, gold and colored gemstones socialized and took selfies and danced to the orchestra's invitation. It was eight thirty. Ry had not shown.

"He promised he'd be here. He will be here."

Or maybe not, the scared, traumatized part of her whispered back.

Maybe it was time she took a break from men altogether. Focused on her business. Ball gowns and tiaras? Only on purchase orders and invoices from now on.

She was wearing the black blingy cat ears tonight. They matched her gown. Janet had requested a selfie STAT in her text a few minutes ago, but Indi had been too disheartened to reply. She wouldn't get to swish around on the dance floor in this gorgeous gown because…

Clutching her skirts, she closed her eyes as a familiar waltz began. She loved to waltz. Her daddy had taught her when she was able to stand on his toes and he'd swirl her about the dance floor like a Beauty to his kind and loving Beast.

"The beast isn't going to arrive tonight," she whispered.

Catching a sigh at the back of her throat, Indi forced a smile to a passing couple, who nodded acknowledgment to her.

Below the three massive crystal chandeliers suspended from the steel beams that arched and created the glass ceiling, the party attendees spun and swirled and laughed and chattered. Unaware that Indi's heart was breaking anew.

She considered looking for the champagne, but nixed that idea. Tonight would not be another replay of the previous Humiliating Experience. If Ry didn't show, she'd lift her head and walk out with shoulders thrust back. Her entire business was based on a woman's confidence and knowing herself. She was a goddess. And goddesses could handle shit, like men who had no idea how important it was to stand by their word.

"Exactly," she muttered.

Whatever trouble Kristine had been in? She hoped it was worth it.

In her next thought, Indi chastised herself for thinking such a thing. Ry would never have jilted her without good reason. As little as she yet knew him, the things she had learned about him proved he was an honorable man. Tonight had simply been Kristine's turn to receive his honor.

Glancing up through the glass ceiling high above, she wished it was darker. Easier to make a quick exit that way, and not be seen by too many.

Maybe it was time to design a sort of breakup survival kit for her website? No. That would defeat the purpose of her brand—imparting strength and confidence to her customers.

Lifting her shoulders and drawing in a breath through her nose, Indi nodded. She was fine. She would not let this tiny moment in her life affect her any more than it should. She'd turn and walk out, go home and strip off her fabulous dress, then shed a few tears. But ultimately, she'd get over it. As quickly as she'd gotten over Todd.

Men could be so thoughtless and self-involved. Why had she allowed herself to pick up with another man so soon after the last? It was her fault she was standing alone right now.

But she didn't want to berate herself. It wasn't her fault. She could date whom she wished, and whenever she wished. And she could have fun with a man for a fling, or longer. She'd find "the one" someday. Probably a werewolf wasn't her best match anyway.

It sounded good when she thought it in her head, but Indi's heart was squeezing. She really liked Ry. And…

Just and.

Indi spun to leave and she walked right into Ry's arms. He hugged her, enveloping her in a sudden and delicious warmth. He smelled like wild and nature and a hint of peppermint. The hard pillar of his body overwhelmed and then offered solace.

Nuzzling his nose aside her ear, he said, "I'm sorry. I had an unavoidable delay."

She hugged him tightly, squeezing her eyelids and knowing a tear ran down her cheek. Tonight she'd used the waterproof mascara. Live and learn.

"Can you forgive me?" he asked, and pulled away to search her face.

She quickly swiped at the tear. "Of course. Nothing's wrong. It's all good."

"No, it's not. I know exactly what you were thinking, standing here all alone. It happened again. Another man treated you like crap."

She shrugged and wasn't able to look him in the eye. He'd guessed it right on the mark.

"It kills me that you had to go there." He stroked his fingers down the curl hugging the side of her head, then tapped her cat ears. "All I can do is try to make the rest of the night as good as it can be."

"It's already improved one hundred percent." And her heart jumped with glee. She'd judged him harshly. He was a man of his word. "You really work the tuxedo. Damn, you are so fine."

"Yeah?" He swept his loose hair over a shoulder. "Well, look at you, Princess Pussycat. You just happen to have that gown hanging in your closet?"

She smoothed her palms over the black taffeta skirt. "Believe it or not, yes. I've not worn it until now. And see." She lifted the skirt a little to reveal the white under-skirt she added.

"That's like the stuff you wore the night I saw you in FaeryTown."

"Tulle. It's princess fabric all the way."

"I do know the fashion was most important to you to-night. But…" He eyed her sweetly, a grin curling his mouth.

"But what?" Indi touched the cat ears. "Is my tiara on crooked?"

"Nope. You're missing something." He reached into his inner suit pocket and pulled out a folded piece of blue tissue paper. "It's nothing fancy. But when I passed it in a store window yesterday, it screamed Indigo DuCharme."

"You got me a gift? I love presents." Her heartbeat jittered for a new and wondrous reason. She took the paper and carefully unfolded it. Inside coiled a delicate silver chain, and the pendant was the tiniest silver paw print. "Oh, my God, this is perfect."

"A little kitty paw," Ry said.

"Oh? Sure. But I was thinking it was a wolf paw. I want it to be a wolf paw, okay?"

"I think a wolf's paw would be bigger—" She met his gaze and his mouth softened. "A wolf's paw it is. Let me help you with it. I practiced because those things are so delicate, but the screw clasp is easier for me."

He took the necklace and when his hand brushed her neck, Indi shivered. A good, so-happy-he-made-it shiver. She should never have doubted him. But she hadn't known him long, and… Enough of that. The man was here. And he'd been thinking of her so much that he'd brought her a gift. The night could not get any better.

But she was open to letting it become the best. It was time to get her dance on.

Ry traced the silver chain around to the front and base of her neck, where the paw rested. "My princess," he said.

He bowed to kiss her, and even though partiers wandered near them, Indi suddenly felt as if they were the only two in the room. The vast airy ballroom suddenly quieted so she could hear her heartbeats mingle with Ry's. And the warm, masculine scent of him permeated her pores, inviting her to tug him closer and deepen the kiss.

Every part of her sparkled with a giddy thrill. She stood up on her Jimmy Choo tiptoes, clasping his lapels. He smelled like earth and fresh grass, with a hint of wild that wrapped about her senses.

"You like to dance?" he asked.

"I do. The waltz is my favorite."

"Mine, too. Shall we?"

He offered her his hooked arm and Indi threaded her arm through it. She had attended many an event and ball, and often on the arm of her date or a handsome friend, but this was the first time one had ever been so gentlemanly. Or had given her a gift.

They descended the half-curved stairs to the main floor. The nervous anticipation over wondering if she had been dumped fled. She walked to the dance floor alongside the sexiest guy in the room. Ry bowed grandly to her, and offered his hand, then whisked her into the music. They danced three waltzes in a row.

Ry was a remarkable dancer, and she was more than impressed that his talents matched hers. And she claimed a good mastery of the dance. His hand held out hers as he led her around the floor, while his other hand hugged her bare back. The back of her dress was cut low to her waist. It offered a connection of skin against skin that curled a giddy warmth over her entire body and tightened her nipples. The two of them so close amongst so many. It felt surreal. Truly, like a Disney scene of the prince and princess dancing. But neither was royalty, and that suited Indi fine. Ry was hers and she was most definitely his.

Six dances later, the orchestra segued into a quickstep. Ry suggested they find refreshment because he never could grasp the syncopations required for the dance. That worked for Indi. Her skirts impeded any frantic steps and she needed a break from the crowded dance floor.

They avoided the wine and champagne and instead tried the craft beer offered by a local brewery. But only a few sips. Because the next dance was a tango, and while Indi was only a little familiar with the steps, it didn't matter. Standing in Ry's arms, following his moves, she felt like the luckiest woman alive. And she noticed the stares from the other women. Or rather, eyeballs focused like lasers on Ry. The man did work the tuxedo. But it might also have been that he was sex on a stick, penguin suit or not.

And she had seen him sans clothes. Pity, all the other women would never have that opportunity. Not while Indi had him in her arms.

At the end of the tango, they lingered in each other's embrace at the edge of the dance floor under subdued lighting.

Ry kissed her and stroked a strand of loose hair over her ear. "You sparkle."

"It's glitter dust. A standard. One must never pass up the chance to sparkle, be it man-made or—" she let her gaze fall to his crotch "—faery-made."

"Oh, I've got some sparkle for you, Princess." He tugged her away from the lights and into a private area against the wall.

"Do you have to leave soon?" she asked.

He checked his watch. "It's only ten thirty. Still got a while before duty calls. Fortunately, the police officer let me keep my sword."

"The police officer?"

"I did say I had good reason for being late." He kissed her again. "But enough about me. I want this whole night to be Indi, Indi and even more Indi. You smell so good. What is that scent? It's almost like candy."

"It's my skin cream, scented with almonds and pistachios."

"Delicious. Food does tend to appeal to we men." He nuzzled his nose into her hair. "I'd like to eat you right here and now."

Now that was a suggestion that she could get behind. Or under. Or however he would like her positioned.

"Remember what I said about getting naked after the ball?" she said.

"Haven't forgotten. As pretty as this dress is, I want to slide it off you and drop it to the floor. Then…" He kissed her earlobe. "I'm going to taste every inch of your delicious skin. Slowly. Deeply."

Indi moaned wantonly. "You are making it difficult to want to head back to the dance floor."

"We can leave early? Stop by your house before I need to take up the sword?"

As much as that suggestion appealed... "No, I love to dance, and you're the first man since my father who actually knows how to dance with me."

She winced at the sudden pain in her back. She'd forgotten about that annoying pain because it hadn't reared up since early this morning when she took a quick dip in the pool.

"Still not feeling one hundred percent?" he asked.

She gave him the standard nod/shrug because she didn't want to complain tonight. "Let's extend this break," she said. "Give me ten minutes and then I'll be ready for another waltz, or maybe even a fox-trot."

"I love the fox-trot. It's fast. Think you can keep up?"

"Just watch me."

"Ryland!"

Ry turned to seek out the man who called to him and nodded. To her, he said, "One of my clients. I fund his charity for rehousing The Wicked, who come here from Faery. He's one himself."

"I'm going to need all the details on that interesting paranormal stuff later. Why don't you say hello to him?" she said. "I'm going to slip out back and wander through the herb gardens. Breathe in some fresh air. Meet me out there?"

"The guy can talk up a storm."

"That's okay. I'm not going anywhere. Come find me when you can."

"Thank you. I'll make it quick." He kissed her cheek and then turned to shake hands with the man.

The Wicked? She couldn't wait to learn about that, or them, or whatever it meant.

Indi followed the hallway out to the gardens. Not many were out in the subtly lit formal gardens. The back courtyard was narrow but long, and a thick line of hedges butted up against the very end and blocked the view of the Seine. The sounds of music from inside segued into the background as Indi inhaled the lush scents and wandered from flower to flower. As she strolled the crushed shell walk, she let her fingers glide across the glossy green leaves of a thigh-high boxwood shrubbery. Everything smelled green and open. And here, the mint and thyme bloomed. The heady scents lured her as if Chanel perfume.

Leaning over, she inhaled the lush sweetness. What had begun as a harrowing will-he-show-or-won't-he-show? was turning out to be the best night of her life. The man could dance! And he had been so apologetic. Easy to forgive him when he was so handsome. And sexy. And smelled like a dream she wanted to linger with between the sheets. Bring on the sparkle! And, well—what *was* wrong with him?

"Not a thing," she whispered, and a smile curled her lips.

The police officer had let him keep his sword? She would need to learn more about that later, as well. But whatever had delayed Ry from getting here on time didn't matter now. He had kept his promise. And she was looking forward to later, when the man intended to taste every inch of her skin. She wished he didn't have to leave her to go slay a couple bad faeries. She wanted him with her all might. But if her superhero had a calling, far be it from her to keep him from that. She would have him later. In his bed. All night long.

"Oh!" The pain at her back stabbed mercilessly.

Indi looked about to see if anyone had remarked her sudden cry. Stumbling forward, she approached the back of the garden, where the lighting was subdued and segued into shadows.

Another sharp pain caused her to misstep on her five-inch heels. Arm thrust out to seek an anchor, Indi sought a bench to sit down. The pain grew fierce. Unrelenting.

"What the hell is wrong with me?"

Ry told Nestor Arch about the international wolf project. Nestor possessed an interest in all paranormal charities—as did Ry. He texted a note to Kristine to arrange to have him speak with Pilot Severo. With more financial backers the project would have an excellent chance at getting off the ground. Checking his watch, he realized he'd been chatting for fifteen minutes. Informing Nestor he had a date he didn't want to leave alone for too long, Ry turned to search for Indi.

His phone rang, and just when he thought to ignore it, some intuition made him tug it out and check the screen. "Princess, what's up?"

"Ry…" She gasped and moaned. "Oh, Ry, hurry. Something's happened."

"Indi, where are you?" He scanned the ballroom floor. All the women were dressed in black and white. It was difficult to home in on her.

"I'm out in the garden. Oh! I don't know what it is. It's… Oh, please come out here. I'm at the back near the hedges, where it's dark. Hurry!"

Dashing toward the hallway that led outdoors, Ry suddenly checked his pace. He didn't want to draw attention. He filed down the hallway and into the garden. His shoes crushed the shell walk and he scanned the low-lit area. Half a dozen couples chatted and sipped champagne.

He lifted his head and sniffed the air. Beyond an intoxicating layer of flowers, he could scent almonds and pistachios. Indi must have stood right here. Following the lingering scent trail, he walked to the back of the garden. A stone bench was placed before a high shrub, and beside that a lonely marble angel bowed her head.

"Indi?" he whispered.

"Back here!"

Back here was… Was she on the other side of the shrubbery?

He noticed a narrow part in the shrubs and slipped through. The street paralleling the Seine flashed with passing headlights, but didn't illuminate this part of the garden. Indi's dark dress camouflaged her body, but the glint from the rhinestones in the cat ears helped him to find her. She was bent over, hand pressed to a tree trunk.

He rushed over and touched her shoulder, leaned down to study her face.

"Something's wrong," she said. "It hurt so bad."

"Your back?" He was about to smooth a palm down her back; the dress was cut low and had allowed him to caress her bare skin as they'd danced, but she stood abruptly. "What is it? Indi?"

"I don't know. I think…something came out of my back."

"What?"

"Will you take a look? It hurt like someone slashed a knife down my spine and then I could feel something… move. Oh, Ry. This is freaking me out."

"Turn around." He glanced over his shoulder, confirming they were alone and no curious bystanders were in the vicinity. Any passing cars would not make them out against the dark shrubs.

Indi turned and the glint from a passing headlight beamed through the tree canopy and caught on the things on her back. Things that had not been there earlier. What the hell? Really? Ry gaped as he looked over her skin and took it all in.

"Ry, what is it? Maybe I scratched myself when I was pushing through the shrubbery. The pain came on so suddenly I wanted to hide in case— I don't know. It's not painful anymore. Ry?"

He pressed a palm to her back but didn't touch the appendages that were so small yet that was probably because they were new and... He didn't have words. How could something like this have occurred?

"Ry, you're freaking me out. What's wrong? What do I have on my back?"

"Wings," he muttered simply. "You've sprouted wings, Indi."

Chapter 12

She couldn't have heard him correctly.

"What are you talking about?" Indi shoved at Ry when he attempted to pull her into his arms. She stumbled backward, but he caught her by the wrist so she wouldn't topple into the shrubs.

Laughter echoed out from the garden on the other side of the hedgerow, but she was feeling no mirth now. "Is that some kind of joke?"

"Princess, you've sprouted wings. I'm telling you the truth." And when she began to protest, he shoved a hand in his suit pocket and pulled out his phone. "I'll show you."

Ry swung around behind her and snapped a shot of her back. "There's poor lighting out here, but with the flash… you can plainly see."

He handed her the phone and she almost dropped it when she realized what she was looking at. It was a dark shot, but the flash lit up the center of her back. And there, looking like crisply unfolded insect appendages, were two small iridescent wings. Each about the size of her hand.

She shoved the phone at him. Grasping frantically for her back, she couldn't reach up high enough to feel them. "What is going on?"

"I don't know. This is..."

"It was that stupid healer you took me to. She did something to me!"

He scratched his jaw. "Maybe..."

"Ry! Really? Your frustrated ex-lover put some kind of weird curse on me?"

"She's not my— I'm sorry, Indi. I don't know what Hestia did to you, but I doubt she could do something like this. I am at a loss. I've never seen anything like this before."

"But you know faeries and all that stuff. Does it look like faery wings to you?"

"They come in all sizes, colors and shapes. But I don't know what else it could be. Can I... I want to touch them. Make sure they're—"

"Real? Oh, Ry, this is crazy!"

"Please, Indi, I'll be careful. Can I do that?"

Releasing a heavy sigh, her shoulders dropping, Indi nodded. Would she ever again attend a ball and *not* have it end disastrously? Who grew wings? This was beyond crazy. Yet she'd been feeling pains in her back since the night she was scratched by the collector creature.

"What if I turn into one of those black sparkly things?" She pressed a palm over her thundering heartbeats. "Oh, my god, this is so not a good night. And I was thinking it was the best night ever."

"The best night? It is, Indi. I mean..." Ry winced. "I got to spend all this time dancing with you and holding you in my arms. It's been so awesome."

"It has been. Truly, the best night. But, Ry..." She

sniffed back a burgeoning tear. "Oh, touch them, then. Tell me they're not real."

He kissed her on the crown of the head, then walked around behind her again. "I'm just going to touch them gently…"

Indi shivered as she suddenly felt a warmth at the junction where the wings clung to her back. It was an intensely visceral touch that seemed to vibrate throughout her system.

"Does that hurt?" Ry asked.

She shook her head. "No. I feel your touch. Intensely. Like you might have touched my hand. That means… Oh, my God, they're real?"

"They seem to be growing out from your back. I haven't studied faery wings up close before…"

He swung around in front of her and pulled her against his chest. The warmth of him was ridiculous. His overwhelming strength and masculinity gave her some solace. She felt safe in his arms. But safe from what?

"Am I turning into a faery?" she whispered.

"I'm sorry, Indi, I don't have answers. But we'll get some. It's…" He checked his watch. "Eleven thirty."

"You've got to get to FaeryTown. And I want to go home and cry."

"I won't have time to bring you home. And I don't want to put you in a cab. I'm bringing you along with me. After the collectors have been dealt with we'll find the healer and ask her about this. Is that all right with you?"

She nodded against his chest. "I do want you to stay with me. I don't want to be alone."

When he stepped away and shrugged off his suit coat, she couldn't prevent a few teardrops. Ry wrapped his coat about her shoulders, to hide the wings, most likely. She tugged it close over her chest and couldn't manage to lift her head to look at him.

"You go ahead and cry," he said. "It's weird. And strange. But I'm here for you. Do you understand that?"

She nodded again and sniffed back the tears. The last thing she wanted was for anyone inside to see her with mascara running down her cheeks. Been there, done that. Had wings been the result of that crazy night after the last charity ball?

"We can get to the valet stand from the garden," Ry said. "We don't have to go back inside. Come on, Princess Pussycat."

Ry parked the Alfa in his usual spot half a block away from where FaeryTown began, and reached behind the seats for the battle sword. The cop had believed his story about donating it to a charity action. Good going with the fast thinking.

But he didn't grasp it, because instead his hand went to Indi's bowed head. A soft tendril of her hair spilled over his wrist. She sat sideways on the passenger seat, facing him, her knees pulled up and an arm wrapped across her legs. Volumes of black taffeta spilled to the floor in a lush puddle. She still wore his suit coat. She'd tugged off the cat ears and there was a tear streak through her blush on the one cheek.

"You going to be okay?"

She shrugged.

"Stupid question. I'll make this fast, then come back for you and we'll go look for the healer. Okay?"

She nodded.

"Stay in the car. I don't want you to get—"

"I got it," she snapped. "If you think I'm eager to go anywhere near that wacky faery stuff, you're mistaken.

I'll be here. Trying to figure this out. Go kill some nasty monsters, then hurry back to me. Please?"

"This will be the fastest the Sidhe Slayer has ever laid his victims to ash. Promise." He kissed the crown of her head, then grabbed the sword and marched down the street.

He hated leaving Indi alone and vulnerable. Not because he expected anyone to wander by and give her trouble. She had been shaking, for heaven's sake. The woman had no idea what was going on with her. Nor did he. Wings? How crazy was that? But he'd touched them. Had seen the skin on her back seamlessly fused into the cartilage and sheer fabric of the tiny wings. They were real.

"If that bitch did something to her," he muttered as he turned into FaeryTown, "she will feel the cut of my blade."

Yet even as he thought it, he didn't believe Hestia would be so vindictive. Not unless it directly affected him. To harm some random human he hadn't even known that night? No, it was impossible to fathom.

He didn't have time to check his watch. The fabric between realms glimmered and spit forth two collectors at once. Ry charged them both. With a swing and a thrust to the left, he took out the first one before it got a chance to see what was coming for it. Turning, he growled...and felt the angry shift to werewolf overtake him. He thrust up his blade into the other collector.

Easy. Quick. He looked at the paw holding the sword hilt—he never had to marvel how easy it was to shift without volition. Outrage and anger always did it for him.

With a shake of his arm, he shifted back to were form and lowered the sword. He couldn't sheathe it because he didn't wear one over his dress shirt and trousers.

"You're getting very efficient at that," Never said as he walked up behind Ry. "Didn't even tear your coat."

Ry swung, lifting his sword to slash.

"Whoa! It's me. Your bro."

He lowered the sword and pushed the hair from his face. "Sorry. Didn't your daddy ever teach you not to walk up behind a guy holding a dangerous weapon?"

"You know my daddy. And there's your answer."

Exactly. Ry could only be thankful he had been raised by his own kind—well, the pack, whom he'd once thought were his own kind.

"You're looking a bit too spiffy for a round of slaying," Never commented. "What's up with the penguin suit?"

"I had a commitment. I'm forced to walk two paths lately with these vicious collectors."

"You're obviously managing." Never nodded down the street toward the section that was always busy with night-clubs and ichor dens. "You remember your meeting with Riske this evening?"

Ah, hell, he had forgotten. If he was going to get any-where in solving this problem, and stop slaying collectors, he did need to speak to the man. Faery. But more impor-tant, he needed to get back to Indi. He'd only been away from the car ten minutes. He didn't want her sitting alone, wondering what had become of him. The poor woman had been through enough rejection, and near rejections, that he didn't need to add to that humiliation. She was so vul-nerable right now.

"I'll take you to him." Never started walking down the street.

"I can't meet the man tonight. Indi is waiting. She can't be alone."

The dark faery swung around, shaking his head and splaying out his hands. "You are going to stand up le Grande Sidhe? I know you're not stupid, Ryland."

Ry winced. "I don't want to. And the last thing I want

is to piss off the leader of a faery Mafia. But something's happened. I need to find Hestia. Indi is…"

"Talk to Riske first. Then you can talk to the healer. Yes?"

Ry glanced down the street. The Alfa was parked just around the corner. When he inhaled, he could smell Indi's sweet scent. Wings?

"Will you do me a favor?" he asked Never.

"Depends." The faery gestured for him to follow as he started to walk again. And when Ry didn't, he stomped a foot. "You shouldn't keep Riske waiting."

Ry said, "I need you to go sit with Indi until I return."

"Babysit your girlfriend? What's going on with her? Why are you so nervous? Because I can feel it coming off you in waves, man. You are not in a good place. This isn't like you."

"I just exterminated two collectors. It's the adrenaline."

"No, it's something more." Never stopped before a building elaborately decorated in violet arabesques resembling something from Chinatown. "What's going on with your woman?"

"She's not my—" Actually, she was his woman. And he would do anything to protect her. "Will you go sit with her, Never? She's had a shock tonight. Don't let her go wandering. Got that?"

Never nodded. "Whatever it takes to get your ass to this meeting." He opened the door and gestured for Ry to walk through. "You should probably leave the sword out here. That's not going to go over well."

With a huff of resignation, Ry set the sword against the outer wall and cast a glance around. Faeries strolled by, but when he met their gazes they quickly looked away. The sword was enchanted with magic from the mortal realm, designed to slay the sidhe. None of them would risk touching it.

He crossed the threshold and Never pointed down a long dark hallway. "End of the hall. Knock twice. Don't speak until you're spoken to."

"Thanks, Never. Now go to the car and sit with Indi."

The dark faery saluted him and strode off.

And Ry hoped this detour would be worth the emotional trauma his absence might create in one very scared and vulnerable human woman.

When the car door opened, Indi lifted her head. Her heartbeats speeded with anticipation. In slid Ry, er...not Ry, but some lanky, dark-haired man with enough spikes on his clothing to cause serious damage, and more mascara under his eyes than she had ever worn.

"Hey, Indigo, right? I'm Never," he said quickly.

"Ry's half brother? Where is he? Did something happen?"

"Everything is cool. Ry wanted me to come sit with you so you're not alone. He'll be back soon enough. Man, this is a nice car. Real leather." He whistled in appreciation.

"Where is he? Did something go wrong with the collectors?"

"Nope. He slayed both in less than ten seconds. That man is incredible with the sword. But he forgot he had a meeting with a very high-ranked sidhe leader that he wouldn't want to disappoint. He might have info for him on the whole stolen-baby thing."

"Oh." She let her leg slide down from the seat, and her foot landed on the car floor, where her dress had puddled. She was tired and wanted to go home and sleep, and hope to wake from this weird nightmare. She wriggled her shoulders but couldn't feel the wings at her back. Had they disappeared?

"So, what's up with you? Ry said you are not doing well."

"He didn't tell you?"

Never adjusted the seat so he could lean back and stretch out his long legs. "He told me you were in the way the other night when he was slaying and got hurt."

"Did he tell you he took me to a healer who fucked me up?"

Now the man turned, curiosity glittering in his violet eyes. "How so?"

Indi narrowed her gaze on his eyes. They weren't exactly violet, maybe a bit of red mixed into the pupils. Such a strange color, but oddly pretty. Also disconcerting.

"Hey." The man snapped his fingers in front of her face.

Indi shook out of the impolite stare. "Right. It happened at the ball tonight. I've…" She twisted her shoulder forward and slipped down Ry's suit coat jacket.

Never leaned forward and inspected her back. "Really? You're faery?"

"No. I'm human. These things just popped out about an hour ago. I'm sure the healer did something to me. Ry told me the two of them had something going on that didn't end well. You men and your lacking insight on we women. He probably broke her heart. And now she's getting back at him through me. I should go look for her right now." Indi gripped the door handle. "If Ry is busy—"

"He said not to let you go wandering. I don't know how or why you have the sight, but apparently you do. And a human walking around FaeryTown alone? Not cool. Turn around again and let me take a look at those things. They're like baby wings."

Indi twisted and she flinched when the man touched one.

"Sorry. Shouldn't have done that," he offered. "It's a freaky thing when someone touches your wings, isn't it?"

"What's freaky is actually having wings. Do you have wings?"

"I do. Even though I'm half vampire."

"You are? Ry didn't mention that. But I guess that makes sense, if you two are half brothers of a father who seems to be some kind of faery gigolo."

"Malrick is a slut, no other way to put it. He likes to make half-breeds. Don't ask me why. Not like any of us want to spend time with the old man in Faery."

"You don't visit him? Go to Faery?"

"Hate that place. Hate the man. Try to avoid it as much as possible. Just like Ry."

"Ry never mentioned why he has such hatred for him. Just that he and his father do not get along."

"Malrick is… The dude has been around forever. He is king of the Unseelies."

"I didn't know that."

"Yeah? And Ry is the Unseelie Prince, or so Malrick would make him that if he would go to live in Faery."

"A prince." Indi clutched the back of the seat and laid her head aside it. "First I learn he's a freakin' billionaire. And then that he's a werewolf."

"With a bit of faery mixed in," Never added.

"And now a prince. And he also has a penchant for playing Batman by slaying wicked creatures from another realm."

"And now his girlfriend is turning into a faery. Mighty strange, all around."

"Do you really think I could turn into a faery? Is that possible? Where does that healer live?" Indi opened the door and shoved out a foot.

She had to get some answers before she fell asleep and

Ry returned to take her home. No more waking in the morning beneath a coffee table without memory of the previous night. She would not leave FaeryTown tonight until she knew what was wrong with her.

As she stepped out of the car, Never shuffled around the front of the hood. He was as tall as Ry but leaner. And the Goth look did not intimidate her. It was just a fashion choice. And she knew her fashion.

"Move," she said. "Or help me."

The man put his palms on her shoulders and bent to study her eyes. Yes, his eyes were eerily beautiful, and yet she didn't feel a sense of safety by looking into them. But not fear, either. More a tense sort of expectation.

Finally, he nodded. "Ry will kill me, but I want to find out what's up with you, too. Let's go find Hestia and get some answers."

Chapter 13

Le Grande Sidhe was the official title for the Seelie faery called Riske. It was a pompous title, and Ry didn't recognize Faery politics or their ways. Hell, this was the mortal realm. But he could respect those from whom he needed answers. And since he was the leader of a powerful Mafia-like organization, Ry did strive to keep the waters as smooth as possible between them.

When he entered a hazy room filled with what he recognized as opioid smoke, he bowed to the man sitting on a pile of tufted pillows on the other side of the small room. It resembled an opium den, decorated in bohemian colors and fabrics. Weird music played, which could only be Faery in origin.

The man's legs were crossed before him and his palms cupped each knee. He wore a black pinstriped business suit. Yet on his head was splayed a massive headdress consisting of tiny bleached skulls, feathers—not mortal realm in origin—and quills.

Riske watched as Ry stood there, acclimating himself to the summery smell of the smoke. It filled his lungs with a swelling that felt like drowning. A wide line of white dashed the man's face from ear to ear. Probably wasn't paint, Ry figured, for many faeries had markings or sigils on their skin, in all colors. Never had a few on his ribs and legs he'd once shown him. They were infused with faery magic.

The sigil on Ry's hip didn't seem to do much more than annoy him that it was there, always reminding him that he was not what his werewolf father wanted him to be. And, of course, made him dust during sex.

"Grande Sidhe," he said to prompt conversation. A slight bow of his head felt necessary.

He was in a hurry. Didn't want to leave Indi sitting in the car with Never too long, and in her state. But he'd focus and get the answers he needed while he had this opportunity.

"Never says you've been asking about stolen human babies," Riske stated simply. No airs in his voice, nor accusation. He gestured with a hand, the iridescent markings on his skin glinting, to a stack of pillows to his left.

Ry sat, awkwardly. The pillows were wobbly, and he was too big and bulky to rest comfortably. He settled by leaning onto his knees and sitting back partially on the pillows.

"Malrick's chosen son, eh?" Riske said.

Ry gave a noncommittal wobble of his head. The label sounded more like an accusation than an accolade to him.

"Your werewolf is stronger than your wasted faery will ever be. Why don't you allow the sidhe in you to rise and embrace both of your natures?"

"Listen, I didn't come here to discuss me. There's a situation in FaeryTown, and I'm not sure you're aware of it."

"While my business operates out of this thin place, I have been spending much time in Faery of late. Never says you've been slaying sidhe? There are consequences."

"Only out of necessity. And if anyone wants to punish me for taking out the collectors, then I challenge them to stand before me and take me out."

"Not many would accept that challenge, I'm sure. Collectors?"

"You're obviously not aware someone has been sending collectors into this realm to steal human infants."

Riske tilted his head. Black-tipped white quills framed his vibrant violet eyes. "It is our right. Is it not?"

If one followed Faery convention. And Ry knew the line between both worlds was smeared, at best, in places like this where they both existed.

"It is a Faery right that harms the humans," he offered carefully. "But it's only ever been a right when a changeling has been left in the stolen infant's place."

That got Riske's attention. He leaned forward, pressing his fingertips together before his lips.

"They are not leaving behind changelings," Ry said. "Every night, at midnight, the fabric between our worlds is breached by one or two collectors intent on assuming a human's soul for the time required to steal an infant and take it back to Faery."

"But that's not how it is done. We take something away. We leave something in its place. It is how the two realms have coexisted over the millennia. And it is how humans can live unaware of our kind. Should an infant go missing, without a changeling left in its place there would be questions. Panic. We don't create ripples."

"Yeah? Well, someone doesn't care how big a ripple they stir. You had no idea this was happening? You don't know who's behind it?"

"I do not. But I will learn. As you should continue to take out the collectors nightly, if what you tell me is true. But why have they stopped bringing changelings to this realm?"

"I don't know. The sacrifice is too great?"

"That doesn't make sense. It throws everything off balance. Besides, changelings are bred for such an exchange."

Ry winced at that statement. Changelings were born to be used as a replacement for a stolen infant? It sounded not cool for the changeling. But he also knew a changeling rarely had memory of its life in Faery, and easily assimilated into the human realm.

Riske suddenly pointed to Ry. "You must ask your father about this. Malrick knows all that occurs."

"In the Unseelie realm. I have no idea where the command to send in the collectors is originating from."

"But you can learn by asking Malrick. I insist you do."

"With all due respect, Grande Sidhe, you don't get to tell me what to do. I'm a free agent. Just trying to look out for the interests of innocent human children."

"Then even more so you should be eager to learn the truth. How long can you continue to slay the collectors without results? Without end to the infiltrations? Someone is sending them here. Collectors are mindless things that need direction."

"I know that." Ry caught his forehead against his palm. He'd hoped for, at the least, a lead from Riske. "So no clue whatsoever?"

"I'm sorry. But whoever is behind this is taking business away from my pockets."

"How so?"

"There is a tariff for bringing a changeling into this realm. It's been…perhaps human decades since it last occurred. I had thought the practice abandoned. Which may explain why this sudden resurgence has gone unnoticed by myself and my staff. Perhaps I'll send Never into Faery to ask around."

"I don't think Never will agree to that. He's not too keen on Faery."

"If the half-breed doesn't do as I ask, there will be consequences."

Ry reached for the sword that should have been at his back, and instead clasped a hand onto his shoulder and rubbed. Damn it.

"You mustn't worry about one insignificant half-breed faery, Sidhe Slayer."

"Never is my brother."

"Half brother."

"No difference to me. Family is those you trust and care about."

"Is not Malrick one of those you trust or care about?"

Ry stood. "I think this conversation is over. I appreciate your time, Grande Sidhe. But please, send one of your more devoted employees to ask around in Faery. I can utilize Never's help here in FaeryTown."

"I wouldn't bring him along when you speak to Malrick," Riske said.

"What makes you think I'd ever purposely speak to the Unseelie king?"

Riske stood now and he was taller than Ry, which surprised him. The smoke in the room seemed to coil toward him and slink along his outline. Ry felt the power hum from him like a cruel summer wind.

"All the answers you seek can be gotten from the Unseelie king."

"You don't know that."

Riske shrugged. "A lifetime of slaying collectors, or a fast resolution to what you deem a problem to the humans and their infants? It's all in your hands, Ryland Alastair James."

Ry winced. He hated when faeries used his full name. There was magic in repeating a person's birth name. And he took Riske's use of it as a threat. But the man didn't know his complete name, so he was safe.

Without another word, he exited the room and stomped down the dark hallway. Once outside, he grabbed his sword and stalked back toward the car.

He didn't get far before a crowd of faeries milling about what sounded like a shouting match between two women made him pause. Ry shook his head and cursed under his breath. He recognized both women's voices.

Pushing through the crowd, Ry stopped beside Never, who stood with arms crossed over his chest, and was watching as Indi dodged to avoid Hestia's swinging fist.

"What the hell?" Ry asked. "I thought I told you to keep her in the car."

"She wasn't in a mind to listen. But I came along with her. I'm keeping an eye on her, eh?"

"I don't consider allowing her to get into a cat fight with Hestia keeping an eye on her."

"Hey, a man learns quickly enough not to get between two women when their claws are out."

"And why are they out?"

"Hestia insists she's not to blame for Indi's wings."

Indi yelled and slashed her fingernails across Hestia's shoulder. The faery hissed at her and lunged. Indi, clad in the black-and-white ball gown with elegant makeup and a certain carriage, going against the stealth and feline healer, whose wild beribboned hair glittered with the promise of her faery magic soon to be unleashed.

It was when Hestia lifted a hand and prepared to blow dust at Indi that Ry decided enough was enough.

He grabbed Indi around the waist and swung her away from the flurry of dust that would likely have landed in her face and eyes. Her tiny wings fluttered across his face as he struggled to contain her.

Hestia lunged for Indi, and Ry yelled, "Grab her, Never!"

"She's lying," Indi shouted. "And she insists you two were lovers."

Ah, hell. He did not need this tonight, on top of all the other things that had decided to tilt his world upside down.

"He was!" Hestia howled. "And he's taken a step down in that department by screwing you, filthy human impostor."

"I am not an impostor! What's she talking about, Ry?"

"Never!" Ry gestured for his brother to get Hestia.

"There's nothing to see here!" Ry called, making eye contact with a few of the residents who were watching eagerly. Some slunk away, others remained defiantly standing ten to twenty feet away.

Never managed to wrangle Hestia and shove her inside the front door to her shop, while Indi settled enough that Ry trusted letting her go. She tugged at her skirt and adjusted her blond curls.

Ry eyed those who still stood watching. He swung out his sword before them. "They call me Sidhe Slayer for a reason!"

The horrified gawkers fled.

And Ry turned to find Indi was no longer standing beside him. He saw her froth of skirt disappear into the healer's shop.

"And here I thought she was tired and wanted to go home to have a good cry."

He dashed inside the shop and encountered Never, standing before Hestia, arms out to stop Indi's approach.

Ry grabbed Indi about the waist. The tiny wings whisked at his shirt and chest while her arms pumped, as did her scrambling legs.

"Would you settle down? We can talk about this like civilized people."

"Civilized? She's the one who tried to turn me into a faery!"

"I can do no such thing!" Hestia shouted back at her. "Ryland, I healed the cut she received from the collector. You saw that! And that is all I did! You know I cannot change a human into a faery."

"All right, ladies, can we all take a breath and settle down? Talk about this?" He looked from one to the other. Never shrugged, still holding his position between the two of them. "Indi?"

Sniffing and crossing her arms, she stomped over to stand beside him. "She's still got it bad for you. She's not going to tell the truth."

"I've never known Hestia to lie," he reassured both women. "And she doesn't…" He exhaled and cast Hestia a look, but he'd expected her to sneer, and instead she glanced away. Was Indi's guess correct? Did the healer still have feelings for him?

"Then how did this happen?" Indi thrust a hand over her shoulder. The wings fluttered madly. Had they grown bigger since he saw them in the car but half an hour earlier?

Ry looked to Hestia.

"I didn't do it!" she insisted.

"I believe you, Hestia. But can you help us here? Since the night you healed Indi, she's been feeling bad. And the pain in her back has grown worse. And now tonight, not two hours ago, those wings popped out."

"Impossible. If she's human."

"Are you saying she's not human?"

"Oh, come on!"

Ry managed to catch Indi about the waist as she stepped forward, arms swinging for a punch. "Princess, holster those claws."

"Princess?" Hestia scoffed. "You've changed, Ry. Never thought you'd go for a poseur like her. You once told me you could see the gold diggers coming. What's with the stupid ears, huh?"

"These ears are my bestselling product," Indi countered. "And they haven't changed anyone into something they are not. Unlike your products. What did you use on me? Some nasty magical herbs? Faery dust?"

Hestia slammed her hands to her hips. "Educate her about faeries, Ry."

"I'm not up on the whole faery lexicon, Hestia. But if you say a human can't be changed to a faery…"

"Not in the mortal realm," the healer said. "But if you take a human infant to Faery, it grows into sidhe. And vice versa— That's it! She's a changeling!"

At that suggestion, Indi stepped back and landed her shoulders up against Ry. He slid an arm across her chest, holding her trembling body before his. The sensation of her wings against his pecs disturbed him. A changeling? That would mean she had been switched at birth. And Riske had said changelings had not been brought to the human realm for decades.

Indi was over a few decades in age. Could it be true?

"She's lying," Indi said quietly. "I was born to Claire and Gerard DuCharme twenty-seven years ago right here in Paris. I've never known anything about faeries or seen…" She gasped, pressing her fingers to her mouth.

Ry recalled her saying she'd seen faeries in her garden. For sure, she had the sight. But that didn't imply she should grow wings because of it.

"How can we learn if that's the truth?" Ry asked Hestia. She shrugged. "No clue."

"Hestia, come on. Give me a break here, will you?"

"I don't need to help you anymore, Ry. We're paid up. Remember? I saved your ungrateful girlfriend's ass from death."

"And I paid you a million euros."

"A million…?" Indi gasped.

Hestia gestured furiously toward Indi. "And now she dares to come into my home and accuse me of something so heinous?"

"I'm sorry," Indi offered suddenly. She turned to Ry and slipped her hand into his. "Can you take me home? I want to get out of here. Please?"

He nodded. "Sorry, Hestia. Never, can you—"

"I'll hang around until everyone is feeling fine," Never offered.

Indi wandered toward the door while Ry held Hestia's gaze a bit longer, seeing her pain. She was hurt. Indi should never have attacked her. But Indi was at odds and out of place.

And he was stuck in the middle.

"Thank you," he said. "I promise I won't bother you again." He turned to leave.

Outside, he followed Indi's swift pace to the Alfa. She slid into the passenger side, and he dashed up to tuck in her dress before closing the door for her. He'd take her to his place tonight. Because he didn't want her to be alone. And because whatever had happened to her, he felt to blame.

He had a new mystery to solve.

Chapter 14

Indi's eyes fluttered open. Sunlight beamed through windows that stretched diagonally to the ceiling above the bed. She spread her hand across crisp sheets. They didn't smell of lavender like hers at home. Where was she?

She sat abruptly, and didn't recognize the bed or the room. But the slanted windows were the same as the ones she'd seen in Ry's living room the one time she was at his place.

"I gotta stop waking in this guy's apartment unawares."

She was still clad in her black taffeta dress, and the tulle underskirt cushed as she rolled her legs off the side of the bed. But the notion to get up and wander didn't appeal. Yet something had woken her. A dream or memory.

She'd been sitting in a sports car with a man wearing far too much guy-liner and he'd said something to her…

"He's a prince?" she whispered.

Ryland James was a prince. Of Faery. His weird Goth brother had definitely said that to her.

And where was Ry? He'd driven her...

Well, she'd lost track of the ride home from FaeryTown because she must have fallen asleep. Exhaustion had literally attacked. But she'd never forget her squabble with the bitch faery healer.

Falling onto her side, her head hitting the überplush pillow, Indi slid a wrist across her forehead and stared out at the brightening sky. The faery woman with strangely pink skin had been downright vicious. She'd snapped at Indi, claiming she wasn't going to talk to Ry's whore. In her lifetime Indi had never been called something so terrible. And who cared if she was dating Ry? The only reason the healer should have been angry about that was if she was still seeing him.

Was Ry two-timing her?

He'd been cagey about his relationship with the healer, but Indi did not think the man would be so cruel to her, another woman.

Yet the argument had only escalated. Incensed, Indi had been the first to swing out with a smack to the woman's face. That was so not her. She'd never fought another woman— except that one time in high school when Amelie Theroux had screwed her boyfriend under the bleachers after a lacrosse game.

That Ry had come along and torn her away from the faery healer was humiliating. What was going on with her? She wasn't herself lately.

And for reasons that had plunged out of her back and now crinkled against the sheets.

Indi didn't know anything more about her condition than she did earlier. She rolled carefully to her back. Her body weight crushed the wings. It didn't hurt, but it didn't feel comfortable, either; they tugged for release, a bit like long hair stuck under the pillow when she tried to shift from side to side.

She rolled back to her side.

The healer had accused her of being a changeling. The word, issued with a sort of hissing hexlike tone, had shivered over Indi's skin. And thinking it now gave her a shudder.

How could she be a faery and not know it? That was the most ridiculous thing she had heard. She'd been raised by loving parents, and had grown up in Paris. In the mortal realm. She'd never once thought about flying or that she might have lived in another place or realm. Nothing in her life could point toward suddenly sprouting wings.

Though she did see faeries in her garden. But that wasn't at all related. Was it?

"I should give Mom a call."

Indi made a point of calling her mom once a week, and visiting her once a month. Claire DuCharme traveled a lot, and seemed to have a new boyfriend every time Indi checked in. The fifty-five-year-old socialite was enjoying her retirement and Indi couldn't offer a single argument against her plunge into adventure and freedom. Claire had always worked hard and after she'd divorced Indi's father, had worked even harder to prove she could survive on her own. Although she'd never snub alimony. And Indi knew her father's monthly payments were footing the bill for his ex-wife's adventurous lifestyle.

Could she tell her mom about the wings? That would freak her out. Claire DuCharme was solidly a nonbeliever. She actually went to church every once in a while and believed in Heaven and Hell. Catholic-girl guilt, she'd once said to Indi, whom she had raised nonreligious simply because by that time Claire hadn't the time or interest in tending to her daughter's religious education.

But maybe Indi could ask about her childhood? Infancy? Had Claire and Gerard DuCharme ever noticed that their daughter was…weird? Not right? Was she crazy to even consider asking such a thing?

She was not a faery!

And yet how had she been able to walk into FaeryTown and see other faeries? She had seen the collectors Ry had insisted a common human could not see.

Maybe she had that thing he'd also mentioned. Seeing? The sight. That was it. Because all her life she had seen faeries in the garden. Of course, she'd never told her mother about those, either. Claire would have laughed and offered her a Xanax. But seeing tiny beings flit amongst the roses did not explain the wings on her back.

Closing her eyes, Indi felt her mind humming busily. Sliding her hand across the crisp white sheet, she wished Ry was lying next to her, and then wondered why he was not.

He'd witnessed her in a chick fight. And he'd had to physically remove her from the ridiculous encounter. Probably wanted to give her some space. Would the man still want to date her now that wings had popped out on her back?

He didn't seem so happy with his own faery side, wasn't willing to tell her much about it. There were things about Faery that offended Ry, she could tell. And until she learned what they were, she wasn't sure where she stood with the man. And she wanted to stand beside him and before him. In his arms.

Because, despite only knowing him a short time, she felt certain she was falling in love with the mighty werewolf warrior. And that was not a faery tale.

Using a thick towel, Ry sponged out most of the water from his wet hair, then popped his head into the bedroom.

Indi was sitting on the opposite side of the bed, her back to him. The wings were— They had definitely grown larger. They had been about the size of his hand last night. This morning? Twice as big.

"Hey," she offered over her shoulder. "Thanks for tucking me in last night. You could have taken me home."

"I wanted to be around for you. I hope you don't mind. I turned on the towel warmer in the bathroom. The shower is all yours."

"Thanks. A shower will feel great. Do you think I can get these things wet?"

"Uh…" She was asking about the wings. "Of course. Faeries do all the time."

She nodded, head bowed.

What Hestia had suggested last night must be weighing heavily on her mind. It was bothering him. How did one discuss with a relatively new girlfriend the fact that she had just sprouted wings? And that she could be a changeling?

"I ordered breakfast from the bistro down the street," he said. "They make a mean goat-cheese-and-asparagus omelet. It'll be here in half an hour. I'll leave you to do your thing. Uh, you can steal some clothes from my closet. I'm sure I have a few T-shirts that you could wear like a dress."

She nodded again. Not talkative.

Ry closed the door slightly and left her to herself. Five minutes later he heard water patter on the marble walls in the bathroom, so he snuck into the bedroom and dropped his towel in the hamper. Pulling on a pair of jeans and forgoing a shirt, he grabbed his iPad and headed out to the living room. It was a workday, and while he didn't expect Kristine to be in the office today after last night's encounter, he figured he should text her and let her know to take the day off.

Everything had been tilted on its head last night. Or at

least, one very important thing. And it hurt him as much as it must hurt Indi. What was up with her? And for as much as he trusted Hestia, had she lied to him? Could she have done something to Indi when she healed her?

He opened a browser and tapped into the para-net, which was like a dark net except it was exclusively known to paranormals. When investigating possible charities and clients, he occasionally visited a board that was open to any and all questions.

In the chat room labeled Sidhe he posed the questions: What can you tell me about changelings? Their origins? Can a human who has only lived in the mortal realm suddenly become faery?

He figured that was enough to garner many replies, so he set the iPad on the coffee table and, just about to put up his feet, jumped when the doorbell rang. He buzzed up the delivery guy, tipped him ten euros and then unpacked the steaming breakfast onto two plates. A side of bright orange papaya and juicy kiwi made his mouth water.

As if on cue, Indi wandered into the living room, flipping her wet hair over a shoulder. She wore one of his gray T-shirts, and it was loose and long, hanging to her thighs. But it was just short enough to make him look to see if anything would be revealed with each step. Nope. Maybe? Ah! The tease!

Ry whistled. "If I knew my shirt was so sexy, I'd wear it every day."

"I prefer you sans shirt." She slid onto a chair before the kitchen counter, which hugged the stovetop and sink area. "That smells great. Madeleine's? Me and my mom used to go there in the summers. You have good taste. Hand me a fork."

"You want water? Or I've got some funky aloe-vera juice stuff."

She lifted an eyebrow.

"I have a personal shopper who gets my groceries for me once a week. She tends to sneak in a new thing once in a while. It's good, but chunky."

"Chunky juice? I think I'll go with water. Don't stand on the other side of the counter. Come sit beside me."

Ry joined her and they ate in silence for a few minutes. Because again, how to casually discuss what seemed to stick out like a pair of wings? The T-shirt bulged across Indi's back where the soft fabric wasn't heavy enough to weigh down the wings.

Out of the blue, she asked, "Do werewolves need blood to survive?"

Her mind must be tracing all the weirdness she'd encountered since first meeting him. Had she not wandered into FaeryTown that night and been attacked by the collector, would she have wings now?

"You mean like vamps?" he asked. "Hell no. We have a distinct disgust for blood. Unless we're in wolf shape, that is. We don't kill for the thrill of it. Only for sustenance."

"Good to know. I think dating a vampire would freak me out."

"Are we dating?" he asked. The label hadn't come up, and he realized he'd probably asked that a bit too quickly.

"Can we be?" she asked with all the sweet innocence of a summer flower.

Ry bowed his head to hers and kissed her lips. She smelled like his brisk male shampoo, which seemed to be mostly cinnamon and clove scents. "I hope so," he said. "I like you, Indigo."

"I like you. Even if it's been a wild ride since meeting you."

"I like my rides wild, if that's any consolation."

"Apparently, I'm growing wilder by the day. Do you think the wings got a little bigger?"

He shoved a forkload of food in his mouth but managed a confirming nod.

"I thought so, too. I can't see them well in the mirror. You don't have a hand mirror to hold up to look at them. Oh, Ry… What am I?"

"I'm not sure, Indi. But I'm going to help you find out."

"Thanks." She squeezed his hand. "I feel lost. My world was so normal and moving along swimmingly. If you consider ball gowns and tiaras normal. Which I do. But now?" She sighed.

Again, he was compelled to kiss her. To be close. To feel her against his skin. He eased his temple beside hers and said, "I hear normal is not what it's cracked up to be."

"I suppose. But at the very least, I would have liked to have a choice in the matter. Do you like asparagus?" She shoved her plate forward on the counter. "I'm not so hungry. Sorry."

"It's all right, Princess. You've had a crazy night. You want some more fruit?"

She plucked a half circle of kiwi from the plastic container it had come in. "I'll just pick at this."

He smiled then and collected their plates, placing them in the sink.

Indi suddenly slapped the counter and exclaimed, "What's this about you being a prince?"

Ah, hell. Really? "That's the last time I ask Never to do me a favor. Did he tell you that?"

"He's kind of strange," she said, inspecting the cut kiwi, "but nice enough. I don't know how it came up— Oh, yes, he was talking about your dad and mentioned you were a prince. Really? I mean, you're a sexy werewolf faery. And a billionaire. And a superhero. And now I learn you're also a prince? I think I've just stepped into the latest romance novel. *The Werewolf Faery Billionaire Prince's Wild Life*."

"Is there a book with that title?"

"No, but I could write one."

"Then the werewolf faery billionaire…"

"Prince," she said, helping him.

"…*prince's* girlfriend would have to be a gorgeous Princess Pussycat with wings."

"That's getting too complicated for a title. And I am not a princess. I just play one in your dreams."

"I have very good dreams about you."

She turned on the chair and leaned an elbow onto the counter. "Does it involve vibrators?"

"You know it."

"You're avoiding the question. Which you have a talent for. But my talent is recognizing that sly move. Tell me about this prince thing. I need all the deets if you're going to be my boyfriend."

"Come here first." He gestured for her to follow him over to the living area, and he sat on the back of the sofa.

Indi sailed across the room and into his arms. This kiss was long and deep and involved as much of their body parts crushing against each other as possible. She felt like a piece of brightness that had escaped to shine on his world. And she tasted like fruit and giggles because she ended the kiss with a laugh.

"What's that about?" he asked.

"The laugh? I've been reading romance novels since I was a teenager. And paranormal romances are some of my favorite. Who would have thought I'd find myself in my own paranormal romance?"

"That's a thing?"

"A very big thing. Women dream about having love affairs with vampires or witches or shape-shifters."

"Really? That's…huh. Have *you* dreamed about it?"

"Not really. I mean, I love the stories, but I know what's real and what isn't."

"I'm real."

She hugged up against his chest and nuzzled her nose along his neck and up to his ear, where she dashed the lobe with her tongue. "I know it. Every bit of you is real and hard, and…if this is a fantasy, I don't want it to end."

He slid a hand up her back, remembered her wings and stopped. "Feels great with your hard tits hugging up against me."

"You're avoiding the question, lover. Now spill." She sat up on his lap, yet thrust forward her chest and winked. "Then I'll let you touch my boobs."

"I can be bribed." He lifted her, and in the process spun over the back of the sofa and slid down, landing with her on his lap, both of them facing the windows. The day was growing bright. Clasping her hands in his lap, Ry explained, "I'm not a prince. I mean, I guess I am. My faery father, Malrick, named me a prince because…" He sighed.

"Never said the guy's an asshole."

"That he is. I don't know him all that well. I told you about the money."

"Right, the leaves that change to cash. I wish I had that problem."

"No, you don't. Malrick thinks by bribing me he'll win me over and I'll move to Faery. I don't want to live in Faery. I was born and raised in this realm and it is my home. As good a home as it'll ever be."

"But you were raised in a pack?"

"I was. I was seventeen when my father, Tomas—my werewolf father—asked me to leave the pack because it wasn't right, a half-breed staying on."

"That's awful. And he had raised you as his son?"

"He thought I was his son. As I did. This sigil—" he tapped his hip "—only appeared when I was seventeen. My father saw it—and another thing, I'd started to dust— and he knew something wasn't right. And it all went to hell after that. My mom confessed her affair with Malrick and then fled. And Tomas ignored me for weeks after that. Stewing. And then he told me to leave."

"Just like that?"

He nodded.

"I'm so sorry, Ry. I can't say that I can understand, but it must have been difficult for you."

"That's when Malrick stepped in with his magical leaves and promises of making me a prince should I move to Faery. I'm thankful I was resistant to it. I only wanted to get away from them all, Tomas and Malrick, and start new. Which is why I'm in Paris now."

"The city suits you."

He shrugged. "I miss the country. I want to go out running every day. It's an innate thing."

"Could you go to your cabin more often?"

"I try to, but I've been so busy with the finances. It seems the more money I give away, the more it grows. It's madness. Some days I want it to stop. And then other days I know I can do so much good with that money, so I admonish myself for feeling sorry for myself. So many have it so much worse than I do. Hell. I don't have it bad at all."

"And you've a good heart, which makes your situation even more impressive. Never stop giving the money to those in need, Ry."

"I won't." He kissed her nose. "Did that answer your question?"

"Are all Malrick's sons princes? You said you had hundreds of half brothers and sisters. Why doesn't he ask some other sibling to move to Faery?"

"Because I am his only werewolf son. And supposedly that makes me his warrior prince, as he calls me. Most desired. Strong and capable of…"

She turned on his lap. He knew she was looking into his eyes, but he avoided meeting her gaze. Finally, he said, "Capable of taking over the reins when Malrick dies and assuming the Unseelie throne."

"You mean like king of the Unseelies?"

Ry nodded. "I don't want that. It's not my place. But Malrick won't make the offer to any other of his by-blows. So he continues to try and seduce me over to Faery."

"Have you ever been to Faery?"

"Once. Briefly. I visited Malrick's kingdom after he'd first introduced himself to me. I didn't know him well then and was curious. I learned my lesson. The Unseelie lands are beautiful and malicious. Faeries are…well, they're not the fluttery sweet things you read about in the children's tales, that's for sure."

"The ones in my garden flutter, and I think they're pretty sweet."

"Be cautious," he warned. "Faeries are never what they seem. And yet they are fierce and strong. I would never judge one too harshly. I talked to Riske last night and he suggested the only way to figure this stolen-baby thing out is to talk to Malrick. I don't think I can do that."

"The Riske guy didn't have any answers for you?"

"He was unaware of what was going on in FaeryTown. In fact, he's kind of pissed about it and is going to send someone to Faery to check in to things."

"Do you really have the time to wait and see what he learns? Ry, if you miss one night, those collector things will take another baby. Oh, my God…"

She slid off his lap and leaned forward, catching her head in her hands.

"What is it, Indi?"

"Was *I* one of those babies? Or rather, was I a faery put in a human infant's crib? Why do they only take babies? Why not adults?"

She subtly shook now and Ry pulled her back onto his lap and hugged her tightly. It hurt him to feel her fear and pain. Her unknowing. How could he reassure her when even he didn't have answers? There were days he felt as lost in the world as she probably did right now.

"They take babies because then they grow into sidhe. Much as the changeling then grows into a human. Yet adults who get lost in Faery remain human, no matter what. No matter what you are, Indi, I've got your back. Promise. You don't have to go through this alone. We're going to figure things out."

"Thank you. I do need the support. I feel like if you let me go I'll fall into a deep pit."

"Never let that happen." He kissed her. Deeply. It was like falling with his arms outstretched and he did not fear landing. With Indi he could be himself. Almost? He would get there with her. He wanted that.

"I need to go home and get changed and…" Indi sighed. "Stare in the mirror a while at these things. I have to call Janet."

"The BFF?"

"She's my bestie. And my business partner. She moved to New York three months ago and is currently setting up a new office for Goddess Goodies. We plan to open that branch before the holiday season. But I can't tell her about this. Not yet."

"Not ever." He waggled a finger at her. "It is never wise to tell humans about what they believe to be myth and fantasy."

"Humans? Am I no longer in that category?"

"Oh, sweetie."

All he could do was hug her. Ry felt her confusion. Her utter inability to accept what had happened. Hell, he was as confused as she was. He didn't know what to say, so he nuzzled his nose against her hair and hugged her even tighter. She felt so good curled on his lap.

When she slid a hand over his abs, he winced as his erection took notice. Didn't take much to get horny with this woman close. But it didn't feel like the time was right…

"You're so hot," she said against his throat as she slid her hand up higher.

Was she in the mood? Because if she was…

"It's hard to walk away from you," she said. "Last night should have been a night to remember. We danced. We kissed. Then we should have topped it off by coming home and making love. Can we do that part that didn't get done last night?"

"The making-love part?" He shifted his hips, and her hand dropped to stroke over his jeans. Not much room left in them now. "If that's what you want?"

"You're thinking it's strange now with these wings on my back?"

"Not at all. I want you, Indi. I just don't want to take advantage of you if you're in a weird place."

"It is a weird place, but I need you to stay beside me in that place. More so, I need to feel you inside me. To just… lose myself right now."

She kissed him, shifting her body as she did, so she straddled him. Sitting fully on his lap, she pumped her mons against his erection as her tongue danced with his.

Ry moaned and set aside any reluctance over having his way with a confused woman. She wasn't mixed up right now. She knew exactly what she wanted and needed.

* * *

They'd moved to Ry's bed, and Indi now sat on top of him, his cock seated deep within her. She rocked on him, drawing up his moans. The man was lost in the moment, and yet he still hadn't forgotten that she liked it when he put pressure on her clit. His thumb altered from a firm to a soft touch right there. And when she increased her rhythm, he read that as a sign to touch her harder, longer, and jitter that touch to milk the burgeoning orgasm.

She felt like a goddess sitting upon him, demanding worship from her follower. And while she knew the strange wings on her back were there, she didn't need to think about them now. Ry's other hand found her breast and teased at her nipple. She tilted back her head, gripping his thighs behind her, and groaned as the intensity of their connection grew her feminine power. She'd never felt more wanted, more desired.

The man gave to her always. And she would take what he offered.

"So close," he said through a tight jaw. His hips bucked up against her thighs. "You almost there?"

"Oh, hell yes." She pressed her hands to his shoulders and met his deep brown gaze. The wolf lived within those irises. She could see his wild, and feel it in his tight muscles and his panting breaths. "Worship me," she whispered.

"Oh, my princess, always."

He suddenly gripped her wrist and dragged her hand to his mouth. His kissed her palm and bit gently as he came forcefully within her. With a squeeze of his fingers at her clit, she went over the edge along with him. Her body tightened and then loosened and she bowed her head to his chest as their combined magic moved through her and burst in a brilliant shimmy of satiation.

And with a glance down, Indi saw the faery dust glimmering about their hips. Something amazing had bonded the two of them.

Now to survive this new adventure without chasing him away.

Chapter 15

After Ry dropped her off at home, Indi strode straight to the bathroom and pulled off his shirt and dropped it to the floor. She stood naked before the vanity mirror to stare at a woman she wasn't sure she recognized anymore.

She could just see the tops of the clear, iridescent wings over her shoulders. They didn't move, but they had made reflexive movements when she pulled off the shirt.

Why was this happening to her?

Or was that the wrong question to ask? It had already happened. She needed to know if they were merely temporary or if she'd have to adjust to having them for the rest of her life.

Wincing, she reached for the hand mirror on the vanity. She turned around and held the mirror high. There were two sets of wings on each side of her spine. They resembled bee wings. The top one was a little larger than the narrower bottom wing. And they grew from her back in a narrow jut and formed a sort of elongated teardrop in shape. They were clear, and looked like delicate paper that could be easily torn if pierced or even bumped. A twist at her waist caught the light in the fabric of the wings and flashed in pinks, blues, emeralds and a deep violet.

Indi sighed. They were pretty. But they did not belong on her.

Sucking in the corner of her lower lip, she wondered how she would ever disguise them. They were already about a foot long. And she hadn't even had them twenty-four hours. Would they grow as large as a real faery's wings? How big were a faery's wings? She'd never be able to hide them if they stretched many feet beyond her body.

Real faeries could put away their wings, yes?

"I have no clue," she muttered. "Is that what I am? Could I really be...?"

She couldn't say the word: changeling. It felt wrong. Not at all like anything that belonged in the comfortable world she knew as her home.

Picking up her phone, she googled *changeling*. The first definition that came up read: "a child believed to have been secretly substituted by faeries for the human parents' real child in infancy."

The entries that followed were similar, yet they were all linked to folklore and myth.

"Not real," she whispered.

And yet proof glimmered just behind her shoulders.

Her phone suddenly rang and it startled Indi so much she almost dropped it. Janet was calling? It had to be middle of the night in New York. Or...maybe early morning. It was past noon here.

"Janet!"

"Hey, chickie baby, what's up?"

"Oh, the usual." She bit the corner of her lip. Ry said

she couldn't tell anyone about this. And why was her hand suddenly shaking?

"Oh, yeah? How did the date with tall, dark and billionaire go last night?"

"Great. You know I'm in my element at fancy balls."

"Hence, your business. But I don't care about what you wore or if you chatted up the movers and shakers."

Indi pressed her shaking fingers to the vanity and leaned forward, eyeing herself in the mirror. "Are you kidding me?"

"I kid you not. I want to hear all about the sexy man."

With a sigh, Indi smiled at her reflection. She could do this—chatter with Janet about Ry and not bring up the fact that she had suddenly sprouted wings. She loved her best friend, but Janet would never believe her. She was also a card-carrying Catholic schoolgirl. The one time Indi had mentioned to her she'd seen a faery in her garden, Janet had laughed and then snorted until she'd started hiccupping.

"This man is one in a billion," Indi said. "And the sex!"

"Ooh! You must tell me all."

"I will." She turned off the bathroom light and wandered into the bedroom to plop down, stomach-first, on the bed. "Where should I start? With his steel abs that could support a ten-story building or with his nice long, thick—"

"The nice long thick one!" Janet insisted.

They always shared the intimate details about sex because it was a BFF privilege. For the next twenty minutes they talked sex, abs and orgasms. And Indi didn't once think about the wings fluttering at her back.

Ry gave Indi a call as he headed out of the office. She was in her backyard, basking in the sun…naked. He wished he could be there for that. The woman was a nudist? He could get behind that. And in front of her. Hell, all over that sweet-smelling skin.

She'd given her mother a call, thinking she might ask her what she'd been like as a baby. Kind of feel her out without actually asking if she suspected her daughter was a changeling. Claire DuCharme was headed out on a midnight flight, but she'd said her daughter could stop in before she left this evening.

Ry had offered to go along, and Indi had appreciated that.

His girlfriend was turning into a faery. Or she already was one. Or...he didn't know. It would be fine by him if she was a faery and had wings. He had no prejudices against any from the paranormal realm. Except maybe witches. Just a little creeped out by witches.

And okay, to get real with himself, *did* he have a pre-conception against faeries?

"No," he muttered.

Any prejudices toward faeries were directed toward the one pompous Unseelie king. Because he'd had the fling with Hestia. That hadn't bothered him. Of course, he'd been heavily drugged at the time. But for sure his eye had been turned by more than a few female faeries while wandering FaeryTown. He could deal with someone not like him. Because he knew what it was like to be different than most.

If the changeling theory was true, Ry wanted to help Indi get the answers she needed. He knew what it felt like to live your life one way, and then to suddenly be told you were not the person you thought you were.

Why had his mother kept that information a secret from him? Because she'd thought he'd tell his father? The man who wasn't actually his blood father, but merely a step-father.

Never *merely*, Ry thought now as he slid into the Alfa and fired it up.

And yet Tomas LeDoux had been able to push his stepson out of the pack with little concern. And Ry had only heard from him twice since leaving when he was seventeen. Once, right after Ry had left, Tomas had sent him a message through another pack member inquiring if he was doing well. And then years later, he'd sent that same pack member with a message that he'd seen him on the news and was proud of his philanthropy. He'd made something of himself!

If Tomas only knew that money was from his real father. Would he be as angered over the faery king's attempts at manipulating the one person he'd spent nearly two decades believing was his son? Tomas had seemed to shuck Ry from his life as easily as pulling off a shirt and tossing it aside.

There was a time when Ry had been close to his werewolf father. Immediately after his first shift, around twelve years of age, Tomas began taking Ry everywhere with him, out for runs through the forest in wolf shape, to secret pack enclaves where only the males showed and where they fought one another for rank in the pack. Tomas had been the only man Ry had to look up to and model himself after as he was growing up. And he'd loved him.

As for his mother? He had no clue where Lisa LeDoux was or if she was even alive. After she'd confessed the affair to Tomas, Ry had woken the next morning only to be told his mother had slipped out in the night, taken a few personal things and hadn't left a note for him. He'd mourned her for months, until his father had finally stepped up to tell him Ry was no longer welcome in the pack.

Everyone he'd thought cared about him had run away or shoved him out of their lives. It wasn't an easy truth, but it was his reality. Now he did the best he could, and tried not to let anyone get so close again. Kristine was truly his only confidante. He hadn't any close male or female friends.

But Indi was another matter. She had insinuated herself into his life without him even noticing. One moment he'd been standing alone in FaeryTown facing down the collectors; the next moment he'd been curled up in bed with a woman and her newly sprouted wings, thinking she was the best thing that had ever happened to him.

And tonight he was going to meet the mother.

He had definitely stepped out of his comfort zone with Indigo DuCharme.

Claire DuCharme was leaving Paris on a midnight flight to New York, but she was always thrilled to give Indi a few minutes of her time. *Minutes* being the key word. Indi didn't mind the brief visits with her mother. They chatted on the phone. And they had never been a huggy-kissy, let's-all-go-to-the-cabin-and-do-the-nature-thing family. Her father always traveled for business, and Claire was also a businesswoman.

Hence, Indi's desire to do the same. Start her own business, that is. It had been natural. Entrepreneurship was in the DuCharme blood.

But faery wings were not. So she'd put on a blue blazer over her white lace sundress before leaving with Ry for her mother's condo. The wings were now so large that they gently folded around her back and halfway toward her chest when flattened. Wearing the blazer gave her the feeling of being strapped down, confined.

"Do you think," Indi said to Ry as they waited for the maid to answer the door buzzer, "if these wings become a permanent thing, I'll be able to make them go away when need be? I can't function in this world if they are going to be a constant." She felt her confidence shrink.

"Faeries do it all the time." Ry's sudden clutch of her hand caught her before she sank too far, and she lifted her head to meet his gaze. "You'll learn to live with them."

The reassurance felt genuine to her, and his hand in hers lifted her spirits.

The door opened and instead of the maid, Claire answered, with champagne goblet in hand. She didn't like flying so always juiced up before leaving.

"Darling! My limo just called and it's going to arrive early. He'll be here in ten minutes. Do come in, come in! I've got champagne!"

Indi followed her mother's clicking footsteps into the vast kitchen decorated in stainless steel and rare violet quartz her mother simply had to have for the countertops. She never cooked and always ordered in or her chef prepared the meals.

"Oh?" Claire stepped around and focused her blue gaze on Ry. With a tap of her real gold fingernails to her lips, she turned on her patented flirtatious grin that didn't annoy Indi so much as confirm her playful yet persistent need to toy with people's reactions. "And who is this handsome piece of hunk and muscle? Indi, you didn't tell me you were bringing along a model. Oh, please, tell me he's more than just a friend. It would be a terrible crime to let all this muscle and pretty go to waste."

Controlling the urge to roll her eyes, Indi squeezed Ry's hand and he stepped up beside her. "This is Ryland James, Mom. This is my mom, Claire. She's already half-wasted. A necessary condition before she boards any plane."

"Not even close to half-wasted," Claire admonished. "I am perfectly sober. Mostly." She tilted back a healthy swallow of champagne. "So, you must have something important to talk about if you couldn't wait until I got back, or talked about it on the phone. Oh, please, Ryland, come sit here on the stool. Would you like champagne?"

Ry looked to Indi and she could sense his discomfort. "No, thank you, Madame DuCharme. Your place is gorgeous. I love the stone for the countertops."

"Oh, he's a charmer." Claire tilted back the rest of her goblet, then nodded toward her six suitcases, packed and ready to go by the door. "If you play your cards right, I'll let you carry down my bags. We'll save the driver a trip, eh?"

"We'll both help," Indi said as she sat on the stool next to Ry.

Claire combed her fingers through her long bleach-blond hair and held her chin just slightly higher than was comfortable. It disguised the wrinkles on her neck, she'd once told Indi. While she wasn't afraid of the plastic surgeon, she hadn't gone quite that far with the adjustments and tightening. Yet.

"What's up, darling mine?"

"Mom, I went in for a regular checkup with the doctor." Indi started on the story she'd decided would be not so terrible a lie, and perhaps get the information she needed from her mother without asking her straight out "Am I a faery?" "Nothing's wrong with me. Just haven't been in for years. You know."

"You really need to go in regularly, darling. Do you want my surgeon's name? It's never too early to consider Botox. That line between your eyebrows will only get deeper."

Indi pressed a finger between her eyes. She had a wrinkle there? She hadn't noticed anything.

"I think Indi is beautiful as she is," Ry said. "When I

first met her, it was her eyes that attracted me. Bright, bold and gemstone-blue. Just like yours."

Claire preened her fingers down her hair and thrust up her breasts, wiggling appreciatively at the compliment. "He's a keeper, Indi. Why does your name sound familiar?" she asked Ry.

He shrugged. "I do some charity work. You might have read about it somewhere."

And if Claire discovered the man was worth billions, her flirtations would only intensify, so Indi rushed to save Ry from that deluge and steer the conversation back on track.

"Mom, I need to know about early childhood stuff for the doctor's records. Do you still have my vaccine records? How was I as a baby? Everything cool? No major sicknesses?"

"Oh, darling, that was so terribly long ago. You're not getting any younger, you know."

"Mother."

"I'm just saying, darling." She winked at Ry. "Though men certainly take on a certain seasoning with age, don't they? Not that you're old, Ry. Mmm, that name."

Indi leaned forward on her elbows, blocking Claire's sight of Ry. "Was I a good baby, Mom? Everything...cool? Nothing, you know...weird?"

"Of course not! Well..." Claire tapped her lips.

"*Well* what?"

"You did have your father and me worried right after you were born. Those first few weeks. Oh, the dramatics!"

"What? I'm not dramatic. Am I?"

"You were, darling. You cried constantly. Day and night. I swear, I thought I would go mad. And I didn't have a nanny then. Your father insisted I had the time to take care of you myself. You were determined to make my life miserable. At least until that one night."

Ry leaned forward and his clutch on Indi's hand tightened. "That one night?"

Claire poured herself another full goblet of champagne and fluttered Ry another wink over the rim as she sipped. "It was the craziest thing, but I'm so thankful it happened."

"Tell me about it," Indi insisted. "I was a crazy baby?"

"Not crazy, just… I never knew what was wrong with you. You burst into this world crying, and didn't stop. I was a walking zombie. I don't think I slept more than twenty minutes at a time those first few weeks. Talk about a need for Botox! And your father wasn't very hands-on. He was always away for business.

"Anyway, that one night I woke, and I couldn't figure out what it was that suddenly jarred me awake. Because there was no crying. I mean, you were always wailing. I was constantly checking for pins or needles in your clothes or weird things in the diapers. There I was, sitting up in bed, thinking maybe something was wrong. Had you died? You know that SIDS thing is a real worry when you're a parent. There's no explanation for it. Babies just suddenly die."

"Mother. Get on with it. What was wrong with me?"

"Right." Claire finished the champagne and grabbed the bottle but didn't pour again. "I rushed into your nursery and there you were, in the crib. Quiet. It was so odd."

Indi and Ry glanced at each other.

"You were completely naked," Claire continued, her gold fingernails rapping the bottle. "Your onesie was on the floor. And a clean diaper lay at the end of your crib. All I could think was I had truly gone over the edge. I'd somehow forgotten to put your diaper on during the last change, and your clothes! Isn't that crazy? That's what sleep deprivation will do to you. I'm sure my hair was a mess that night."

"Mother, continue!"

"You're very testy today, Indigo Paisley. What's up with you?"

Ry pushed the champagne bottle toward Claire. "I think you need a refill, Madame DuCharme."

"Oh, aren't you delicious?" she cooed as Ry refilled her goblet. Claire took a long sip before tapping her lips. "Where was I?"

"I was lying in my crib naked and quiet," Indi prompted.

"Yes, naked as a baby bird. I think that's when your nudity thing began. She's a bit of a nudist, you know?" she said to Ry.

"I've—"

Indi rushed a hand over Ry's mouth. Her mother didn't need the salacious details, and she would never hear the weird truth about her as a baby if they didn't keep Claire on track.

"What happened next?" Indi asked.

"Hmm… Oh, I leaned over to make sure you were all right and you just beamed up at me. It was the weirdest moment. The light from the baby lamp shone across your cute little face and it was as if you were smiling at me. Sort of reassuring me." Claire placed a hand over her heart. "I'll never forget that moment. I cried. All the anxiety and uncertainty whether I was a good mom over the past weeks melted away. I put your onesie and diaper on you and sang a little tune until you fell asleep. And then I didn't wake until morning. That was six hours later. You'd never slept that long. I couldn't believe it."

"What was that about?" Indi asked. "Did I start crying all the time again?"

"No. After that night you suddenly became the perfect

baby. I told your father it was as if you were a different baby. The doctor suggested you probably had gas or some unresolved issue from the birth that finally worked itself out. You've been the perfect child ever since. Though you do still have a tendency toward dramatics. Oh, and the nudity."

Indi's mouth dropped open, but she didn't know what to say. Her mother had thought she was a different baby. Because she had been? Had that wailing, crying baby not been her? Had a faery taken her to this realm and placed her in the crib while whisking away the crying infant? Was she even related to Claire DuCharme?

A sickening feeling curdled in her gut and she swallowed down the need to gasp, to cry, to clutch at her chest and scream.

"That must have been difficult for you," Ry offered to Claire. "Babies can be a handful. Your daughter grew up to look just like you. A stunner."

"Oh, darling, if you keep that up, you'll have to come along with me to New York. I know my lover enjoys three-somes."

"Mother!"

Claire chuckled and this time took a chug of champagne directly from the bottle. Her cell phone rang and she checked the rhinestone-studded monstrosity. "The driver is here. I'll text him to wait while I have my daughter's studly boyfriend bring down the bags."

"I'm on." Ry stood and squeezed Indi's shoulders from behind. He whispered to her, "You good if I do that?"

She nodded. "I think I've heard what I needed to hear. We'll be down in two shakes."

Ry grabbed a bag, then another, then another, and managed four of them without so much as a wince of struggle.

"Where did you find him?" Claire asked as the door closed behind him.

"I ran in to him the night Todd broke up with me."

"Oh, a rebound man. I love it!"

"He's not a rebound. I like him, Mom. I want to keep him around for a while."

"I second that idea. Sorry. Do you think I flirted too much?"

"No need to apologize, Mom. If you hadn't flirted with him I would have thought something was wrong with you. Thanks for telling me about how I was as a baby."

"You can tell your doctor there's nothing at all wrong with you. You were such a good child. Never once got sick. Seriously. Not even a sniffle."

Indi nodded. She had been remarkably illness-free over her lifetime, and had often wished for a cold or flu just to miss some school. Yet another twist to the bizarre scenario that had suddenly become her life.

"Darling, where did you get that awful blazer? Is that cotton?" Claire shuddered. "And really, when did you start wearing blazers?"

"I'm cleaning out my closet, seeing what fits and what doesn't work."

"Well, that shroud does not work. Toss it in the charity bin. Your man does charity work, huh?"

"He's…" If she let Claire know Ry's financial status, the woman would hire the wedding planner right now. And if she let her know he was a werewolf faery? No amount of champagne would ever get the woman to stop laughing. "He's a good man."

"And sexy as fuck. Grab my purse. I think I can manage another goblet of champagne on the elevator ride down." Claire poured the remainder of the bottle into her glass and then pointed to the remaining two suitcases as she opened the door. "You got those, too, darling?"

"Yes, Mom. Right behind you."

Chapter 16

Ry pulled the car in front of Indi's place, then leaned over to cup the back of her head and kissed her. She'd been a little off since they left her mother's home, and for good reason. The things Claire had told her about Indi's sudden change in behavior really did lean toward a changeling being placed in a crib.

He held his mouth against hers, lingering in her sweet warmth, her pistachio-and-almond scent, then kissed her nose and each of her eyelids. "Can I come back and crawl into bed with you when I'm done with the big bads?"

"Will you have strange black sparkly stuff all over you?"

"I can take a shower."

"Deal. I'll leave the door open. I'd love to roll over and find your warm body lying next to mine."

He dipped his head and nuzzled his nose against her ear. "Please be naked."

"That's not going to be a problem. Apparently that was a thing for me right from the start."

He kissed her again, then asked, "Are you okay?"

She shrugged. "Probably not. My mom just laid some heavy information on me. And there's only one way to take it."

"Don't forget what I said about being here for you. I promise you that, Indi."

"Why are you so good to me?"

"Do I need a reason?"

"Maybe."

"I can't *not* be nice to you. It's not how I am. And you're so cute and cuddly. And you've got those pretty new wings that I find very sexy."

"You're just saying that to make me feel better."

"No, I mean it. You're not up on faeries and their wings, are you?"

"What do you think?"

"Would it make you feel a little better if I found someone for you to talk to? A faery? How about Never?"

"Like ask him questions about faeries and their wings? Maybe. I still need to confirm this changeling thing. Because much as it all seems to point in that direction, I'm the sort that needs a solid."

"I thought you believed once you saw something."

"Right. And I can see them. I just…"

He understood. It had been difficult for him to accept he wasn't completely werewolf in those days following the upset in his family. "We'll take things slowly. But I think it might not hurt for you to chat with Never. Just let me know if you want to."

"Thanks, lover. You'd better get going. It's eleven thirty."

"See you, and all those vibrators, soon."

"If you don't hurry," she said as she got out of the car,

"I might start without you!" She blew him a kiss and wandered up to the front door.

When she was inside, Ry pulled away from the curb and headed toward the eighteenth arrondissement.

Had he been truthful by telling her the wings appealed to him? He wasn't sure. He'd denied his faery heritage all his life. At least, ever since he'd found out he wasn't full werewolf. Being ousted from one's pack by the man he thought had been his real father was not something a guy took lightly. Or could ever forget.

He did everything he possibly could to push down his faery attributes, and was thankful he didn't have wings. That would cement the fact that his life was not what he'd expected or wanted it to be. He was not the wolf he'd thought he was.

Stopping at a light, Ry had the sudden realization that Indi must feel the same way. Her life had been going fine and dandy up until those wings had popped out. Then… wham! Life as she knew it would never again be the same, and the life she had led had all been a lie.

They were two alike. They could share things no others could. The realization was so immense he could but sit there at the light, not driving forward, as he choked back a heavy swallow and bowed his head.

He'd never felt like this about a woman before. Was he falling in love with the Princess Pussycat who wore wings and rhinestone ears?

Indi rolled over in bed, and her hand slapped against a hard, hot stretch of skin that then moved and growled in a seductive tone. Without opening her eyes, she snuggled up against Ry's body, her body reacting like a magnet snapping firmly to iron. She was still drowsing in dreams, but the closer she snugged to him, the quicker some parts of her body strived to come awake.

"You smell like you got into my body cream," she whispered, and kissed the body part closest to her mouth, which pulsed once under her lips. "Mmm, now I know why you like it so much. I could eat you up." His stone-hard pectoral muscle felt like steamed rock. She dashed out her tongue and landed it on the tiny jewel of his nipple.

"You want to sleep?" he asked on a whisper.

"No. Do you?"

"Couldn't sleep against your beautiful body if I tried."

His hand glided down her side, pushing the sheet below her waist and exposing her skin to the warm summer breeze that sifted the sheers before the open window. Indi arched her back, pressing her breasts against his chest, and he urged her forward by the hip. They entwined legs, and a crush of his hard-on against her pussy started her engine.

Now she was awake.

She kissed his neck and nuzzled up against the stubble that shadowed under his jaw. He felt like an inferno and she wanted to burn herself out within him. Against her mons, his erection tightened and he pumped it slowly, wantingly; the heavy head of it tugged at her clit.

"Mmm…" His growl crooned to her like dirty song lyrics.

Entwined in kisses, and skin hugging, Ry embedded himself deep within her. They barely moved yet managed to find a slow pumping rhythm that fed the exquisite spin of burgeoning orgasm in her core. It felt like she could come, and then she did not because it seemed ungraspable. And she fed that sensation because it teased and promised and tempted.

"I could stay inside you always," he whispered. "Indi, you're a new home I want to keep only for myself."

"You can stay. I'll never ask you to leave." Their clasp slowed even more until their bodies were still, yet she squeezed him inside her with pulses of her muscles. "Feel that?"

He nodded against her forehead. His hand released hold of her hip and slid upward until she felt a strange shimmer course through her system. It was as if her whole body was her clitoris and he'd licked it lavishly. She gasped.

"That okay?" he asked. "If I touch your wings?"

"Oh, yes, please, Ry, that makes everything… Oh…"

The next stroke of his fingers lightly gliding along a wing scurried all sensation directly to her core. Crashing into bliss, Indi cried out and came powerfully, her muscles tensing and relaxing and tensing again. She clung to Ry's body, her fingernails clutching into his skin as she gritted her teeth. Wave upon wave of pleasure rolled through her body and shivered her system in a joyous surrender.

Ry moaned out a low cry of triumph as he, too, came. His hips bucked against hers as he filled her.

"What the hell was that?" she gasped against him as they settled into a panting, elated loose embrace.

"That was what happens when you touch a faery's wings," he offered.

"I think I don't mind these things so much if that's going to happen when I have sex."

Ry chuckled and lifted himself to lean onto an elbow. Pale light from the bathroom shone into the room and barely lit the bed, but she could see his face and his glistening skin. He studied his hand, then slid it along her hip.

He slicked his fingers along his softening erection, then showed them to Indi.

"Is that from you again?"

"Actually," he said in a gentle tone, "I think you're starting to put out dust. My dick is sparkling. Heh!"

"Does that mean I've got a glitter pussy? Oh, my God, that's…"

"That will be our little secret. The half faery and the changeling." He turned to sit up on the bed and ran a hand over his hair. "Be right back."

Ry wandered into the bathroom and Indi slid her fingers between her legs. Sparkle orgasms?

"This is crazy," she whispered.

Ry didn't turn on the bathroom light. His vision was honed so he could see shadows of his reflection in the vanity mirror. And the glints of dust sparkled on his skin in a weird rendition of the collector's sparkly skin, only his was in shades of gray.

He winced and bowed his head. He'd come with her before and the sheets had sparkled softly afterward. But not quite so much as tonight. It had startled him in a surprising way. He hadn't wanted to upset Indi, but seeing the dust had instantly shot him back to that night at the pack compound.

Seventeen and randy as hell, he had dated a few human females but hadn't been able to tell them he was werewolf, so he'd been eyeing the one eighteen-year-old female in the pack, yet she had been his friend since they were kids. He'd wanted to keep their friendship and not complicate it with sex. And yet there had been only so much a guy could do to stave off those feelings of desire.

That night he'd jacked off and had been startled when his hand had sparkled. Had that stuff come out of him? What the hell?

He'd not had a moment to consider what was up when he heard footsteps, and scented his father's approach. Tomas had laughed at catching his son in the act, then had punched him on the shoulder. It was something men did. Wasn't anything to be ashamed of. Except…his father's eyes had veered to Ry's shaking hand.

"What the hell is that?" Tomas had asked. "You're sparkling like some kind of…"

"I don't know. It's never happened before."

"Don't tell me." Tomas's jaw had tightened and he'd turned to face the compound, half a mile off through the forest. "That bitch!"

Ry had followed his father back to the compound but had found him arguing with his mother. Only then had she broken down and confessed that she'd had an affair with a faery and that Ry was actually that man's son.

The betrayal and shame Ry had felt that night to learn such a thing had tightened his throat and dropped his heart to his gut.

And he felt the same thing now. He gripped his chest and looked out toward the bedroom, where Indi was lying on the bed, glittering with faery dust.

Could he do this with Indi? It was bringing up all this… stuff. Issues. Bad memories from his past, which wasn't really his past but something that he had to face very day. And his life had been going smoothly until recently, when he'd started slaying the collectors. Everything had been cool. He'd had no worries.

A man shouldn't run away from the trouble that reared its head and defied him to step up and change and evolve. But how to resolve the big empty hole that had formed in his heart that night he learned about his real parentage? And then, months later, when he'd been ousted from the pack by the man he had only ever known as his father?

"Ry? You okay in there?"

"Be right out," he called.

He closed the bathroom door and took a piss.

It was either walk away from Indi right now, mark it

off as a great time and focus on stopping the collectors, or face the shame that still clung to him and teased with the sigil at his hip.

He pressed a hand over the sigil. It warmed. Faery magic? If he used it, he was submitting to the reality that he had never been a son of a werewolf.

Chapter 17

Ry woke early to head into work today. Indi still slept and he was inclined to let her bask in the soft morning light showering her half-covered body. Hair strewn across her face and wings spread over her bare back, she looked like a fallen faery someone might have batted out of the sky.

He wiped a hand over his abdomen where some of the faery dust had settled. His dick no longer sparkled. Most of that had rubbed off on the sheets. He wasn't going to dwell on the dark feelings that had attacked him last night. At least, he would try not to.

He collected his clothes and wandered into the bathroom to dress. On the way out, he took a moment to glance out the patio door.

Indi had told him this place had been in her family for centuries. She had probably been raised in this house. Or rather, if she truly was a changeling, she'd have been brought to this very house and placed in the crib of that wailing baby Claire DuCharme had told them about. And if a faery had come into this home, that meant there could be a thin place nearby.

Sliding on his sunglasses, he opened the patio door and walked out. The sun heated his face and he tugged back his hair, wishing for something to tie it away from his face. He wandered along the pool edge, focusing his senses to the air, the smells and the pressure of the world falling against him. Felt like a backyard to him. He smelled the roses growing wildly along the fence and shrubs. That was Indi's innate scent, and he smiled to realize it came from her garden. Earth and grass sweetened the air. And a neighbor must have cats, because he smelled the fur and urine of a marked territory close by.

Cats. They were so obstinate.

He followed the pool around to the long and narrow yard and toward the copse of frothy chestnuts at the back. Suddenly a tug of something stopped him. He spread out his arms and closed his eyes, sniffing and noticing the waving vibrations in the air.

"A thin place," he whispered.

It had to be. It felt as it did when he entered FaeryTown. An ineffable tug at his musculature, and then the awareness that the air was lighter and…then it was gone.

He stepped back, feeling the tug as if he was stepping out of what could be a portal. Indi might have been brought through this very area twenty-seven years earlier.

And if a guy wanted to communicate with a particular faery, he might call him out here. Not that he wanted to. But it was good to know this place existed.

Ry turned and marched back into the house, made sure the patio door was locked and quietly left through the front door.

He glanced back to the house before getting into the Alfa. He might have to use that thin place. Like it or not.

Working on the spreadsheet for the vibrator samples, Indi had narrowed it down to three. Even with all the data, she still felt she was missing something. A factor that wasn't terribly important to most vibrator users, she felt sure, but she wanted to discover anyway. The data point regarding usage with a male partner. Ry had seemed interested in helping her. But it hadn't come up last night.

The wing sex had been amazing enough. That she'd gotten a shock of sensation when he touched her wings was stunning. It had served like a supercharge to her orgasm.

Did all faeries experience such when their wings were touched?

She'd ask Never that question when he stopped by tomorrow. Ry had called her to let her know his half brother was willing to talk to her and she agreed. While she was still freaking about it, the smart thing to do would be to learn as much as she could about being a faery.

Because all evidence pointed to that truth.

It was weird. It was awful. It was horrifying.

Yet at the same time, it was wondrous. It was interesting. And it was kind of cool. She had wings! Did that mean she could fly? Could she change to a small size like those faeries she had seen in her garden? And the faery dust during sex. What was that about? Would she start to sparkle and glitter constantly? And would she ever be able to make her wings disappear so she could go out in public and act like a normal human woman?

After a long afternoon and into the evening, Indi texted Ry that she would make him supper if he was interested. He had a late meeting with the man he'd spoken to the other night at the ball, so he took a rain check.

Gathering up the vibrators she'd decided were unworthy of inclusion in the catalog, she packed them away. Three remained.

"Guess it's just us tonight, folks. A movie and then an orgasm? Sounds like a plan."

The next morning Indi flitted about the house, straightening up and dusting. So many questions, and she was eager to have them answered. Ry's brother was stopping by today. Normally the faery would insist she come to him, but Ry had mentioned she had a pool. Apparently his half brother loved to swim, so he was bringing his trunks and would be here soon.

Thinking she should prepare a snack or drinks, she veered toward the kitchen, and set to making a welcome feast for a faery. Grocery shopping was tops on her list after seeing all she had was some cheese, crunchy baguettes in need of the garlic she didn't have and a box of Pierre Hermé's macarons that had been in the fridge for a week.

"So much for a welcome spread," she muttered. "Maybe he doesn't eat normal food. What do faeries eat?"

Yet another question to add to her list.

When the doorbell rang, she panicked and checked her hair, then tugged at her skirt. The long, flowy maxi skirt was the same color as the roses out back. And she'd panicked over which shirt to wear to top it off, and had settled for a T-shirt from a Soundgarden concert she'd been to years ago. Not quite her style, but the Goth faery might appreciate it.

She'd met Never before, but for some reason inviting a faery into her home felt momentous. A concession to the reality she had found herself shoved into.

"You're so weird," she muttered as she approached the

front door. "Get over it. Your boyfriend is werewolf and faery. It doesn't get more awesome than that."

She opened the door with a big smile and was greeted by a somber, sulking dark faery. Streaks of guy-liner stretched out from the corner of each eye. Coal-black hair was spiked all over his head and had begun a party-in-the-back shag. Dressed all in black and sporting a nose ring, he dangled a pair of bright red swim trunks from his forefinger.

"Let's party," he said, and wandered inside her house.

Indi set a tray of lemonades and macarons on the table by the lounge chair and then settled in. Never toweled off and stretched his lean figure, which was surprisingly muscled. A doggie-style shake sent water flying from his skin and hair in all directions.

"That was awesome," he announced. His guy-liner had washed off and the hair was spiked about his head at awkward angles, until he rubbed the towel over it, making it even more awkward, yet strangely appropriate for his style. "I need to get a place with a pool. Or rather, a girlfriend with a pool. Ry really made out by hooking up with you."

"You don't think Ry can afford his own pool if he wanted one?" she asked as he sat on the edge of the double lounge chaise. She handed him a lemonade, which he tilted back. "Or even ten pools, for that matter."

"He gives all that tainted money away. My brother lives very spare, save for the sports car and that fancy watch. This is good. What's it called?"

"Lemonade. It's a popular human drink," she said, unable to prevent the mocking tone.

"Really? You think I don't know what lemonade is, changeling?"

"Don't say it like that."

"Like what?"

"Like it's an accusation." Indi pulled up her knees and propped her chin on them. "Sorry. I was teasing about the lemonade. You're…different."

"Way to compliment a guy."

"I mean… I've not been around your sort much. I'm not sure how to act."

"My sort? Is that the faery sort? The vampire sort? Or the Goth sort?" He snorted. "You and Ry make the perfect pair. Silver spoons and limousines."

"I don't think Ry was born with a silver spoon."

"Doesn't matter. He's got the bucks now."

"Are you jealous?"

"No. Yes." He shrugged. "I thought we were talking about you."

"We are. All right, here goes. Is being a changeling a bad thing?"

"No. Maybe. I don't know." He settled beside her and stretched out his legs before him. "Depends on who you ask. Doesn't bother me. I pretty much hate everyone until I get to know them. You're cool. If Ry likes you, I like you."

"Despite the silver spoon?"

"You got it."

She met his lemonade glass with a *ting* and they both drank.

"Hand me that plate of cookies," he said.

She did and his movement flicked water across her face. She wiped it away and said, "I've never seen a man enjoy the water so much."

"Maybe I've got a bit of mermaid in me, eh?"

"Ry mentioned mermaids are real and vicious."

"Every myth, fable and legend is real. Including unicorns. And mermaids are assholes, so avoid them."

"You mean they're not like Ariel?"

"Who's that chick?"

She dismissed bringing a fictional character into a conversation she wanted to be real and honest. She sat next to a man who was half faery and half vampire. "Tell me about yourself. The half stuff. You're a faery and you have wings, and…fangs?"

He took a bite of a macaron, then opened his mouth to reveal fangs lowering amongst the pink crumbs. "That I do. And one of the advantages of not completely being vamp is I can eat human food. These cookies rock. They're crunchy but soft. Funky."

"I can't believe you live in Paris and have never tasted a macaron."

"I live all over. But when in Paris I spend most of my time in FaeryTown. Macaron, eh? Nice."

"Do you bite people and drink their blood?"

"I do not." Never leaned against the back of the chair. He set the plate of macarons on his bare abs. The man's skin was pale. Indi suspected a flash of sun might instantly burn him. "Human blood makes me sick. It's the iron in it. It fucks with the faery side of me. Faeries and iron do not mix."

"How so?"

"Meaning, iron can kill us if it's in the proper form and we consume it or it's stabbed into our organs."

"Will it harm me?"

"I don't know. If you're just coming into the whole faery thing, it could be gradual. Or not. Who knows?"

She would like to know for certain. But if he couldn't tell her what she was, she could at least get more information from him.

"Then if you're a vampire don't you need to drink blood? To survive?"

"I drink ichor."

"What's…isn't that like the blood of the gods?"

"Could be. It's what we faeries call our blood. But our blood isn't red like humans'. It's clear and sparkly."

"Really? That's kind of cool. And that's coming from a woman who lives for the sparkle."

He smirked and downed another macaron. "Ichor tastes great. But I don't need it as often as a vamp needs blood. Maybe once a month. And the weird thing? Full-blooded vampires can't drink faery ichor. Or they can, but ichor is addictive to them. It's like a drug. FaeryTown is where dust addicts go to get their fix. But for some reason it doesn't have that effect on me. Which is good, but also so wrong. I'd like to know that high."

"Sounds complicated. And a little twisted."

He delivered her a smirk that told her all she needed to know about how he felt about twisted.

"I thought vampires couldn't go in the sun."

"A myth. Mostly. The sun will burn a vamp, slowly, but it's not an instant thing. I myself love the sun."

"You'd never know."

"I can't tan. Maybe that's a faery thing."

"No worry of skin cancer, then."

"We don't get human diseases."

"That's one less thing to worry about. What about wooden stakes and crosses?"

"A wooden stake through the heart will pretty much kill anyone or thing. But there's a legend of a vamp who got staked and the thing was left in. Slowly, over weeks, the stake worked its way out and he survived. Freaky. And crosses? They can give a vampire a serious life-threatening burn *if* the vamp has been baptized. Me? No sacraments were ever said for me. Bless whatever freakin' god or goddess for that."

"So if I have a vampire chasing me, I should ask if he's been baptized before whipping out the cross?"

"If you have a vampire chasing you I'd suggest running faster, not pausing to chat."

"I suppose so. So that's the vampire side of you. Tell me about faeries. About…me. I mean, I think I'm still human, but I'm not sure. But just in case I'm not, I need to know what to look for, to recognize. Oh. Just tell me what you can, please?"

"You know I'm doing this as a favor to Ry? I don't normally spend my afternoons drinking lemonade with a fancy woman and answering all her probing questions."

"I need this, Never. I'm trying to figure out what I'm becoming. Or have I been this all my life?"

"If you're changeling? You've been that way all your life. Changelings are born in Faery and taken to the mortal realm. As I understand it, the changeling, when left in this realm, becomes like human. But once a faery always a faery. I wonder if Hestia's healing did something to awaken your true self."

"Maybe?"

"Herne knows what the hell kind of herbs that bitch healer used on you. It's a good thing Ry didn't hang around her too long."

"Were they close?"

He shook his head. "Just a quick fuck, as far as I understand. Couple nights, then so long, see ya later. Heh. Sorry."

"I'm a big girl. You can say things to me."

"Yeah, but you're shivering, sweetie. You're not cool with all this, so don't get too big for your britches. How are you adjusting to the wings?"

She reached over her shoulder and stroked the top of one. "They're getting bigger every day. Will I be able to control them? Put them away? I can't live with wings, Never. I couldn't go into a store again. Or an event. I have business meetings I need to attend. Fashion shows to watch. Negotiations with designers to make. I don't see showing up with wings as a positive."

"All faeries have control over their wings. Unless you're a sprite. Those things have wings out all the time. And they are nasty little critters. Mark them on your *stay-away* list, too."

"Sprites and mermaids. Check. Now tell me how to control my wings."

"You should be able to fold them down and put them away so they furl into you. It's hard to explain, but you sort of think them away and then think them back out."

She cast him a doubtful look.

"Want me to show you?"

"Please."

He nabbed another cookie and stood, then checked the sides of the yard. "Any neighbors watching?"

"The neighbor to the right is on vacation for the summer in Austria. The neighbor to the left is an invalid and lives on the lower floor. She can't see over the fence and shrubs."

He lifted an eyebrow.

"I walk around naked out here all the time. There's nothing to worry about."

"Naked. Nice. Did I mention Ry found himself a good one?"

"You did. Now back to the important stuff."

"All right. Prepare—" he splayed out his arms in a showman's pose "—to be dazzled."

With a dramatic stomp of his foot and thrusting back of his shoulders, wings suddenly unfurled at Never's back. They were huge and elegant and…black. They resembled bat's wings to Indi, yet they gleamed with a silver and violet iridescence and were much finer and more delicate than a leathery wing.

"Nice, huh?" He winked at her. "Tell me you're dazzled."

"Very fitting for a vampire faery," she said. "I am dazzled."

"That's faery vamp. My faery nature is most prominent. And unlike Ry, I'm not afraid to admit that."

His wings stretched behind him, then spread wide. Then he curled them forward to hug about his arms and they wrapped across his thighs.

"You've got such control over them. Can you fly?"

"Of course I can fly. What good are wings if you can't take to air?"

The man leaped up and the wings flapped. He soared over the pool and to the back of the yard, then circled and landed back before her. "Never wise to fly in the city. Someone could see. And I don't trust that your little old lady might not spend her days with a spyglass."

"Do you think I can fly?" She stood, reaching back to touch the wing that seemed to shiver. Clasping at the thin fabric, she felt it slide through her fingers like fine silk.

"Maybe. They probably need to grow to full size first. Those are baby wings."

"How big will they get?"

"Big as mine? Bigger? Smaller? Every faery is different. But look. Once you learn to control them—" he folded down his wings so they dusted the tiled deck floor "—you'll be more confident. And you should be able to put them away, too." As he gestured with one arm in display, suddenly his wings curled toward his back.

Indi walked around behind him. His back was bare of wings or any sign he'd had them out. "That's amazing."

"You should be able to fold yours down now and put them away. You just have to concentrate."

"Concentrate on what? You said it was a feeling. That's so vague."

"Maybe think to yourself 'wings down' or 'wings away'? I don't know. I've been doing this all my life. I was born this way. It's like trying to explain how to breathe to someone."

She nodded. "I'll try it. But can you turn into a small faery like the ones I see in my garden?"

"I can. But I don't do it often. Takes a lot of energy. That's another thing you have to feel to do. And you will get control over your dust, if you have any. Faeries put out dust at all levels and amounts. Some put out a lot, others not so much. Like me. I'm stingy with my dust. And that works fine for me."

"What about when you have sex?"

"Ah, so we're getting into the true confessions now?"

"When Ry and I have sex…there is dust."

"Ry *is* half-faery."

"Yes, but he thought it came from me last night. Is that something I'll be able to control?"

"Not when the orgasm is good," Never said with a wink. "Have your wings started reacting to touch?"

"Oh, my god, yes." Indi realized that was an overly enthusiastic answer and pressed her fingers to her lips.

Again, Never winked. "It's only a good thing. That's why I'd never invite you to touch my wings, and vice versa. You should not allow anyone you don't trust or feel intimate with to do the same."

"This is so much to take in." Indi sat heavily on the end of the chaise.

Never joined her and gave her knee a friendly nudge with his. "You've got Ry on your side. And me, I guess. Any friend of Ry's is a friend of mine. Even if me and the half bro aren't best buds. I wish we were closer. I like the guy. He's one of the good ones."

"He is. You're not so bad yourself."

"Don't go letting people hear that. I do have a reputation to protect. Mad, bad and slightly crazy faery vamp. I work for le Grande Sidhe and do some questionable things, let me tell you."

"I don't want to hear about them. I want you to be the guy in the red swim trunks with a greedy penchant for macarons."

He caught his head in his hands and shook it. Then he looked up. "Yeah, I suppose. But don't tell anyone I was wearing red. It would shatter my rep. You have any more questions?"

"Is there any way to confirm that I was brought here when I was an infant? That I'm not really Claire and Gerard DuCharme's real daughter?"

"I don't think you should go down that path. I mean, listen." He took her hand and met her gaze. "Parents are the people who raise you, right? Doesn't matter who gave birth to you or how you ended up in this life. What does matter is who took care of you, who loved you, who caught you when you fell and encouraged you when you wanted to race."

"That's very profound coming from a mad, bad and slightly crazy faery vamp."

"Don't tell anyone, okay?"

"You have a lot of secrets to keep. But deal. Thanks, Never. I do believe that family is and are the people who care about you. I care about you. So that makes us family."

"Don't get all mushy on me."

"I won't. But you're Ry's family, so I'm going to adopt you as mine as well. I have more macarons in the kitchen if you're interested?"

"Promise you won't tell Ry I like the pink ones?"

"Yet another secret!"

Chapter 18

The next day, Ry called and said he was bringing over something for supper, so when Indi opened the front door she expected to see her tall, handsome lover holding some takeaway bags. Instead, what she saw was a huge burst of red and violet roses. There must be dozens.

"Oh, my gosh." Overwhelmed by the lush colors and fragrance, she stepped back.

The flower spray moved a bit and she heard Ry's voice. "Are you okay? Indi? Can I come in? These are getting heavy."

"Oh, yes, come in! Ry, these are so beautiful. I've never seen so many."

"I bought all the florist had. Didn't want any other woman getting them but you. You like them? They're the colors I see in your wings."

She absently reached for the bottom of one of the wings that she'd had to wear a low-cut sundress for so they didn't rub against her clothes. "Really? I thought they were sort of shimmery clear."

"They are deepening in color. They're pretty." He managed a kiss to her cheek while holding the massive bouquet. "But not as pretty as you."

The gesture was so amazing Indi wanted to hug him and tell him she loved him. But that felt abrupt. And was it true? Did she love him? Not that fast. Maybe?

"You are the best boyfriend a girl could have. I might have a vase big enough to fit these."

"You don't need one. They threw a vase in for free. It's in here, hidden by all the flowers. Let me set them on the coffee table before I drop them."

He set down the bouquet and then ran out to retrieve the food he'd left in the car. Cucumber and dill filled the air as Indi unpacked the food and plated it. She kept looking at the roses. They were more lush than those small ones she had climbing the fence in her garden, and their perfume filled the entire living room and kitchen.

As Ry stood up from searching her fridge for some beer, she lunged into his arms and wrapped her legs about his hips and kissed him. "Thank you, lover. You really know how to make a girl feel special."

He turned her against the fridge and held her there, kissing her deeper and longer. A cold beer pressed against her thigh, but the shiver was sexy cool. When he finished she sighed and let her fingers toy with the ends of his hair, which fell against his chest.

"Let's eat fast, then have sex in the pool."

He raised an eyebrow at that. "Didn't my brother go for a swim yesterday?"

"He did. I don't think I've seen a grown man more excited about swimming. He's a character."

"Did he answer all your questions?"

"Some of them. Others he gave me a lot to think about. I'm going to practice folding down my wings and maybe I can make them disappear."

"Not forever. I do think they are gorgeous. And I'm not saying that to make you feel better."

"Thank you." She kissed him again, then shuffled down from his clutch to sit by the counter. That compliment she would accept without argument. Goddesses were strong like that. It would take a while to accept this big life change, but Ry made it easier. "So, about the sex?"

"I'm in." He sat next to her and popped open a can of beer. "But first…"

He stopped speaking for so long, Indi bent to study his face, bent over the plate, fork lifted high. "Ry?"

"Right. I need to do something when we're done eating. I, uh, checked out your yard the other morning before I left."

"For what?"

"I was thinking about what your mother said. And I guessed that you were probably raised in this house?"

"I was. I told you this property has been in the family a long time. I did a total remodel a few years ago when the place officially became mine."

"I was thinking that if a faery came through with a changeling baby twenty-seven years ago, there had to be a portal or a thin place close by. And after walking around in your yard I found one back near the trees."

"A thin place? Like FaeryTown?"

"Yes. It could be a portal even. It's a very small, concentrated area."

"What does that mean? A portal?"

"It means it's a spot where faeries can enter and leave this realm. And… I can make contact with my father from there. I think it's time I did. Last night four collectors came through from Faery."

"Four?"

"Yes, they are increasing in numbers. And I almost let one get by. It was a close call. I need to end this, Indi. And as much as I don't want to talk to my father, he seems the only option. Someone who might have information."

"Sounds like a good plan to me. So, you just stand in the thin place and call him out?"

"Basically. If I'm correct about that area of your yard, then it should work. I'll run out in a bit. But would you do me a favor and stay inside when I do so?"

"Oh."

"I don't want Malrick getting distracted. And whatever is said is something I need to keep between the two of us."

"Oh, sure. I'm good with that. I have some work on my spreadsheets to do. Though I'm still missing some important data for making a decision on which vibrator the catalog will feature."

He cocked his head her way and grinned that sexy charmer smile.

"Yes, it involves getting a man's assistance."

"Well, I have offered to assist."

"I'll put it on the schedule for tonight?"

He winked. "Let's be crazy and spontaneous about it. Why not? Like maybe later after I've talked to my dad."

"Spontaneous it is. Now, tell me what this is I'm eating."

"That's a falafel. Made with chickpeas."

"It's very good."

"It's even better with cucumber sauce." He handed her the little plastic sauce container and she gave it a try. "Yeah?"

"Num. Do werewolves have a cultural or traditional meal?"

"Raw meat," he said without a blink. When Ry looked to her, his jaw dropped. "Sorry. It's a wolf thing."

"All righty, then. Promise not to invite me along on any forest-foraging excursions, 'kay?"

"Deal."

Ry strode through the yard close to the area he'd noticed as a thin place. He brushed against it, feeling it tug. Rubbing an arm, he vacillated over what he intended to do. He'd never thought he would ask Malrick for help. And he suspected there would be strings attached.

"Hell. In for the dive, right?"

He stepped forward. The air about him lightened. His heartbeat raced. His fingers clenched and unclenched by his sides as his breathing quickened.

Inhaling a deep breath, he found his calm. The wolf inside him didn't like the Faery air, and he growled as if warning an approaching predator. Shoulders stiffening, he attempted to quell his anxiety.

The last time he'd spoken to Malrick, the man handed him the leaves and told him he was always welcome in Faery.

It could never be his home. It was just the place where his biological father lived. The man was a mere sperm donor. His contribution to Ry's existence had probably taken all of five seconds. Over the years, he'd reasoned it was truly those who raised a man who were his parents, blood or not. His mother had been blood. And the pack leader, Tomas LeDoux— Ry tried not to go there. It was too painful.

Tomas had turned his head away the day Ry walked away from the pack. He had told him he wished him well and knew he would succeed on his own, but then had merely shaken his hand. Not a fatherly hug. Not that Ry had expected one. Though he missed that final contact now. Something to show him all those years had been real. That Tomas did not regret raising him as his own.

He'd never have the answer to that question. Because much as he did not want to go to Faery, the idea of returning to his pack was even more outrageous. He hadn't been banished, permanently marked as an unwanted, but it felt much the same.

Glancing back to the house, he couldn't see if Indi was peeking out the kitchen window. It wasn't that he didn't want her to see him talking to Malrick, he just didn't want her to get upset. Because if anyone could piss off another with a few words or even an obstinate look, it was the bratty Unseelie king.

Exhaling heavily and shaking his arms loose at his sides, Ry nodded decisively. Tilting his head from side to side, he worked up his courage. And then he blew out a few huffs and planted his boots on the grass.

And quietly, ever so softly, he whispered, "Malrick."

Because it wasn't as if he was overly excited about this plan.

Before he could second-guess his decision, the air shook in waves and the fabric between worlds opened to allow a tall man with black hair and silver eyes to walk through. Dressed in a tailored green suit that sported beading along the sleeve cuffs and hem, and which had been cut to allow his massive silver wings freedom, he bowed his head to Ry.

"My warrior prince has finally called for me. I am honored, Ryland Alastair James LeDoux."

That Malrick knew his full name did not sit well with Ry. But he'd not used it to control him. Yet.

"I have a few questions for you, Malrick. Don't get all excited. I'm not coming for a visit."

The man's upper lip twitched, but he maintained decorum. He wielded a cane that looked fashioned from a dark yet clear crystal, and which was capped by metal that probably wasn't silver but something faery in composition. Many rings hugged his long, graceful fingers, and one glinted fluorescently. At his neck, violet sigils curled up and back into his dark hair.

"You do know what's been going on in FaeryTown every midnight, yes?"

Malrick turned his head to face the wind and it blew his hair to reveal his skeletal bone structure. Some faeries were alien in appearance to Ry, and his father was one of them. His eyes were silver. They didn't exactly glow, rather they glinted like chrome, and it disturbed Ry to look at them. Most faery eyes were violet. Only the eldest's eyes turned silver with age.

With a splay of one beringed hand, Malrick finally said, "Enlighten me."

Ry had a hard time believing the man—a king of the Unseelie—was naive regarding the goings-on, but if that was what he had to do, he'd spell it out.

"Someone is sending collectors to this realm to steal human babies and take them back to Faery."

Malrick shrugged. "It is what is done."

"Not without leaving a changeling in its place. And even then, it's just wrong."

"There is no right or wrong, son. Only perception."

"Don't go New Agey on me. You know about this situation. That is apparent."

"No changelings, eh? That is…a novelty."

Ry narrowed his gaze at the man. He wasn't lying, but he wasn't telling the truth, either. He could feel it as his werewolf growled warningly within him.

"Settle your wolf," Malrick admonished. "I don't like it when your sort sniff at me like I'm a strange being."

"My sort? I thought you favored werewolves."

"I do. You are the strongest and the bravest of all my children. But I don't abide any who would treat me as something they must fear."

"Somehow I think that's exactly what you enjoy. Without others to fear you, what power would you have?"

Malrick's smile was so tiny it barely curled the corner of his mouth. "Why won't you come to Faery and assume the title of Unseelie prince, as you should? I need you there, son. I won't live forever."

Ry scoffed. The sound almost turned to full-out laughter, but he toed the grass and shook off the sudden urge to show his disgust. "You've got many centuries ahead of you, I'm sure. And in Faery years that's a long time."

"What if I told you I was dying?"

"That would be a lie spoken in an attempt to manipulate me."

Malrick tilted his head down. His upper lip flinched. When he looked at Ry, the man's power seemed to creep out and grasp Ry by both shoulders and hold him in an aura of fierce enchantment. He could not look away from Malrick. Didn't want to. He did honor his position as a great king of Faery. Despite his rumored wicked ways.

On the other hand, weren't all faeries wicked? At the very least malicious or mischievous to a fault?

"It is my doing," Malrick announced boldly. "The collectors. The Unseelie have developed a need for human offspring to populate our dying numbers. We are fading, Ryland. You must believe me. There's something wrong with the Unseelie. Perhaps too much inbreeding over the years? I cannot know. Much as it belittles our great race, we require the infusion of human blood into our species to keep it strong."

"You have no right to steal innocent human babies."

"Should I resume the practice of leaving a changeling

in its place? Tit for tat? The human families are never the wiser. Although…we've no longer the resources for those nasty changeling beings."

"Changelings aren't—" Ry stopped himself from giving the man too much information. Stuff he didn't need to know about. "Stop sending your collectors. Now. Or I will come after you if that's what it takes to stop it."

Malrick's wings unfurled with a hiss, stretching at least eight feet out on each side of his body and glistening in the sunlight. The high cartilage along the tops of each of the four-sectioned wings gleamed like steel, and perhaps it was solid and adamant with age. The sheer silver fabric reflected the light and made Ry blink.

"Do not threaten your father, boy."

"Your ichor might run in my veins, but my father was the man who raised me, Tomas LeDoux. You will never earn the right to call me son!"

The faery lashed out and gripped Ry by the throat. His fingers seemed to stretch all the way around until his nails clicked together at Ry's nape. The faery king lifted his feet from the ground with ease, yet Ry did not struggle. Let him power-play. He wouldn't condescend to such theatrics.

"You do not want to make an enemy of me, Ryland," Malrick said, looking up at him. "I can accept your faulty mortal-realm beliefs about parentage, but know that indeed my ichor runs in your veins, and you will be called to your homeland. Sooner, rather than later."

He set down Ry and his wings swept up to a snapping close behind his back. "Is that all you wanted from me?"

"I want you to stop," Ry insisted. "I can go out every night and slay those mindless idiot collectors forever if I have to. But that will get neither of us where we wish to stand. Can we come to terms on this, Malrick?"

"You're not listening to me, boy. The Unseelies need

the infusion of human DNA. And if you had ever the time and interest to visit, as I've requested, you would see how we are failing. Another few winters and we may simply fade away."

"Impossible. The Unseelie lands are vast. Or is it just your kingdom you are focused on?"

The Unseelie king lifted his jaw at that statement. Ry's guess was correct. The man was only concerned for his subjects and closest of servants, surely.

"What do I have to do to make you stop?" Ry asked, knowing what the answer would be, but hoping the man might surprise him.

"Come to me in Faery. Sit on the throne beside me."

As he'd suspected. "Never."

"Ry!"

Turning at the sound of Indi's voice, Ry hissed an oath. Malrick opened his wings wide at her approach and put up his cane to stop her from approaching too closely.

"Who is this one?" Malrick asked.

"I'm sorry, Ry. I had to come out here," Indi said. "I realized your father could be the one who can verify for me what I am."

"What you are?" Malrick sniffed. His upper lip curled. "You mean a nasty changeling?"

Indi's jaw dropped open. She caught her palms against her chest.

Ry stepped toward her, but she took two steps back.

"Is this your woman, Ryland? You would choose a changeling?" Malrick's lips crimped. "She is beneath you. Changelings are dirt. Meant to be cast away for a more valued prize."

"Enough, Malrick. Be gone with you!"

At that powerful entreaty the faery king took a step

back. With a *whoosh* of his wings, he swept backward through the portal.

Indi dropped to her knees in the grass, catching her face in her hands. "Is it true?" she asked on a wobbly voice.

"Princess, no." Ry kneeled before her. "I told you Malrick is an asshole. He said that to you because he's mean. It's what he does best."

"But he knew what I was. That confirms things. Am I…less than dirt?"

"That is merely the opinion of a stupid, pompous king speaking from his position of false power. Don't listen to him. You are valuable and beautiful and I care about you, Indi."

"Can you care about me even though you hate the faery part of yourself?"

"I—" He'd never told her that about himself. Had she gleaned as much from him?

"Indi, faeries are…they are a fearsome breed. Strong and powerful. Warriors. You should not be afraid that you are one."

"I'm not afraid. But you are. Why do you try to hide that part of you? Why not talk to your father more? If the only reason you hate him is something your parents did—because none of that was your fault—then you might be missing out on something that could be truly amazing."

He'd never heard it put that way before. Yet it had been his fault. His mother had fled because his father had learned that Ry was not completely werewolf. And then when he hadn't been what Tomas had expected, he'd been kicked out of the pack. If his father had never stumbled on to him that night, he might still be in the pack.

"Ry?"

He pulled Indi into a hug and caught her soft sobs against his shoulder. This had gone over as well as he'd expected. The faery king had confirmed his worst nightmare about the source of his struggles. And he'd given his girl-friend the truth, which was that in Faery she could never be viewed as anything but the lowest of the low. Truly, she had been born to be cast out for something more valuable.

But this was the mortal realm. And he didn't subscribe to Faery beliefs. He only hoped Malrick's words would not sink too deeply into Indi's psyche.

Chapter 19

Indi curled up in a ball on the couch. Ry had walked her inside after Malrick had left, but then had wanted to return to the thin place and speak a few words to cleanse the area. She'd left him to it.

What that awful faery king had said to her. Was it true? Changelings were dirt, the lowest of the low, abandoned here in the mortal realm?

But this was her realm. Her home.

Or was it?

Now she was more confused than ever. And she didn't know how to process it all. And with the overwhelming scent of the roses Ry had given her filling the air, she felt dizzy and not at all on balance with the world.

Closing her eyes, she thought she should be crying about this, but the tears didn't fall. Instead, a heavy emptiness filled her chest. And the crush of her wings against the back of the sofa annoyed her, so she stretched out to lie on her stomach.

"Stupid wings," she muttered. "Stupid changeling. I hate this! I want it to all go away."

But she knew that could never happen. She'd lived her life thus far as something she was not. Only now was she turning into what she really was. And was that a despicable thing?

Despite Ry's comforting words, it was difficult to grasp hope.

"It's starting to rain," Ry announced as he walked into the living room. "Hey, Princess, you going to be okay?"

"No," she answered flatly.

He kneeled before the sofa, their faces inches apart. "You get to pout about this for the rest of the night. It's a lot to take in. Then tomorrow morning you're going to lift your head and accept it. This is you now, Indi. There's no going back."

"I know that. But what about you?"

"What about me?"

"When are you going to accept your faery side?"

He bowed his head. She knew this was something he'd been dealing with for a long time, and she could never relate to being literally kicked out of house and home by a man he'd once believed was his real father. But Ry had told her faeries were fierce and strong. The description fit him to a tee. If he wanted her to believe that she could weather this storm in her life, then he'd better help her by showing her he could do the same.

"You've given me something to think about," he finally said. "You're right. And I don't hate faeries. It's a manipulative father that makes accepting the idea of them difficult."

"I'm sorry your werewolf father wasn't more supportive when you needed him most," she said. "I'm very lucky to have loving parents. Even after they divorced, both have remained key in my life." She slid a hand into his. "Maybe we can do this together?"

"I'd like that," he said.

"But I still get the night to pout?" She jutted out her lower lip.

Which he kissed. "Absolutely. You're going to start practicing folding and putting away your wings tomorrow, too. Promise me?"

She nodded.

"What do you need, Indi?"

"What do you mean?"

"I don't know. Most women like ice cream or chocolate when they're depressed. Kristine goes for the vanilla mochi. I'll get you whatever you need to wallow in."

She had to laugh at that one. What a sweet man. He was trying to make her feel better. And he wasn't doing a terrible job at it. "I do have a tendency to drown my sorrows in fig jam."

"That sounds…weird. You want me to get some?"

"I have ample stores in the kitchen. And it does sound good slathered on some crunchy shortbread. Do you have to leave soon?"

"It's still early." Ry sat on the floor, his back to the sofa, and tapped the rose petals that hung lowest in the bunch.

"Malrick is not a nice man. Faery." Indi toyed with Ry's hair, which spilled down his back. "What did you learn from him? If you want to tell me."

"He's behind sending the collectors to this realm. He gave me some excuse about needing humans to repopulate the dying Unseelie race."

"Are they dying?"

"I don't know. Doubtful. I suspect Malrick is merely populating his inner circle. Of course, he agreed to stop if I move to Faery."

"Oh."

"I'm never going to live in Faery. It is not my home. And he can't force me to do anything."

"But then the collectors won't stop coming. And eventually one or more of them will get past you. Especially if they start arriving in greater numbers."

"I'll figure something out. It's going to be a fight. But I'm up for it." He kissed her forehead. "Those flowers are full of fragrance."

"Yes, they're making me dizzy. I might fix myself some fig snacks and go out to the patio for fresh air. I think I need to be alone tonight, Ry. Is that okay?"

"Of course. But will you call or text me later to update me on how you're feeling?"

She nodded. He was made that way. Kind and caring. A warrior protector to her Princess Pussycat.

"I'll see you tomorrow," she offered. "Maybe I'll stop by again with lunch for you and Kristine. I just need the night to wallow and feel bad about myself."

"Fresh start in the morning. The both of us. Promise?"

"Agreed."

He stood and she tugged at his jeans. "Ry?"

"Yes?"

The words *I love you* sat on the tip of her tongue, but they didn't quite trip out. "Thank you."

"I'll see you tomorrow." He started toward the door. "Don't forget to call before you go to bed!"

He closed the door behind him and Indi sat up, wiping away the tears that had fallen. He was right. She was pouting about something she couldn't change. But she was allowed a good pout. If not, she'd never be able to move beyond.

She headed to the kitchen to prepare her sad-girl supplies and then headed outside to the chaise, where she devoured half a jar of fig jam. And when the sun was completely below the horizon, lightning bugs glinted in the roses climbing the fence.

And Indi had to wonder if any of them were faeries. And if so, were they like her? Or rather, was she like them?

Ry took a hit to his back, right in the kidney. It never ceased to amaze him that the collectors, which appeared as if made of mist and a substance of blackest black, could deliver a physical blow. He swung around, battle sword sweeping the air, but the sudden twist felt as if something punctured inside him. He dropped to his knees, clutching his side. Blood oozed over his fingers. Had one of those bastards managed to stab a talon into him?

He'd slain three collectors—as had Never—and two remained. Malrick was increasing their numbers.

His brother aimed a small, specially designed bow loaded with arrows toward a collector. Direct hit in the heart. The thing spun and yowled silently, clawing the air. When it soared above Never's head, the dark faery thrust up with his other arm, slashing a small sword across the collector's throat, and succeeded in decapitating the nasty thing.

Never turned to pump his fist, yet Ry pointed behind him, and yelled, "That one! He's almost out of FaeryTown!"

Pulling himself up, yet staggering, Ry winced at the incredible pain in his kidney. He might have internal bleeding, but his werewolf nature usually allowed for rapid healing. As Never turned, and with a flap of wings took to flight after the collector, Ry staggered down the cobblestone street. Neither was swift enough to catch the creature before it exited FaeryTown.

When the collector broke through the skein that demarcated FaeryTown from regular Paris, the creature's body glittered like millions of stars and then soared down the street.

"It's going to latch on to the first human it sees," Ry said.

Never landed near him, shoving the sword back in a holster on his thigh. He wielded the crossbow at the ready. "Let's do this!"

Both ran full speed after the thing.

Ahead, a nightclub blasting techno tunes began a long stretch of clubs, theaters and sex shops. The streets teemed with partiers, both residents and tourists. While Ry and Never could see the collector, they knew a human would not see it. And if anyone saw them, running down the street with swords wielded high, the police—who, he noted, were parked a few blocks ahead—would be on them swiftly.

"How we going to do this?" Never asked as he shoved the crossbow at the back of his waistband. He glanced to Ry's side, where he bled, but didn't comment.

Ry sheathed the sword at his back. "We don't have much choice but to follow the thing. It's going for that man in the red shirt. We'll never make it—"

Both Ry and Never stopped as they witnessed, fifty yards ahead of them, the collector insinuate itself into a particularly burly man standing in line, holding a drink and chatting and laughing with a circle of men and women. He suddenly handed his drink to the person next to him, made a gesture like he was going to take a leak, then strode off, down the sidewalk, away from the nightclub. Purposefully.

"Do we grab him?" Never asked.

"I don't know." Ry increased his strides, wincing at the pain in his kidney. "We can't kill the human. We'll have to wait until it leaves the body."

"Then I guess we're going to play follow the leader."

Heartbeats thundering, Ry crossed the street before oncoming traffic, following the human body that was no longer human in thought. The collector controlled it completely, yet the body functioned as a human and couldn't fly or run any faster than a normal man, so this would be an easy follow.

The thing wove through the streets, focused as it headed toward the Seine and the main island. When it paralleled the river and headed east, the destination became obvious to Ry.

"I think he's headed to the Hôtel-Dieu," he said.

"The hospital?"

"Where else to find a baby?"

"How the hell can a creature from Faery manage to steal a baby in a place like that? There's security. Cameras, and maybe even tracking ID technology."

"I'm not sure."

But he was going to find out.

Soaking in the bathtub filled to the steaming surface with bubbles, Indi decided to take what Ry had said to heart. She got to pout about the whole changeling thing for a little longer. The rest of this night. But then she had to pull herself up and move forward. It was what she did. She'd not established a successful business by wallowing over her defeats.

Besides, they were not defeats, but rather challenges.

And her new condition was not something that was going to suddenly change. She. Was. A. Changeling.

The Unseelie king had confirmed that fact.

Now what was she going to do about this challenge?

When life got tough, she put down a couple goblets of champagne, cried about it, then moved on. Just as she had with Todd.

She had moved on. In a very strange way.

If she had never been cut by the collector that night, and Ry had not taken her to be healed, might she still be the same old normal human she'd once been?

"But you've never been human," she reasoned with a blow at a handful of bubbles.

And besides, had she not been healed that night, it sounded as though she would have died. So the result had been to uncover her truth—and live. Which she should be happy about.

And she would get there. As soon as she figured out how to control her wings.

She had to admit, this hot bath made her wings feel great. It was as though they channeled the heat through her system like a luxurious spa treatment. She'd never felt so relaxed.

Grabbing her cell phone from the shelf beside the tub, she texted Ry, thinking he was probably finished with tonight's slayage, but just in case he wasn't, she didn't want to interrupt him while he was busy with a call.

Doing much better. Taking a bath, then heading to bed. See you tomorrow, my sexy werewolf lover.

She set aside the phone and settled deeper into the water and bubbles. Sitting on the edge of the tub was a pink silicone vibrator designed for use in the water. She'd get to that soon.

For a woman who had easily accepted that the man she was dating was werewolf, she should find accepting her wings as easy. She wanted to see Ry in all his werewolf glory. To meet that part of him that he kept from this crazy rat race of a world. She'd love to go to his cabin and watch him dash through the fields and forest in wolf form.

While in that shape, would he know she was his girl-friend? Or would he be more like a wild and feral animal?

He'd said something about being in his animal and human mind at the same time when he was werewolf. And two werewolves could have sex? That was interesting. As well, he'd said something about a werewolf having sex with a human. Even more interesting. Also, squicky.

She wouldn't judge. She did have wings. And that could prove very weird in bed. Sparkles flying every time she came?

She smiled to remember Ry's dick glittering with faery dust. That was not something he'd ever let his male friends know about. But she thought it was spectacular.

Apparently, there were some good things that came with being faery. And from this point forward, she intended to embrace and accept them.

Her phone rang. It was Janet. Indi still wasn't ready to tell her bestie about learning that she was a change-ling. But that didn't mean they couldn't discuss Janet's date last night with the drummer from a minor yet known rock band.

Indi connected and said, "Tell me everything."

"Oh, girl!"

Ry and Never followed the collector inhabiting the human's body in through the ER doors at the Hôtel-Dieu, a city hospital located in the shadow of Notre Dame. Ry had not been inside a hospital before. He'd no need because wolves didn't get human ailments, and when they were injured the rapid healing process negated any need for a doctor.

And if the wound was serious? He knew a certain healer in Faery who— Nope, he had to stop considering Hestia as a convenient fix for his problems. He had hurt her. Unknowingly. Best he stayed as far from her as he could. For her emotional healing.

While the wound on his side still pained him, he knew it was healing from within, and he should be top form soon enough. He wore a dark shirt, so the blood wouldn't be noticeable. The faery dust was another issue.

Did anyone notice his subtle sparkle? Wasn't making it any easier for him to embrace that side of himself, that was for sure.

The antiseptic smells in the ER hit him hard. He dialed down his senses, then noticed the strange look Never got from a patient seated on one of the waiting-room chairs.

"We stand out," he muttered.

"You think?" Never ran a hand along his thigh holster. "I give it two minutes before we're forcibly tossed out for the weapons alone. He's going right."

They picked up their pace and followed the man, who, as he neared a nurse walking toward him, paused to ask her a question. He touched her arm, and the nurse's eyes fluttered. She clutched a clipboard to her chest. The man stepped back, leaned against the wall and shook his head in bewilderment. The nurse turned and walked with purpose in the direction from which she had come.

"I think it just switched bodies," Never said.

"Me, too. Don't lose that nurse."

As they passed the man who had initially been standing outside the nightclub, he muttered, "Where am I?" and then he wandered down the hallway.

"He'll be okay."

"If we take out the nurse," Never said, "we kill the human as well."

"We're not going to harm any humans today. Don't let her out of your sight."

The nurse walked through a ward painted soft green

and Ry smelled the sweetness of innocence and new life. And anxiety. This was definitely the maternity ward. The nurse walked into a nursery and he and Never stopped in front of it. Behind the glass viewing window were two neat rows of babies in cribs. The nurse walked up to one wrapped in a blue blanket, cradled it in her arms with no emotion, then walked out.

"She can't walk out of the building with a baby in arm."

"I'm not sure," Ry said. "Can humans see her? I don't know."

"They can see the human baby."

"Maybe. The collector might have some enchantment to conceal the infant. We let her get outside, then grab her. You take the baby and I'll take care of the collector," Ry commanded.

"Why do I have to grab the kid? I don't know what to do with a baby."

"I don't know, either," Ry said testily. "Just bring it back inside. Hand it to someone in the ER. But don't drop it."

"You think I'd drop a baby?" Never swore. "Maybe. I haven't touched one of them before. They look so…delicate. She's heading outside!"

Once the nurse broached the outside, Ry saw that she began to shudder. The collector was leaving her body, forming in black mist all about her, still clutching the baby.

"Now!" Ry ordered.

Never ran up and grabbed the baby from a swirl of black mist. The nurse screamed. And the collector swept toward Ry. It slashed its talons, catching him across the jaw. Bending and twisting at the waist, Ry spun around, dragging his sword through the collector's torso. Its maw opened in the toothy silent yowl and it dissipated.

"What are you doing with that baby?" the nurse cried.

"She's in her body. Give it back to her," Ry said.

Never shoved the infant into the nurse's arms. "It belongs in the maternity ward. You took it out for a walk."

"That's not something I would—"

But Ry and Never did not wait around for an argument. They ran across the street, insinuating themselves into the shadows caressing the buildings, and didn't stop until they reached the river.

"That was close." Never jumped onto the concrete balustrade before the river and sat, legs dangling.

"Yes. But how many will Malrick send tomorrow night?" Ry eased his fingers along the cut healing on his jaw. "We won't be able to hold off the invasion for long. I have to make Malrick stop this."

"You said he wanted you to sit the throne beside him in Faery? You cool with that to save some human babies?"

"No. But what other choice do I have?"

Chapter 20

Ry was on the phone in his office when Indi arrived with lunch for the threesome. When Kristine suggested they head to the nearby park, Ry nodded that he'd follow as soon as he got off the phone.

The Jardin des Plantes was a massive garden that had existed for four centuries. It consisted of many themed gardens devoted to various flowers, insects, a zoo, a gallery of mineralogy and geology, even a labyrinth.

Kristine, marching like an Amazon goddess on her six-inch bright yellow pumps, led Indi to her favorite lunch spot in the garden of bees and birds under the shade of a chestnut tree. She kept a blanket at the office for such adventures. Indi settled next to her and opened her salad.

"Ry has been distracted today," Kristine said after they'd eaten for a few minutes. "He actually growled at me when I asked him how things went last night."

"Really? I haven't had a chance to talk to him since he

left for FaeryTown last night. I hope everything went all right. Has he, uh, told you about…me?"

"Your wings?" Kristine made a show of peering around Indi's back, but she'd put on the blazer again today and figured she'd only get another few days' use out of that before her wings stretched below the hem. "He told me the day after the ball. What's up with that, sweetie? You a faery?"

Kristine leaned against the tree trunk and crossed her legs at the ankles. Her skintight dress matched the shoes, and she accessorized with copper jewelry. Against her dark skin tone, she worked it.

"A faery," Indi said. "Maybe? Probably." She set her lunch on the blanket. Ry trusted Kristine, and even though Indi knew her not at all, she could use some girl talk. She could not talk to Janet about this. "I met Ry's father yesterday. It was not a happy event."

"Really?" Enthralled, Kristine munched a carrot stick while granting her a rapt ear.

"Ry found a thin place in my backyard, which is where he suspects I was brought through when I was a baby. And then his father, Malrick, confirmed it. He said I was a changeling. He also called me nasty and lowest of the low."

"I've heard that sparkly-lipped king is an asshole. I wouldn't take his opinion on anything for gospel. A changeling, eh? That's interesting. That means you get to keep the wings forever?"

"I guess so. Seems whatever that healer did to me she must have awakened my true self. I'm trying to accept it. It's just… Kristine, all my life I've thought I was one thing, and now I suddenly learn I'm not that at all. I'm not sure who or what I am anymore. And Ry can relate, having always thought he was full werewolf, only to learn about his crazy family background. Though I think he struggles with his faery side more than he'll let me know."

Kristine tutted and wiped her lips with a napkin. "You paranormal sorts. So mixed up. I think the only one of us who has a firm grasp on who she is, is me. And who would have thought the transgender chick would ever say that?"

Indi laughed. "You do have it all together. Any advice for someone who has had it all pulled apart?"

"Don't look at it that way, sweetie. This is just you, progressing. Moving forward. Hmm…" She tapped her lips in thought. "Look at it like this. You're emerging from a chrysalis the mortal realm wrapped around you when you were brought here as an infant. Now you're spreading your wings."

Indi liked the sound of that. Of a butterfly emerging to spread her wings.

"You've got to grow into those wings and become the faery you were born to be," Kristine said. "You're pretty and smart. Ry tells me you have a million-dollar business that caters to goddesses?"

"It's called Goddess Goodies. It's focused on renting used designer gowns to those who might not be able to afford a dress for prom or an event. We only charge for shipping and cleaning. We make the money to buy those gowns from my accessories line. We also buy vintage gowns, which I and a handful of seamstresses fix up and resell. Those we sell for the big bucks."

"Ooh, I'm all about the dresses and goodies."

"I'm excited about the accessories line. I want it to encompass all the things we women want and need to feel good about ourselves. Like the cat ears I wear. They're one of my best sellers."

"I love those cat ears. I need some leopard-print ones myself."

"I have those. I'll bring you a pair next time I stop by."

"Ooh!" Kristine wiggled the toes of her shoes gleefully. "Oh, here comes Ry. He's got his pouty face on."

"Ladies." He sat on the blanket and opened the untouched boxed lunch. "What did I miss?"

"Just girl talk," Indi said. "Things not go well last night?"

He sighed heavily and stabbed his fork into the sausage-laden pasta Indi had figured he'd prefer over a girlie salad. The man was a carnivore, after all. "Malrick sent eight collectors last night, and Never and I missed one. It escaped into the mortal realm."

Kristine and Indi exchanged wide-eyed looks before they said in unison, "What happened?"

"We followed it to the Hôtel-Dieu and watched it kidnap a baby. The collector can assume the body of any human it touches, and it took over a nurse's body. We stopped it. The baby is safe. I'm not sure Malrick is going to let up, though. He's going to send more and more, and I'm just one man. Even with Never's help, we won't be able to hold them off in numbers for much longer."

"Don't you dare succumb to your daddy's bribes," Kristine said. "We want you here in this realm. It's the only home you've ever known."

"I want that, too, but I'm not sure how to get around it." He stabbed at the pasta. "Can we…not talk about this right now? I've got a headache trying to sort this all out."

"Of course. You want this?" Indi offered him an olive on the end of her fork and he ate it.

"Did you see the invitation that I left on your desk this morning?" Kristine asked.

"Invitation?" Indi searched Ry's face.

He shrugged. "I did. I'm not sure about it."

"Another ball?" Indi asked hopefully.

He smirked at her enthusiasm. "A Midsummer's Eve

masked ball. I'm not sure about attending if I'm going to be busy slaying collectors."

"It's an early party," Kristine offered hopefully, with a wink to Indi. "Starts at seven."

"Oh, Ry, can we go, please? You know how much I love a fancy party."

"I do know that."

"And costumes!" Indi cooed. "You know, I do have a nice set of wings I could wear."

He lifted an eyebrow and exchanged a look with Kristine. "Why don't the two of you go?"

"Why not all three of us?" Kristine offered. "I'd love to arrive on the arm of a handsome man. But I can share." She fluttered her lashes at Indi. "You okay with that?"

"Of course! Oh, please, Ry? Taking two women to a costume ball? We don't have to stay long. And you can ditch out early to fight the big bads while Kristine and I close the place down."

"Now you're talking." Kristine met Indi with a fist bump.

Ry shook his head and laughed. "I know when I'm outnumbered. Fine. But it's not for another week or more."

Indi clapped and squealed. "That'll give me time to put together a costume. What are you going to go as, Kristine?"

"Probably something feral, like my heart." She curled her claws at them and purred. "A sexy wildcat."

And Ry laughed, though Indi sensed he wasn't completely on board with the idea. He was worried about saving the world. Or at the very least, a bunch of innocent babies. The man was honorable.

And she was falling in love with him.

Ry took the rest of the day off. It was near quitting time by the time they finished lunch. He wasn't about to drop

off Indi at home, either. She breezed into his apartment, wings shimmering at her back. When she turned and fluttered her lashes at him, he quirked his gaze at her.

"I brought something along we might like to play with." From her purse she pulled out a hot pink vibrator.

Ry took the intriguing object, clicked it on to a steady rhythm, then waggled his eyebrows. "Let the games begin."

With a giggle, Indi turned and raced toward his bedroom, sundress dropping in her wake. She jumped onto the bed and crooked a finger at him. She was in a good mood. And with a humming vibrator in hand, he was the man to oblige her anything she wished.

"You know how to operate one of those things?" she asked as she dropped to her knees. Her pale skin lured him closer and the glint of the sun in her wings appealed.

"Can't say I've used one before." He held it up before him, going cross-eyed to look at it. "But I'm willing to learn."

"Then shut it off for now. First, we warm up."

"Oh, I'm warm, Princess."

She unbuttoned his dress shirt and shoved it down his biceps. Ry cast aside the vibrator to the pillow and dropped his trousers. The grip of her fingers about his erection made him hiss.

"You're more than warm," she cooed.

He slipped his fingers between her legs, where she was as hot as he was. "I don't think a warm-up round is going to be necessary."

"Probably not." He bowed to suck her nipple in between his tight lips, and her wanting moan dripped with need. "Oh, mercy, you make me go from zero to ten like that."

"I think I saw the controls on this thing only go to three." He leaned aside to grab the vibrator, without leav-

ing her breast—he did have talent—and blindly clicked it on. He teased it over her wet nipple. "Is this where you like it?"

Her gasp was accompanied by a rotating maybe-yes-maybe-no head shake.

"You're going to have to speak up," he said, moving the vibrator about the tightly ruched nipple. "Or I'll figure this thing out on my own."

"Oh, yes, please. You...do that."

She clutched his shoulders. The scent of her arousal wilded him. Ry wanted nothing more than to push her back onto the pillows and bury his face between her legs to sup at her heat. But her sudden inability to speak a full sentence intrigued him.

"That's..." She bowed her head over his as he licked at her other breast. "Wow. Uh-huh."

"Did your spreadsheet cover this kind of usage?" he asked, looking up to catch her open mouth and closed eyes. So beautiful. And completely at his command right now.

She shook her head and sucked in her lower lip.

"Hmm, this one is getting all the attention." He laved his tongue over her nipple, then placed the humming pink vibrator over the wet bud. And Indi groaned deeply.

He kissed her there at her throat, where her pleasure found voice. And when he leaned in close, his chest connected with the little vibrator and it played over his nipple. He jumped, and then...leaned in closer. Whew! That *was* interesting.

Indi managed to find her senses and she kissed his neck, then under his jaw, where he kept his beard trimmed close. "Lower," she whispered. "Please."

He trailed the vibrator down her abdomen and as he did she leaned back and sat, opening her legs for him. Displaying herself like a lush goddess.

"Not inside," she said quickly. "I don't like that. Just… everywhere else!" Her last syllable ended on a high note as Ry touched the vibe at her clit.

Nestling his face between her breasts, he licked and kissed and suckled at her while playing the vibrator all over and along her delicious edges and folds and rises and swells. She moved so lusciously beneath him, undulating and moaning. The wings swept the sheets, fluttering rapidly at the tips. He was so hard, and could come—but he needed to watch her, to hold her as she shook in his arms. To own her.

He noticed she liked it when he let the nicely weighted vibe rest outside her swells for a while, and it seemed to get her off even more. Her body began to pulse. He heard her heartbeats quicken. Her fingers clenched and unclenched at the sheets. And…then she gave herself to him.

Powerfully. Unabashedly. Sweetly. And with a cry of utter pleasure that invited him to finally let go as well. As he clutched at Indi's arm and buried his nose against her neck, his body tremored. The bedsheets were dusted.

And his heart surrendered.

Indi rolled over on the bed to face Ry's back. It was broad and suntanned and his ab muscles curled around his torso. Like a sculpture. She stroked his skin, devouring the warmth radiating from him.

At the center of his back, she traced where she decided wings would sprout were his faery side more prominent. Her own wings were folded down against the mattress, a skill she was proud of. Now to master putting them away so they wouldn't hamper her everyday routine. Like shopping. Going out and about. And sex.

Ry had mastered the use of a vibrator like a pro. Whew! That model was going on the website for sure. And she noticed sparkle on the sheets and Ry's skin. Not like a night-club glitter disaster. Just a glint here and there. Imagine how much money she'd save on glitter now.

That was a bright side to suddenly learning one was a faery, yes?

There were plenty of bright sides. And she had to start moving toward them instead of always going with the neg-ativity. Because, yes, there was the sex. And she might be able to fly someday. That could be cool. If she was out in the country with no one around to witness such an odd thing as a grown woman flying. If Ry shifted to wolf shape and she flew, they could race through a forest together. That was a weird yet intriguing goal to set. But why not?

Ry stirred and rolled to face her with eyes closed but a smile on his face. She slid a palm up his abs and leaned in to kiss his chest. "You get in late last night?"

He yawned mightily. "There were so many of them."

"Did you get them all?"

"Thanks to Never's help, yes. Hell, this has got to stop. I'm going to take a shower and brush my teeth before I kiss you." He rolled over and sat up. His hair spilled down his back and Indi just managed to brush her fingertips over the tops of his buttocks before he stood and wandered into the bathroom.

He was outnumbered, fighting the collectors. And it was his father's doing. The mean old faery king. Indi wished there was something she could do to help. Could she wield a sword and stand beside him every midnight? She might have to give it a try because the man could not fend off the denizens without a crew of his own.

She rolled to her back and shook her head. Weeks ago she would never have had thoughts about faeries and deni-zens of evil come to steal human children before getting slain by a heroic werewolf whose half brother faery vampire stood by his side.

What a wild ride her life had become.

And…it was a ride she wanted to stay on. So she'd grip the reins and see where it took her.

Ry wandered back to the bedside. He was naked, and he smelled like toothpaste.

"God, that's so big," Indi said, eyeing his hard-on.

He rocked his hips, setting the sizable attribute to a swing.

"Really?" she said. "Do that again."

He obliged her by pumping his hips again. "It's what I've got to offer. But, uh…maybe you prefer that?" He nodded toward the vibrator sitting on the nightstand.

"You're skilled with it, but I do prefer how you operate your own equipment to an auxiliary device any day."

"I am familiar with its operation." He waggled his hips, setting his erection to a bounce.

"I want to gain more experience operating that tool." She patted the bed. "Come here, wolf."

Chapter 21

Ry parked in front of Indi's place and walked her up to the door. He had intended to slip into the office this afternoon, but when she took his hand and led him inside, he abandoned that plan without another thought.

The woman dropped his hand and wandered ahead of him, dropping her dress in her wake. She never wore a bra or panties, and her heart-shaped derriere wiggled as she strode toward the patio doors. With a glance over her shoulder at him, and a wink, she went outside.

Pulling off his shirt, he tossed it on top of Indi's dress as he stepped outside. He unzipped and shuffled down his jeans. She hadn't jumped in the pool. Where was she? Kicking off his pants, he wandered out naked, searching the yard. When a woman whistled from behind him, he spun to find Indi sitting on the lounge chair, one hand between her legs, and a coy smile inviting him closer.

* * *

"If you wanted to go to Faery," Indi said as she stretched out her bare limbs on the lounge chair, her hair falling across Ry's thigh, "could you go from my yard? Through that thin place?"

"Yes. But I'll never go there. I have no desire to be a prince."

"Sounds like a good time to me."

"Not if I have to sit on a throne next to Malrick."

"You think he actually has a throne?"

"I know he does. Never has visited. He told me about the palace and the throne and the servants. Many servants. And his courtesans."

"Sounds so eighteenth century."

"Fashion-wise and social norms-wise, Faery is a weird mix of human centuries. You know they say that time is happening all at once? And if there's a good example of that, it's Faery."

"I'd love to see it someday. Just for a visit."

He stroked her hair. They lay on the chaise longue naked after some exhilarating sex and a quick dip in the pool. Indi tilted her head to check his expression but couldn't read his face, for he stared off across the backyard.

"I fear if I go," he finally said, "there will be no return. This mortal realm means too much to me. I have friends and family here. And even if my never going to Faery means Malrick stays pissed and continues to send the collectors through? I'll fight those bastards forever if I have to."

"I want to help. You know, I took a fencing class when I was in high school. I was actually good at it."

"Is that so? You think you could wield a broadsword against the collectors?"

"I'll give anything a try."

"My sword is out in the car. You want a lesson?"

"Yes!" She flipped over on the chaise and propped her chin on his thigh.

"But not naked." He kissed her forehead. "You don't want to damage any of these pretty parts I love so much."

"I'll get dressed."

"I'll run and get my sword."

Indi had changed into a slim-fit sundress, and Ry had protested her choice of attire. Didn't she have a pair of jeans or leggings? When she insisted that her standard wear was a dress, and if she was ever going to be enlisted to fight with a sword she would likely be wearing one, he acquiesced.

The broadsword he showed her was long and heavy, and the blade was slightly curved and featured some pretty etching.

"It's enchanted to kill sidhe," Ry explained as he held it before her to inspect.

Indi ran her fingers along the smooth, cold blade. "But doesn't that include you? And me?"

"It's also focused to the wielder's intent. I couldn't harm myself with it if I tried."

"But someone else could?"

"No one is going to lay their hands on this."

"Except me?" she asked with hope.

He winked. "Except you."

Initially, he showed her some correct grips, and helped her to balance the heavy sword, but it only took her a few minutes to get a feel for the weapon and now Indi swung it through the air with expertise. At least, she was going to claim expertise. She'd hacked off a section of the rose shrub, but had told Ry that was on purpose, though she suspected he knew the truth.

"All I have to do with the collectors is thrust and drag, right?" She performed the move in front of her while Ry stood back a good fifteen feet.

"You need to stab them in the chest, where I think they have a heart. Not positive on that one, but seems to be the sweet spot. Either that, or decapitate them."

She swung the sword over her head, both hands to the hilt, and slashed an imaginary head off a wicked sparkling villain. "Gotcha!"

"You do have some skill, Princess Pussycat."

"I have my secret talents. This sword is heavy, though. You got anything lighter?"

"I've a few weapons at home. I have an épée that would be perfect for you. The blade is three-sided. An excellent but light weapon. I'll bring it over next time I stop by and you can give it some more practice. How's that?"

She performed a giddy jump, then handed the sword over to him.

"I have never seen someone so thrilled at the promise of a weapon." Ry sheathed the weapon in the thin leather holder. "You never cease to surprise me."

"I wouldn't want you to become bored by me." She spun and when her twirl took her into a strange-feeling area of the yard, she suddenly stopped and put out her hands as if to balance. "What's that? Is this the thin place? Ry, I can feel it."

"Yeah?"

"It's…lighter? And…" She shook her shoulders and her wings trembled. "I feel like I could fly."

"Can you?"

"No. I tried this morning. I try every morning."

"I think they've still a bit of growing to do."

She sulked. "I have to learn how to put them away. I need a shopping fix. And I cannot march into Hermés with these things sweeping the security guards as I make my entrance."

"Did Never give you the lowdown on how to do that?"

"He said it was just a feeling."

Ry swept her into his embrace with one arm across her back. His fingers traced the bottom of one of her wings. "Like this feeling?"

The sensual strokes arched Indi's body forward against his. "That is so good. Never said I shouldn't let anyone touch my wings."

"No one?"

"Not unless I want to have sex with him."

"Then I hope I'm the only one you'll ever let touch these pretty wings." He kissed her. "If you want to visit Faery someday I'll…see what I can do about that."

"Really?" She bounced in his embrace. "As long as I could return here. I wouldn't want to stay. I'm like you. I have a home and family here."

"Do you wonder about your family in Faery?"

"I have a little. Did my mother have me merely to send me off to another realm? That sounds callous. But maybe she needed to? Did she get paid for it? She might have needed the money. That's all I've thought about it. Not sure I'd ever want to meet her. I mean, my human parents are my parents. No matter what."

He kissed her. "You've accepted this, haven't you?"

She nodded. "Mostly. I'm moving forward. And it's my new reality, so I'm starting to put my arms about it. I wish you could accept your—"

He kissed her again. "It's getting late. I should get a move on. I have to run by the office before heading to FaeryTown. See you later?"

"Of course."

* * *

Days later, Indi put a pair of leopard-print cat ears in a gift bag, along with the Girl Power enamel pin, which was a Goddess Goodies bestseller. She'd give it to Kristine next time she saw her.

Ry had left an hour ago for another meeting. He was not looking forward to it because the man was a celebrity and he expected cameras to be flashing. But the celebrity was also half-vampire, so he knew the drill. He owned a charity devoted to blood diseases that Ry wanted to contribute to.

Now she stood before the dressmaker's dummy, which she'd been using to work on her costume for the masked ball. She'd started with a vintage McQueen chiffon gown in violet and soft rose and had shredded the four-level hem. It now looked like something Tinkerbell would wear to a summer faery bash. Rhinestones and moiré ribbon added the perfect touch here and there.

"And I have just the pair of wings that'll go with it."

She folded down her wings and then took great delight in stretching them out wide. She'd become talented at the tuck and fold, yet the complete putting away of wings was still out of her grasp.

"Not something I need to worry about for the ball. But I may never get invited to another brunch again if I insist on sporting wings and claiming them a new accessory for my business."

She touched the delicate chain around her neck where the tiny silver paw hung. She was the werewolf's girlfriend. The billionaire werewolf prince's girlfriend.

Ry's riches didn't matter to her. She was a self-supporting woman. She didn't need a man to take care of her financially. Never did she want to rely on a man for that. She invested wisely and had started a nest egg from her trust fund.

What she really wanted from a man was closeness and companionship. Trust and honesty. And toe-curling sex. Which she got in spades from Ry. He was the perfect man. And even his faults—always having to leave for midnight slayings, unsure about his faery side, camera-shy—were lovable enough to overlook.

So why did she feel a weird twinge of anxiety that this was all too good to be true? As if she was standing on the outside looking in at a world of creatures she might never be a part of. How to truly belong?

"I need him to embrace his faery side," she said, thinking out loud. "Maybe?"

Leaving the dress, she decided to head out and bask in the setting sunlight in the garden. Plucking her gardening gloves from the drawer at the end of the kitchen counter, she also grabbed the small pruning shears and headed out the patio doors to check on the roses. The spent blooms needed deadheading.

Surrounded by lush perfume and the golden glow of the setting sunlight, she got lost in the mindless task of snipping and dropping the flower heads to the dirt bed to compost. Fat, furry bees hummed about the flowers, and an emerald dragonfly flitted by, its wings glinting.

Indi felt the sun on her wings move through her body in a warm rush. They were a part of her. Maybe being a member of the faery race simply required her to say *yes*?

"Yes," she said with resolution.

When something much larger than a dragonfly but smaller than a bird fluttered close, Indi didn't make a sudden move. She focused on beheading another dead blossom while aware the tiny faery landed on her shoulder and stood there, perhaps observing her work.

"Hey, friend," she said quietly. She supposed such a small creature might feel as though she was blasting its ears if she spoke in a normal voice. "Suppose you noticed those fancy wings on my back, eh? No wonder I've always been able to see you. I just wish I could learn to put them away."

The faery on her shoulder alighted and hovered to a stop above a thick rose bloom. The tiny thing was shaped as a human, with a diaphanous petal dress she must have fashioned from these very roses. Her pink hair stuck out straight from her head like a spent dandelion bloom, and she fisted her tiny hands at her hips and made a face, as if concentrating. Of a sudden her wings furled and disappeared, dropping her to land, legs straddling the rose bloom. She looked to Indi and spread her arms as if to say "See? I can do it."

"You can understand me?"

The faery nodded.

"Oh, I wish I could hear you speak. Then you could teach me how to do that."

The faery tapped her temple and furrowed her brow.

"I know. It takes concentration. A feeling. Easier said than done."

Standing, the faery unfurled her wings and buzzed up and around Indi's head. With a wave, she fluttered off, leaving a faint trail of faery dust glistening in her wake.

"That was cool," Indi whispered. That they were communicating with her meant they must realize she had changed and was one of them. The acceptance felt immense.

Closing her eyes and dropping her hands to her sides, Indi curled her gloved fingers about the cutting shears as she focused her thoughts toward where her wings met her back. Imagining them and the blood, or was it ichor, that flowed through them, she folded them down with ease.

And then she unfolded them but tried to pull them in. And…of a sudden they did just that.

Indi sucked in a gasp as she felt as if the wings entered her back and became a part of her. "I did it?"

She reached over a shoulder and couldn't feel any part of her wing. "I did it!"

Jumping and pumping the air with a fist, she performed a hip shimmy. And in her excitement, her concentration faltered. With a sudden tug and a whoosh, her wings unfurled to full glory.

But she had managed it for a few seconds.

"I am so good."

Turning to twist into another victory dance, Indi stopped abruptly at sight of the silver-eyed faery staring snidely at her from five feet away. Dressed in purple velvet with a silver lace cravat, he shook his head and sniffed.

"Changeling," Malrick said. "You disgust me."

Chapter 22

Indi sucked in a breath and stepped backward. A rose thorn scraped her elbow and she flinched. Folding down her wings, she felt the action as a tremble that shivered through her body, and the feeling did not relent.

"Why are you here?" She'd had to muster the courage to ask the question to the imperious faery standing before her. "Ry's not here. He doesn't want to speak to you anyway."

"You have not the right to speak for my son. Do not besmirch his integrity by attempting to do so."

She puffed up her chest and lifted her chin. The man was intimidating, but she wasn't about to shrink before him. "What do you want? If I disgust you so much I can't imagine why you would waste your time standing in my air."

"It is a rather interesting air." Malrick stretched out an arm to the side, palm curled over the cap of his cane, which regally displayed his physique. Even beneath the hippie velvet, he was long and built, most likely a force that could bring a strong man to his knees. "The enchantments in this little yard are many. Curious."

Indi looked about. Sure, the roses grew rampant and she rarely found a weed to pull. And there were the faeries. But enchanted?

"I wonder over your parentage," Malrick said. His silver eyes were hard to look at. They were metallic and reflective. "Most changelings are born to their fate." He narrowed his black eyebrows and tilted his head as he took her in with a sniff of disdain. "There's something more to you."

"You mean I may not be the disgusting changeling you claim me to be?" Was there hope that the wings were temporary?

"Oh, you're a changeling, no doubt."

Indi's shoulders dropped.

"But what I wonder is this—were you born to be brought to this realm or were you taken away from one who would have preferred you remain in Faery?"

"I don't understand."

Malrick sighed, and in two seconds he stood but a foot before her, looking down into her eyes. He hadn't moved his legs, but had rather flown toward her. Indi inhaled his sweet perfume. Citrus, vanilla, pepper, a softer hint of something unnamable. He was…alluring. Like a creature of myth that one might only dream to see. To possibly touch.

His eyes darted over her shoulder, taking in her wings. "They have a distinct color to them," he said. "The violet on the upper wings and ruby on the lower. Much like… well, hmm…"

"Tell me what you're not telling me."

"No." He stepped back and with a flick of his wrist the cane slid up his grasp until he held it by the black crystal center. He turned it to shove the silver head against her chest. "You are not fit to be my son's menial maid, let alone his consort. And I will not allow this silly romance to continue."

Indi shoved away the cane. "You don't have a right to tell me what to do. Or to decide what is right for Ry. He's a big boy. And he seems to have done quite well for himself in life."

"With my donation."

She'd forgotten about the gift from Malrick that Ry was constantly trying to give away. But she had no intention of rocking the boat. She had no idea of what this man—a faery king—was capable.

"Ry gets to choose whom he dates. Right now? That's me. You don't like it? It's not as if you've ever given your son any of your time, or showed him that you care. Go back to Faery."

"Strong words, which you cannot stand behind, foolish changeling. In this instance, it is you who must be the one to step away and allow my son to resume his life in the manner which it was proceeding before he met you."

She crossed her arms and defied him with a stare. Janet called it her don't-fuck-with-me look. A girl had to hone that talent to survive in the business world. She could stand up for her words, but she sensed the minute trembles in her wings would give her away, so she quickly folded them back and away.

"My son fights valiantly to rescue human babies," Malrick said.

"Because of you! You are the one sending the collectors to steal the babies. You can stop it. Why don't you?"

"I am sure Ryland has told you my reasons."

"To repopulate your kind?" Indi shook her head. "Pitiful. Don't you have enough babies by now?"

"Indeed." Malrick again shoved the cane head against

her chest and she gripped it but could not push it away. "I offer you a bargain."

"Which is?"

"I will stop sending my collectors through FaeryTown. You need only do one simple thing."

"And what is that?"

"Walk away from my son. Break his heart. End the relationship."

"But I—"

Malrick lifted a beringed finger before her. "It's entirely up to you, Indigo Paisley DuCharme. Make sure my son never wants to see you again. The moment that occurs, I will cease to send in my collectors."

He pulled the cane from her grasp, and it seared her skin as it slipped away. Indi hissed and clutched her hand against her heart as the faery king turned and strolled away, alongside the pool, and back toward the thin place. When he appeared to walk through the sky and disappear, Indi finally let out a gasp of pain.

She looked at the cut on her palm, which sparkled with faery dust and…her red blood had lightened. It was becoming ichor. As she watched, it healed. A shiver of relief softened her wings and they fluttered forward around her arms as if to provide the hug she desperately needed.

"Break up with Ry?" she muttered. "To save the babies."

Her heart thudded double-time. Indi fell to her knees, there before the roses. Tears spattered her cheeks, and she realized just how much she loved Ryland James.

Ry returned home after a long day at the office spent confirming many donations. When his doorbell rang and Indi's voice asked to be let in, he couldn't get to the door fast enough to buzz her up. When she reached his floor he rushed out to embrace her and lift her into his arms. Her legs wrapped about his hips and she met his kiss with as much passion and hunger as he felt.

"I miss you when more than a day passes that I see you," he confessed. And it didn't feel weird to admit that neediness. The woman had gotten into his veins and he didn't mind that at all. "Want me to take you out and wine and dine you?"

"No, I want you to pull off all my clothes and have sex with me."

"The second option sounds much more appealing."

He closed the front door and didn't set her down. As he veered toward the bedroom, Indi pulled off her top. And as Ry held her there before the bed, he realized something.

"Where are your wings?"

She beamed and kissed him quickly. "I mastered the art of putting them away. It really is a sort of feeling, like Never explained to me. And I can keep them that way. At least for a few hours. Pretty cool, huh?"

"That's awesome. But I do love your wings. They are like your hair or your eyes and your soft lips. They fit you. And they look right on you."

"You're a sweetie." She curled her fingers over his shoulder and he felt her nails dig in. "Let's see if I can bring out your wild. I'm horny, wolf. And your hard pecs against my tits feel so freakin' good."

Ry laid her on the bed. She spread out her arms, closing her eyes and tilting forward a hip. She seemed to revel in her newfound ability to put away her wings. It had to be an accomplishment that bolstered her confidence. And it was evident as she arched her back, lifting her breasts in an irresistible tease.

He kissed one luscious breast and laved his tongue over the rigid nipple. He loved teasing them about in his mouth, toying and playing with them. Sucking them as if she could feed him life and brightness and love.

Love? Where was his mind heading? It wasn't love. Not so fast. Maybe?

Ry leaned over and sucked in her other nipple, while tweaking the wet one he'd left behind. She squirmed and rocked her hips beneath him. His erection strained for escape and she pushed up his shirt to under his pits. Pausing from the delicious feast of her breasts, he pulled off the shirt and tossed it aside.

Meanwhile, Indi unzipped her miniskirt and shuffled it down to reveal she wore no panties beneath.

"Either you dressed fast today," he muttered as he shoved down his jeans and boxers, "or you planned ahead."

"I'll never tell," she said with a wink and a grab for his cock. "Oh, yeah, bring that big boy back down to me. It's so hot and hard. And it's all mine."

Being claimed had never felt so awesome. Ry leaned over Indi and she took control of him with a masterful clutch about his cock. She was in a hurry as her actions lured him between her legs. Using him as a sort of paintbrush, she rubbed the head of his erection against her folds. Mmm, so hot and already wet. He groaned and pushed harder, showing her his impatience to get inside her.

Yet she kept him firmly in hand and slicked him up and down over her clit. So he let her play, knowing she was feeding her desires. Bowing to her chest, he kissed her throat, then nipped his way down to tease each of her nipples. If he bit a little too firmly she squeezed his cock, which he didn't take as a warning but rather a reaction to the intensity of what she was feeling.

She had wanted to see his wild.

Sunlight threatened to spoil a good sleep, but Indi resolved to surrender to the day. She spread her arms across the sheets, hearing the shower shut off in the other room.

Ry was an early riser. Of course, the man was a philanthropist who took pride in his work. She was thankful that her job could be done from her home or anywhere she could get Wi-Fi.

She rolled to her stomach and closed her eyes. Last night after he'd returned from slaying the collectors, she'd heard him muttering how they were still increasing in numbers. It was getting harder to stop them. He needed help. He needed to do something to make it stop.

And she could do that for him.

Malrick's bargain had not been forgotten. She'd come here last night with intent.

"Hey, Princess." Ry breezed into the bedroom, buttoning up a pale green dress shirt, then found his shoes and stepped into them. "I'm late. Have an early meeting today with a client, so I gotta run." He bent and kissed the crown of her head. "Text me later, okay?"

She nodded as he was leaving the bedroom. A lump formed in her throat, but she forced herself to call after him, "Goodbye, Ry!"

"'Bye, Princess!"

She heard the front door open and close.

And Indi sat up on the bed and began to bawl. That had been their last goodbye.

Chapter 23

Ry swung by the flower shop on his way home from work, but they had already closed.

No flowers? He tugged out his phone and texted Indi. Done with work. Want to go out for Italian?

It took her a minute to reply: Sorry. Not home. Business issues. Will be busy…all night. Rain check.

"Rain check," he muttered.

He texted back. I can wait for you in your bed?

He reached the Alfa and slid inside. Three or four minutes passed and still no reply from Indi.

"She must be really busy. All right. This wolf can deal."

He'd pick up something on the way home and make it bachelor's night. Time to give a good think to how he was going to resolve the collector issue. Last night, he and Never had let another slip through to the mortal realm. If they ever let more than one slip, they'd not be able to track them both, and thus rescue the baby before the collector could bring it back to Faery. It was a two-man job.

Was it time to consider Malrick's plea that Ry abandon his only home to live in Faery? He was no prince. And even if Malrick's days were numbered, Ry had no desire to become king of a bunch of faeries. He didn't do king. He didn't want to do it. He just…did not.

His phone rang and he answered. "Kristine. What did I forget?"

"Your briefcase with the file you were supposed to read tonight and fax back before you come in to work tomorrow morning. I've scanned the file and will email it to you."

"What would I do without you?"

"You'd be living in that sweet castle, making babies with your faery princess and not having a care about all this real-world stuff."

"Someone's gotta give that money away, Kristine. It's not going to happen by itself."

"I have a pretty good handle on it, Ry."

She did. Ry knew his foundation would do just fine if he left it in her capable hands a day or two.

"Take a vacation, why don't you?" she suggested. "Why not after the ball this weekend you head up to the cabin? It is the full moon that night."

"It is? Shit." He hadn't realized it was coming up so quickly. This past month had been a whirlwind. He couldn't go to a ball on that night. Could he?

"I figured you forgot, otherwise you never would have agreed to take us out that night."

"I'll have to make it an early evening."

"Bring Indi along with you to the cabin, *mon cher*. I mean it."

"Maybe."

It would present a good time for him to show her his

true colors. Make that fur. But there were also the collectors to worry about. Damn it. The night of the masked ball was going to be a challenge.

"You two have plans this evening?"

"Indi is…busy. Just me and a frozen dinner from Picard."

"I could pick up some sushi and head over to your place with the documents that you need to sign."

"Sounds like a plan. Thanks, Kristine. See you in a bit."

He hung up and veered toward his place. Full moon this weekend? And still the collectors to deal with. Could he get a break?

On Thursday morning Indi stood before the dressmaker's dummy staring at the costume that she would never wear. Pastel chiffon hung like the softest feathers in dagged tiers to form a long and flowing skirt. The ivory-beaded bodice was strapless and laced up in the back to the point where her wings could comfortably rest on top. Overall, tiny rhinestones—which she had added—glittered on the skirt. And she'd imbued her own dust—possible with a shake of her wings—into the chiffon to make the entire creation shimmer.

It was so pretty. She hated to take it apart.

"I could sell it. Never sold costumes before. Could be a test and trial. Maybe."

Though it was certainly a beautiful dress that could be worn as a noncostume. She stroked her fingers over the skirt. Ry would have loved to see her in this. And while she didn't know what his plans were for a costume, it didn't matter now. He could be a wolf, a superhero, or even a regular guy and he'd win her heart.

A heart that was cracking open wider and wider.

She'd lied to him last night in the text about being busy

with work. And what would she say to him today when he texted or called?

"You have to do this before Saturday," she said. "Rip off the Band-Aid. Just do it so the man can be free of the responsibility of trying to save so many."

With a nod, and a wince, she decided. Despite every inch of her body screaming against it, she would officially break it off with Ryland. But she didn't want to do it face-to-face. How could she? Yet the thought of being so unfeeling only reminded her of how cruel Todd had been to her. She wasn't that person.

"You have to be."

Because if she saw Ry again she wouldn't be able to go through with it. She'd wrap her arms and legs about him and kiss him and forget there were more important things in this world than her happiness.

Wings falling to hang behind her, Indi could but shake her head. Yeah, it was like that.

When her cell phone rang she grabbed it, but then stared at the screen. It was him.

"I can't do this."

Another ring vibrated the phone in her hand.

"I have to do this."

One more ring and it would forward to messages…

Indi clicked on. "Hey, Ry."

"Indi. Princess. How'd work go last night? I missed you. Me and Kristine ate Indian food and watched reruns of *Game of Thrones*."

"You and Kristine are awesome together."

"She's my sis. So when can I come over? After work? I want to take you to a new place in the seventh. It opened last month. Supposed to be organic, fresh from the farm to table kind of food."

"Ry, I…"

"Please don't tell me you're busy again. I will come over there and physically pull you away from your work if I have to."

"Ry, stop."

"Uh…okay. What's up, Indi?"

Her fingers dug into the back of the sofa, and her heart dropped to her gut. The subtle shivers she'd experienced when facing down Malrick returned and her wings trembled against the backs of her thighs. It was all she could do to speak clearly and not burst out into tears.

"Ry, it's over. You and me? It's not going to work."

"What the—"

"Just listen. I'm so sorry. You are the nicest man. Truly, an amazing person. But I'm not right for you. You've got things to concentrate on, like protecting innocent babies. And… Batman never had a real girlfriend. Not for long, anyway. That man could never settle down. And for good reason. So much hero stuff to do. I'm holding you back."

"No, you're not. Indi, where is this coming from?"

"From my heart, Ry." She sucked in a breath as she felt something stab mercilessly at her heart. "I'm trying to do this fast and as painlessly as possible. I care about you, but…it won't work. I'm going to ask that you don't come over here. Just…please, try to walk away from this. Love you."

She clicked off and tossed the phone to the sofa. Then she pressed her fingers to her mouth. She'd ended by saying she loved him! What the hell?

"I don't. I can't. Do I?"

Her heart knew the truth, and that sent her running for her purse and car keys. She had to get out of the house. Away from the possibility that he might hop in his car and head over here to talk to her. Because he would. She'd just delivered him the worst dump of all. He deserved more from her.

But she didn't know how to do that convincingly.

Fleeing her home, she had no idea where to go or what to do, but she couldn't sit and wait for him. Her heart wasn't that strong. She left the phone on the sofa, locked the front door and with tears blurring her vision, ran for the car.

Ry raced up to Indi's front door and rang the bell. He peered through the side window but didn't see any movement inside. The silhouette of a dressmaker's dummy stood before a far window. He glanced down the street and didn't see her car. She wasn't home.

Turning and kicking the door behind him, he cursed none too quietly. He'd missed her.

How could she have done that to him? Break up with him over the phone? It hadn't felt right. Like she had been forcing the breakup. She'd spoken so quickly and hadn't given him a solid reason why she didn't want to see him again. He was too good for her? What a load of crap.

Batman had a girlfriend. Vicki Vale and Catwoman and…so many others. All right, so the man had never truly settled down.

Why the hell was he thinking about Batman anyway?

Something was up with Indi, and he wasn't about to walk away without talking to her face-to-face.

He kicked the door again and marched down the sidewalk to the Alfa. He could sit in it and wait for her return, but he had no idea where she was. She wasn't replying to his texts. And if he sent another one he'd tilt over into stalker column.

Gripping his fingers at his temple, he squeezed them through his hair. "What did I do wrong?"

* * *

Seven texts, each asking for her to meet him so they could talk. Indi set down the phone after she'd returned to the house. After dark. And with a slow drive down the street to make sure Ry wasn't parked out front waiting for her. The last text had been sent half an hour ago.

He wasn't giving up.

Which only deepened her love for him. He didn't want to let her go easily. And much as that would prove difficult for her to stand against him and do as his father demanded, she had to. For Ry's sake.

She wasn't doing this to make the faery king happy. She was doing it to make life easier for Ry. And to save the babies.

When she tossed the phone angrily across the room, it hit the dressmaker's dummy and bounced off, landing on the floor. Indi headed upstairs to run a tub. If Ry came over, she would not answer the door. She couldn't. It hurt too much to do this, but she had to be strong.

Chapter 24

Ry had fallen asleep on his sofa, phone in hand. After waking, the first thing he did was check his messages. No return texts from Indi.

She'd really done it. Walked away from him. And he couldn't figure it out.

"What did I do?"

His foot slid across the hardwood floor, shoving the broadsword under the coffee table. He'd gone to Faery-Town last night, as usual. And…nothing had happened. Not a single collector had come through. He'd stayed there an hour beyond the time they normally arrived. Never had joined him in searching the sky for the tear between the realms that would signal their arrival.

Had it finally stopped? It didn't feel right to Ry. Malrick would never stop sending the collectors. He was too greedy. The old man had simply missed a night. They'd be back tonight.

Ry would hope for the best. That it truly was the end.

The phone rattled in his grasp and, answering quickly, he said, "Indi?"

"Sorry, *cher*, it's just me. You bringing in those signed forms today?"

"Right." After he'd signed them, Kristine had forgotten to bring them back with her. "Yes. I'll be in soon." He hung up and tossed the phone aside on the sofa.

Summoning the energy to rise and take a shower and eat something was a monumental task. He felt defeated. Not in control. And as if, once again, he'd been rejected by someone he'd thought had cared about him.

It wasn't like when his werewolf father had told him to leave the pack, and yet his heart hurt the same way it had then.

Had he fallen in love with Indi?

He needn't consider the answer. He knew it without question.

But life continued to move and exist around his aching heart and romantic entanglements. He did have to bring in those forms. He'd drop them off, then immerse himself in work. Maybe Indi needed a few days to work out whatever had scared her away from him.

He nodded but wasn't buying his logic. It was the best he could manage right now.

An hour later Kristine stood in the doorway to his office holding the forms he'd handed her. She wasn't about to move aside and let him through. And he recognized that steely glint in her brown eyes.

"Something's up with you, Ry. And I think it has to do with Indi. Tell. Or I'm not letting you into your office."

"Not today, Kristine."

"It's that bad, is it?" She cocked a hip to the right, effectively filling up the whole doorway. "Talk."

* * *

Around eight in the evening, Indi checked her text messages. Ry had texted three times today, and the last one had been over six hours ago. He must be busy with work.

Or he had finally given up.

It had only taken him twenty-four hours to accept their breakup.

She wasn't sure how long it would take her. Forever felt about right.

Catching her face in her palms, she sniffed back tears. Out the corner of her eye she spied the pile of tissues that had collected during the day as she paced, sat and wept, paced some more, went out to the backyard to curse the faery king, cried some more, tried to do some work, then ultimately ransacked the fig jam and now had a terrible stomachache and sore eyes. At her feet, the discarded tissues glittered with ichor.

Swiping a finger along her eye, she studied the tears wetting her finger. Faery dust sparkled in her pain. It was dreadfully pretty, and only made the lump in her stomach all the harder. Who would help her to understand and grow into the faery she had become now that Ry was out of her life?

Could she do this alone? Janet might be able to understand. Eventually. But Indi thought of Ry's insistent warnings that she tell no humans about them. She needed a Paranormal 101 class to know how to function now that she had become one of the myths.

When the doorbell rang, she froze, her flight-or-fight instincts begging her to crawl behind the sofa and hide.

Of course Ry wouldn't give up on her. Not so fast.

She could not look into his beautiful brown eyes and then not fall into his arms and confess her deep love for him.

"Indi?"

He'd sent his secretary to talk to her?

"Indi, we need to talk," Kristine called from behind the door. "Ry doesn't know I'm here. Come on, sweetie, open up. I brought mochi."

With a sigh, Indi waded through the tissue piles and opened the door. When Kristine saw her red eyes and tousled hair, the woman bent and pulled her into a hug.

"I knew this would require mochi."

Half an hour later, and after a lot more tears, Indi was done dodging Kristine's questions about why she'd broken up with Ry. She couldn't do it anymore. She had to tell the truth.

"I love him, Kristine."

"Oh, I know that, sweetie. And he loves you."

"He does?"

"Of course he does. He hasn't told you yet? I can smell it on the two of you when you're together. All flowery and hope and romantic pink sparkles. I've never seen Ry fall so hard so fast. And look at you with your puffy red eyes, trying to convince me you don't care about the man. You are a terrible liar. And you definitely need to clean up all these tissues."

Indi plucked another mochi ball from the container Kristine had brought along. She'd not tried the sweet balls of dough-wrapped ice cream until tonight, and oh, they were delicious.

Kristine nudged a tissue aside Indi's cheek, then showed her the sparkle. "That's some serious dust, sweetie."

"Who would have thought such heart-deep pain could be so pretty?"

"Oh, don't do this to your heart. You two deserve each other. Can you tell me why you don't want to see Ry anymore?"

"No. Yes. Oh!" She needed to spill everything. Faery king, be damned.

"Okay, here's the truth," Indi said. "But if you tell Ry I swear I will come for you. I will sneak into your house and break all the heels off your shoes. And don't even get me started on the Chanel I've seen you wear."

Kristine gasped. She crossed her heart with her forefinger. "Girl's honor. I'll stay mum. But I can't promise not to convince Ry that you're worth going after."

Indi sighed and her shoulders dropped. "You can't do that. Or the collectors will start coming again."

"Say what? Ry told me he went out on the hunt last night and not a single collector came through. Can you believe that? Maybe it's over?"

"It is over. Because of me. Kristine, Ry's dad came to me and told me if I wanted it to stop all I had to do was stay away from his son. To break his heart. Malrick hates me because I'm a low-life changeling. I'm not good enough for his prince of a son. So…as much as I adore Ry and know I really do love him, I couldn't imagine him fighting those things forever. And if I can help him by walking away from him?"

Indi quickly grabbed another tissue and caught a stream of tears with it.

"Daddy dearest blackmailed you? The asshole. You did the right thing. I mean, not really. You broke Ry's heart. But you did stop the baby stealers. That was unselfish of you."

"Thanks. I hate myself for it. Because I had to be so cruel to Ry."

"You were. He's suffering. But, sweetie, do you really want to stand back and let Malrick tell you what to do? Don't let him control you like that."

"But…you said the collectors have stopped."

"Do you love Ry?"

"Yes." Her response came out much quicker than Indi imagined it would. But she nodded, following up with another firm and very true "Yes."

"Then tell him."

"I can't! Malrick will send back the forces to collect more babies."

"We'll stop that when it happens."

"No, that's— It's impossible. Ry was having a tough enough time as it was holding them off. He can't fight them forever. And I've put an end to it by breaking up with him. Done deal."

"It sounds good. In theory." Kristine fluttered her spangled manicure before her. "Oh, this is a tangled mess. You're damned if you do and damned if you don't. I hate to see two people with broken hearts like this. It's not fair."

"Maybe Malrick is right. Maybe I'm not good enough for Ry. He's an important man. He's got a billion-dollar business."

"It's charity, sweetie, and you know how he loathes that money."

"Even better reason for him to give it away. He needs to do that as a means to slap his father in the face."

"True. Oh, what are we going to do?"

"There's nothing to do."

"The ball is tomorrow night."

Indi shrugged. "The two of you go and don't think about me. I'll be fine."

"Sure, but that dress—" Kristine gestured over her shoulder "—is stunning. A dress like that demands you make an entrance."

"There are more important things to consider than how I look in a dress. Although, I confess, it makes me feel like a faery princess."

"I bet it does. Aggh! This is crazy. Are there any more mochi left?"

"Sorry, I ate the last one. Those are the best."

"My go-to for breakups and missed seasonal sales. Always picks me up."

Indi slid sideways across the back of the couch, landing her head against the woman's muscled shoulder. "Kristine, do you think you can convince Ry to stop thinking about me? To let it go?"

"I'll do no such thing. But I won't encourage him to go after you, either. As promised. This is between the two of you. I'm glad I have both sides of the story, though. I was starting to hate you for being mean to my big brother."

"I hope we can stay friends, but I'm afraid that would keep me too close to Ry. I can't ever see him again, Kristine. It's too hard on my heart."

"It'll get easier. With time. I should probably go. It's past eleven! Wow. I want to call Ry later and see how it went in FaeryTown. If he doesn't find any critters to slay, then we know that old asshole of a father has kept his word. Oh, sweetie, I wish you could come to the ball tomorrow night. Ry was worried about it, but I think he figured out a plan."

"A plan?"

"You know it's the full moon tomorrow night. Midnight chimes and he doesn't turn into a pumpkin but rather a raging werewolf. He was going to whisk you off with him to the countryside."

"Really? I dreamed about going to his cabin with him." Indi touched the delicate silver wolf's paw dangling about her neck.

"You do know that cabin is actually a castle, right?"

"I didn't know that. Wow." Indi put up both palms. "Don't tell me any more, Kristine. I'm going to donate the dress to Goddess Goodies and be done with it. Paris is a big city. Ry and I can both live here and not ever worry about seeing each other. If only it weren't for—" She sighed. "Maybe I'll find myself a place out in the country, where I can run my business and not worry about people seeing me walking around with wings."

"Hiding from the snoopy people. Just like Ry and the paparazzi. Did I mention you and Ry were meant for each other?"

"Enough!" Indi stood and picked up Kristine's red leather Gucci purse. "It's time for you to leave. I don't want you to leave. But this is another Band-Aid I have to rip off."

"I hate that bastard Malrick for doing this to the two of you."

"Me, too." Indi wrapped her arms around Kristine, and the woman's hug nearly squeezed the breath from her. "I love you, Kristine. Take care of Ry. Promise?"

Tears wobbled at the corners of her eyes and the woman tipped her red-lacquered fingernail to catch one. "Promise. God, you make your own sparkles now. That is so crazy. Oh! I love you too, Indigo DuCharme. If I text you, promise you won't block me. It'll be hard walking away from you."

"Nonsense. You've got the swagger, girl. Just put one of those five-inch heels in front of the other and keep doing it." She opened the front door and watched as Kristine left. Waving, she sniffed back tears.

The woman was going to tell Ry everything.

And secretly, Indi was relieved for that.

Chapter 25

Ry charged through the office doorway and bypassed Kristine's desk. Last night had been almost perfect. He'd waited in FaeryTown until well after 1:00 a.m. No collectors had shown. Again. Malrick had stopped sending them. Hallelujah!

The only thing that hadn't made it perfect was that Indi had broken up with him. And much as he'd wanted to go to her house after waiting for the collectors, he'd had to force himself to return home. Alone.

He wasn't done with her. But he wasn't sure what was up with her, either. It killed him to stay away from her, but something inside him told him to give her the space.

He'd slept fitfully. And this morning an old friend from Ireland had rung him. That call had knocked him off his short-lived confidence regarding the baby trafficking. So much so, he'd checked in with another friend from Berlin. And one in California.

What the hell was going on?

"I'd offer to brew you a coffee, *mon cher*," Kristine said, "but I don't think any amount of caffeine is going to chill that anger vibe you've got going on. Is it Indi?"

He almost slammed his door on her but then decided she didn't deserve to feel his anger. When she clicked into his office on a pair of towering red heels, he could but sit in his chair and shove the laptop across the desk. Kristine caught it before it could slip off and land on the floor.

"Talk," she said simply.

Ry grasped the air before him, imagining his fingers clutched about Malrick's neck. He shook his hands, then growled.

"That bad? I know you're in love with her, but—"

"This is not about Indi. And I'm not in love."

"Oh, yes, you are." She tapped her lips and shook her head. "But we'll table that discussion for the more pressing concern. What's got you so tight and angry?"

"It's happening everywhere, Kristine. The collectors are coming through all over the world."

"What? Are they back in FaeryTown?"

"No. Last night was calm and collector-free. I don't know why they've stopped coming through in Paris, but I'm glad for it. And I was thinking, at least something was going right in my life until a friend called me this morning. He knew I was having trouble with collectors here and wanted to compare notes. Seems they are coming through in Ireland. And Berlin. And I verified the same with another friend in the States. They are coming through all over, Kristine!"

"Shit. That is so not what Malrick—" Kristine pressed her lips together and her eyes grew wide.

Ry stood and leaned across the desk. "Malrick what? What do you know?"

She shook her head, then closed her eyes tightly, then dramatically let out a breath and dropped her shoulders. "Oh, the girlfriend code just can't apply now. I have to tell you."

"Tell me what?"

"Ry, I went to see Indi last night."

"What? Why would you do that?" Then he straightened. "What did she say? Is she okay? How does she look? Did she give you any clue what is going on with her and me?" He thrust up a palm. "No. Sorry. It's not my business if she told you things in confidence."

"She did, and I do respect the girlfriend code made over emergency mochi and tears."

"You brought her mochi?" He couldn't help a small smile. He wanted to hug Kristine for that one.

"Of course! I raided my secret stash for her. Let me tell you, that girl had so many tissues scattered about I could have swum through them. Her tears sparkle, you know? It was such a pretty mess. Anyway, whatever is spoken in confidence from one girlfriend to another must be kept sacred. But, Ry. Now that I know about collectors coming through everywhere else?" Kristine made a show of looking over her shoulder, then directly back at him. "I have to tell you what Indi told me. She didn't dump you because she wanted to. She thought she was helping you. And your father lied big-time to her. That asshole!"

"Malrick talked to Indi?"

Kristine nodded and brushed her fingernails against the lapel of her white business suit.

"Shit." Now he was beginning to understand. If Malrick had spoken with Indi, the faery king must have convinced her to stop seeing his son. A son he deemed unworthy of a lowly being such as a changeling. "Why didn't I make that connection? Malrick must have threatened her."

"It wasn't a threat he made, but a promise. Which he's not upholding if the collectors are coming through everywhere but here."

"I don't understand."

"Sit down, *cher*. What I'm going to tell you is for information about fighting the good fight only. What you and Indi do romance-wise is between the two of you. But you have to promise me you won't go running back to her. That would betray the trust she has for me."

"But if she didn't want to break it off?"

"Just sit. We'll figure this out. You need to know exactly what a sleazeball your father is."

On Saturday morning Indi stood in the kitchen staring at the front door. The doorbell had just rung, and she'd heard footsteps walking away, followed by the roar of a delivery vehicle. Something had been dropped off on her stoop. Or…? Ry could be out there, waiting to talk to her.

She wanted to see him.

She couldn't see him.

Kristine had verified to her that the collectors had stopped coming through in FaeryTown. Malrick had upheld his part of the bargain. She would uphold hers.

With a nod, she went back to unloading the dishwasher. A mindless task that she hadn't taken care of for days. She'd been so busy with…

No, she wouldn't think about him. But how not to?

Another glass placed in the cupboard. Another plate…

"Did he eat off this plate the night he brought over takeaway?"

She clutched the plate to her stomach, then turned to eye the front door. Three minutes had passed. Setting the plate aside, she decided no one was out there, and made a beeline through the living room. She opened the door to find a flat white box tied with a pale green ribbon sitting on the step. Her name was lavishly scrawled on a thick ivory card tucked under the ribbon.

A mystery present left on her stoop? That was too fabulous to resist. Even though she suspected it could be from Ry. No one else would be so generous. And she'd not heard from Todd since that fateful night. Not that he'd ever been generous with gifts or surprises.

She carried the box inside and sat on the sofa. She'd yet to clear away her tissues, so she had to wade to get there. What a pitiful case she'd become. Time to call for a one-day maid touch-up on the whole house.

The card was just that. No message on the back. She tugged the ribbon loose and then pressed the soft satin against her cheek. Ry hadn't kissed her for days. She missed the heat of his mouth against hers. Of feeling it glide over her skin as he devoured her want and need and gave to her so easily. Unconditionally. He was a man who would never ask her to do something for a favor in return. He was not his father.

Tears threatened, but she shook her head. She was a big girl. And she would get through this. But whatever was inside the box, she suspected it was because Kristine had talked to Ry.

Indi had been hoping she would.

Inside, under a folded layer of pale green tissue paper, lay a gorgeous engraved invitation for tonight's costume ball. It was for Ry's plus one. She picked it up and rubbed it against her lips. The paper was satiny and smooth and emitted the slightest scent of clove. Nice.

But she wasn't going to the ball. She'd already packed the faery costume in a box in preparation to send it to the warehouse for a photo session and to ultimately sell online.

"Has to be done," she said decisively.

Why had her heart become so involved? She had managed to forget about Todd in less than twenty-four hours. Ry? She felt sure she'd never shuck his presence from her heart.

Ready to set the invite back in the box and toss it away along with the flood of tearstained tissues, she noticed a piece of white blue-lined paper at the bottom of the box and pulled it out. Torn from a notebook and written on with blue ballpoint pen. In Ry's handwriting.

Her wings shivered. She didn't want to read it. But she couldn't crumple it up and toss it aside. He hadn't called her. He'd respected her enough not to do that. This was his way to communicate with her.

Sighing heavily, she read the note.

Talked to Kristine. Malrick lied to you. More on that later. What's important is that I get to see you one more time. It can be the last time we see each other. If that is what you want. But please, Indi, allow me one last moment with you. One last dance. One last hug. One last kiss.

Please, be my faery princess tonight.

I'll be waiting at the ball.

Tears streaming down her cheeks, Indi shook her head and clutched the note to her chest.

It was what she wanted more than anything: one last hug, one last kiss. One last moment.

But if he touched her again, could she walk away from him? If his mouth kissed hers, how then could she manage to turn away from him? If she felt the heat of his body up against hers, how to push away and deny that deliriously delicious sensation?

And yet… She reread the second line he'd written. Malrick had lied to her? What was that about?

"Oh." She leaned forward, eyeing the invitation. "You're only asking for heartache if you go, Indigo. You know that. You and fancy balls lately. Nothing good ever seems to come of them."

And if she was to tell Ry how she really felt about him—that she loved him—that would break her bargain with Malrick. The collectors would return to FaeryTown. Ry's nightmare would begin again.

But she wanted to see him this one last time. Maybe that would make the end easier? She didn't need to tell him she loved him. She could go to the ball, give him that one last dance and then confirm that the break-off was indeed what was best for them. Let him kiss her. And then walk away.

"Aggh!"

Indi wished she'd never opened the front door.

Chapter 26

It hurt Ry's heart to be the one standing at the ball, alone, wondering if the girl would show up. Would Indi walk in and stand at the top of the stairs, looking for him? All eyes would land on her and everyone would wonder who that beautiful woman was. And why was she alone?

He should have sent a limo for her.

But no. Ry had wanted to give Indi the *option* of showing tonight. He hadn't wanted to force or cajole her into coming. It was entirely her choice to show up. And if she did? He prayed it would be for that last kiss he'd requested.

Or it could be for much longer. Dare he hope?

He checked his watch. Sixteen minutes, two seconds after 10:00 p.m. It was getting late. Tonight he needn't dash out at midnight to check for collectors; he had backup. Never was standing watch right now. Because things could go many ways tonight. And Ry had prepared for one or two of those instances.

Would she show?

Feeling as if his heart was a heavy lump in his chest, he pressed a hand over the crisp white tuxedo shirt. Most of the men wore tuxedos to these fancy costume balls, along with masks or other accessories to make the costume part. The focus was on the gorgeous women and their elaborate costumes. Ry wore a quarter mask that covered his left eye and was furred like a wolf and had one wolf's ear. It was all he'd wanted to do for a costume. Kristine had called it understated but sexy.

And where was Kristine right now? She, in all her glorious leopard-print girl power, had wandered off to find champagne.

And Ry had never felt more vulnerable. Sure, he could stroll about, find some familiar faces to chat with, laugh at some jokes. But...no. He didn't feel right tonight. And he would not unless and until she showed.

"She's not coming," he whispered as he clenched his fingers near his thighs. Were people staring at him? Why did he feel as if he stood alone in the center of a vast ballroom with all eyes on him? He hated this feeling.

Indi had felt that way when he had arrived late for the Grand Palais ball. The night her world had changed and she had sprouted wings.

"A faery," Ry whispered to himself.

That word had only ever been a cruel judgment against him—faery. But how could he think that when seeing Indi in all her glory with wings spread and smile beaming, and dust glittering in the air about her?

He would never have wings. But he did dust and he knew some faery magic lived within him. What sort of magic, he wasn't sure. He'd always denied it and turned his back on all things Faery.

If he embraced his faery side, would Indi come back to

him? He had never been a man to make measures to win other people, to change in hopes of gaining the advantage.

And yet…how could it hurt to truly explore that weak part of him that might only enhance his life? Magic? What man wouldn't want to tap into a little of that now and then?

Ry winced. Was this what desperation felt like? Forming concessions in hopes of a more positive outcome?

"Champagne!" Kristine announced grandly.

Saved from his dark thoughts, Ry spun to take a goblet from his catty assistant. She wore a long leopard-print gown that was slit up to the thigh to reveal some crazy tall heels. Her nails were black and sharpened to points, and on her head of bouffant hair she wore leopard-print cat ears that Indi had given her.

"You want to take a spin around the dance floor, *cher*?"

He probably should. To get his mind off the fact that he'd been jilted. For real. And for reasons that tore him apart. Indi believed Malrick's lies.

"Oh, Ry, she might still show."

He tried a smile, but it came out as a straight line. "I don't deserve someone like Indigo DuCharme."

"Why would you say something so ridiculous as that?"

He shrugged. "She's an independent woman. Smart, talented. She doesn't need a man."

"Needing and wanting are two different things. And I happen to know she wants you. You feeling sorry for yourself? You? The man with all the looks, charm and money?"

Kristine's indignant flare of nostril and that judgmental side-eye always clued Ry he needed to climb down a step. Or two. She was his compass, and he was wise enough to know that.

"You're right. As usual. I've never been on the getting-dumped side of a relationship before. It hurts."

"Oh." Kristine's eyes suddenly widened and she smiled

widely. "The hurt is about to go away. I do believe the faery princess has arrived."

Ry followed the gesture of her long, wicked nails. Turning, he glanced up the staircase. And standing at the top, looking down over the crowd, was a faery princess in pastel silks with wings that swept in lush waves of color behind her.

Ry handed the champagne goblet aside, blindly letting it go, and didn't care if anyone caught it. She had come for him. He took the stairs two at a time, but stopped on the one stair below the main floor, putting him eye level to the beaming princess who had stolen his heart.

"You came," he whispered. It was the stupidest thing to say, but he was happy and relieved and…in love.

Indi's smile beamed. "A girl can't miss an opportunity to wear a pretty dress, can she?"

"It's the prettiest dress in the whole room. But you are prettier." He tilted his head, taking in her blue gaze, which… "Your eyes are violet." The color had deepened. Had they become the color they were when she had been born in Faery? And everywhere, her skin sparkled with natural faery dust. "My gorgeous faery princess, you are truly in your element tonight."

She bowed her head shyly, and Ry felt compelled to touch her under the chin and gently tilt up her head. "And some sparkly cat ears to finish the look," he said of the rhinestone-studded ears she wore. "You've stolen my heart, Indi. I want you to know that. Whether you've come to give me a final kiss or a kiss that'll last forever."

"Actually, I'm not sure what I've come for," she said.

"You don't have to know. I'm just thankful you're here. Can we… Would you like to dance?"

"More than anything."

Offering her his arm, Ry escorted Indi down the stairs

to the dance floor. By luck, a waltz began and he swept her along with the other fancily clothed couples. Beneath the twinkle of a half-dozen chandeliers, the room and the mood of the partiers alchemized into a wonderland. And Ry, the reluctant prince, had found his princess. He might never take her to Faery, but he would love and honor and care for her here in the mortal realm. If she would give him a second chance.

Yet she had said she wasn't sure why she'd come. To dump him or to take him back? He'd leave it to her. And he'd have to accept whatever decision she made. He wouldn't try to influence her. Right now he wanted to enjoy her in his arms. For the short time they had. Because before midnight, this wolf had to get the hell out of here. Collectors or not, the moon was high and full. And his wolf was already champing at the bit for release. Faery-Town would be his best bet to make the shift without being noticed by humans, and that was his plan.

"You've mastered the wings," he said as they slowed to spin about the curving end of the dance floor. "They move as if dancing with you."

Indi beamed at him. "They are mine now. They are no longer some strange appendages I must learn to accept. I'm a faery. And I'm cool with that. About ninety percent cool with it. I've still got a lot to learn. Your costume is perfect. Only revealing a little bit of yourself, right?"

"I'm not big on costumes. I prefer to see what's behind the mask. No secrets."

"Some secrets are necessary. How's your wolf doing?"

He squeezed her hand, leaned close and whispered, "He's ready to run, but I'm good. I won't howl in the middle of this tony crowd."

"I was surprised when you sent the invitation," she said. "Kristine told you she stopped by, didn't she?"

"She did, but she didn't tell me everything you two talked about. She invoked the girl code. Or so I was firmly told that some things are sacred."

Indi laughed, and Ry took the moment to spin her toward the center of the floor, where it wasn't so crowded with dancers. She felt like air and light in his arms. He desperately wanted to kiss her. But he didn't want to share that moment with others.

"You understand I had to do it, then?" she asked as they slowed while the music segued to something more like a rumba.

"I do," he said. He slid his hand around to her back and rested it at the base of her back, where the flutter of her wings brushed his skin.

"Malrick said I'm not good enough for you. You're a prince, after all. I'm just a fake faery princess. I'm not even a princess. That's just a name you call me."

"What Malrick said was a whole lot of fiction. There's something you need to know about the Unseelie king. But I don't want to talk about it now. I want to hold you, Indi. To feel your heart beating against mine. Because I'm not sure if this will be the last night I get to do this."

She stepped up to hug him and they swayed to the music. As she tilted her head onto his shoulder, her hair tickled the underside of his jaw.

She said softly, "I remember the first time you kissed me. I forgot my name."

He recalled a moment of losing memory of his name when looking at her as well. An amazing feeling, actually.

"I'm going to make sure I don't forget a moment of tonight," Indi added.

Ry slid his hand up her back and when he touched her wings they flinched, then folded over his hand. And he hugged her until her heartbeats pounded against his chest. Nothing felt more right. Or more frightening.

He couldn't lose her.

When Indi looked up at him, tears quivered at the corner of her eyes. The teardrops sparkled. "Ry..."

He bowed his forehead to hers. He didn't want to hear what she was going to say. Damn his father for making that awful bargain with her!

She gasped and pushed her hands up to clutch at the back of his neck. "I don't want this to end."

"It doesn't have to."

"It does. Kristine told me the collectors have stopped coming through in FaeryTown. I made a bargain with your father."

"She told me about the bargain. It's a bargain Malrick didn't keep."

"What?"

He'd not wanted to get into this during these precious moments he had with her, but it was now or never. And the clock was ticking closer to his need to pull a Cinderella.

"Come with me." Ry clasped Indi's hand and walked her off the dance floor. He weaved around a massive marble column and behind it found some quiet, though partiers were everywhere.

A woman dressed as an Egyptian goddess leaned close to Indi and said, "The wings are stunning. And they must be animatronic. Gorgeous costume!"

"Thank you," Indi said, then bowed her head.

Ry lifted her head with a tip of his finger under her chin. "Be the goddess you are," he said.

She smiled. "I do feel amazing in this dress and with these wings. And on your arm." She snuggled up aside him. "But I'm freaking about what you just said. How has Malrick lied to me?"

Ry leaned in, putting his hand to the marble column above Indi's head, closing them in a private moment. He said quietly, "I learned this morning that Malrick has been sending collectors through portals and thin places all over the world. He's stopped sending them in Paris, but not everywhere else."

"I don't understand. There are collectors stealing babies elsewhere?"

Ry nodded.

"That bastard. We had a deal. I—I walked away from you because I thought it would stop things."

"Please walk back into my arms, Indi," he said. "These past few days without you have been the worst. I need you in my life. I love you."

"Oh, Ry, I love you, too. But…if we get back together, Malrick will send the collectors through FaeryTown."

"I'm ready for that. It'll happen tonight. Malrick knows everything about me and what I'm doing. He'll know if I kiss you and make you mine. Are you willing to stand by my side and accept whatever comes because of our feelings for each other?"

"But those poor babies…"

"All across the world. Not just Paris. Indi, your sacrifice did not stop a thing."

"I feel like such a fool. But, oh, Ry." She pressed her hands to his jaw and tilted up to kiss him. "I want you back."

Her mouth fit to his like nothing else could. They were made for each other. Two strange souls thrust into this realm and led to believe one thing, then surprised with something else. He could accept his faery side with Indi to support him. Because he wanted to help her accept her life just as much. He would do it. He needed her.

And he hoped she needed him.

"I love you so much, my werewolf prince."

"Will you be my faery princess?"

She smiled against his mouth. "That's not a proposal, is it?"

"Oh, uh…"

"Because it's too soon for that."

And he hadn't meant it as that, either. Whew!

"Just be my girl," he said. "My lover. My faery. My Princess Pussycat." He pressed his hand against her bodice, over her breast. "My heart."

"I can do that."

And with a tug up of her skirts, she jumped to wrap her legs about his hips and they kissed all through the next song, and the next. Lost in her was the best place. A place Ry never wanted to leave.

When Ry's cell phone buzzed in his inner pocket, his heart dropped. It was a call he'd been expecting. He'd kissed Indi. He'd sealed their fates. Malrick knew. The time was eleven forty-five. He answered Never's call and was told exactly what he'd expected to hear.

"I'll be there as quick as I can," Ry said, and tucked away the phone.

"What is it?" Indi asked.

"Never just slayed a collector in FaeryTown. And we don't expect one or two or even a dozen tonight. Malrick will send multitudes. I've got to go."

She grabbed his hand. "I'm going with you."

He didn't argue because he wanted her by his side so he could protect her, and know that she was back in his life. "You better believe you are. I'm going to need all the backup I can get. Good thing we trained for this." He kissed her forehead and scanned the area for a quick escape.

Kristine spun as Ry approached and she saw the fierceness in his demeanor. "Got the call?"

"You know it."

"I'm right behind you." Kristine fell in and the three-some left the ballroom and headed for the rental Ry had picked up earlier.

"This car is not yours," Indi said as he held the passenger door open for her and she got in.

"Needed something with a bigger trunk," he said, and closed the door, then held the back door open for Kristine. "Time to go kick some collector ass!"

Chapter 27

"It's the full moon," Indi said as Ry parked the car close to where FaeryTown merged with the mortal realm. "You can't be here, Ry."

"Once in werewolf shape I'll go unnoticed in Faery-Town. And I will shift. Just a warning. You should probably stay in the car."

"Oh, hell no. You're not leaving me alone."

"Hey!" Kristine called from the back seat. "I know you two are in love and all, but look beyond those rose-colored glasses, faery girl. I am here!"

Ry spoke up before a girl fight could break out. "I need you both. If you're willing?"

"Hell yeah!"

Ry looked back at Kristine in the rearview mirror. "You use that ointment I gave you to see faeries?"

The woman tapped the side of her elaborately made-up eye. "Mixed it in with the eye shadow. I can see your sparkle, big boy. And Indi's, too."

Indi, surprised by that, gave Ry a good once-over. Sure enough, he did sparkle. But was that from her touching him or his innate faeryness? She was starting to see as a faery now? Cool.

"Everyone out!" Ry swung around to the trunk and opened it to display the contents.

Indi leaned over to inspect the assortment within. "Wow. You really did plan ahead. No wonder you needed a bigger trunk."

Inside the trunk were swords, knives, a battle-ax with spikes on it and even a whip. Ry grasped a sword that hummed when he pulled it out, and the whip.

"What is that?" she asked.

"It's my sword."

"But I've never heard it hum." Indi turned to Kristine, who shrugged because she obviously hadn't heard it. And the realization struck Indi. "I'm totally faery. I can hear swords!"

"It's got a song, that's for sure." Ry sheathed the sword behind his back. "Now for you, Miss I Took One Brief Lesson on Swordfighting, I think this will be perfect."

He handed Indi an épée that wasn't at all heavy. The hilt sat nicely in her grip and it felt like an extension of her arm as she gave it a practice thrust. "I like it. Feels right."

"Good. It's perfectly balanced. It was made by a friend of mine from the States, Malakai Saint-Pierre. You won't have to work very hard with that one. It knows what it's meant to do. And that is slay the big bads."

"Works for me."

Kristine perused the collection, her fingernails fluttering over the remaining assortment. Finally she grabbed the battle-ax and a short-blade sword.

Ry glanced down at Kristine's shoes. "You might want to slip into something a little less…precarious."

"Are you kidding me?" Kristine pointed out a toe of her glossy black shoe. "*Cher*, I wear shoes bigger than your dick. I can run a mile in them, top speed, and kick your sorry ass to the curb." She tilted the sword blade against her shoulder and looked askance at him. "What's your super power?"

Indi looked to Ry, who blanched, but then nodded in concession. "Knowing when to hold my tongue." He bowed before the two of them. "Ladies first."

"Oh, you know it!" Kristine marched forward.

And with a wink to Indi, Ry asked, "Are you ready for this?"

"Dressed in faery finery and reunited with the man I love? Hell yes. I want to poke some sparkly bad guys with a sword."

"Remember to avoid their talons. And stay close to me. I'll protect you."

"I know you will. What about when you shift to werewolf? Will you…know me?"

"I will. But don't expect me to be able to speak. Just… trust me?"

"I do, Ry." She kissed him. "I do."

They arrived in FaeryTown to find Never battling three collectors, a short sword in one hand and a loaded crossbow in the other. He signaled to Ry, then pointed toward a mass of darkness oozing through the torn fabric in the sky.

This was going to be a battle. And Indi wasn't so much scared as pumped with the adrenaline racing and stirring in her wings. So much so that her feet lifted from the ground, and as Ry gave the battle charge, she soared toward the approaching collectors.

Ry kept an eye toward Indi as he slashed his way through the horde of collectors that blackened the sky.

She was flying about a foot off the ground. Never for more than a few seconds, but those wings at her back were certainly trying. And she dodged more than a few lunges from the taloned collectors with a swift beat of wing. Good girl.

Never winked at him and pointed toward Indi. "I've got her in my sights as well. We can do this, man!"

They could do this. And as black mist hailed about them with each collector death, Ry surrendered to his werewolf and shifted, gripping the weapons in each paw with fierce determination.

It was not easy swinging an épée while wearing a ball gown, but Indi found that with a leap she was able to flutter her wings and fly briefly, which freed her from getting tangled in anything on the ground.

Another dash of the blade straight up into one of the creature's chests rained down black sparkly ash over her head. She remembered the cut that had almost killed her, so she closed her eyes and mouth so as not to swallow any of it. But she didn't stay unaware for long. Swinging about, and with a battle cry that pushed up from her very soul, Indi charged toward a pair of collectors that were giving Kristine some difficulty.

The creatures blackening the sky came at him swiftly and with teeth exposed. The werewolf, who experienced it all in his most primal state, and yet also with the sharp cunning of a man, used the enchanted sword in one paw, and its claws on the other paw to bash through the enemies.

It howled at the moonlight. It howled for the release and freedom in this shape. And it howled because it knew it was fighting for a good reason, and not for some means to satiate a hunger.

But it needed something more. And the burning at its

hip answered that need. With an innate sense of what it must do, the werewolf allowed the faery power to course through its system. It tightened in its muscles and expanded its chest. It made his growl deeper and more forceful. And with a glow of faery dust surrounding it, the mighty creature marched forth, leading its troops toward victory.

What seemed like an hour later, but was probably half that time, the black dust from slain collectors settled in a strange, sparkling mist about them. Indi took stock of their motley crew. Never, covered in ichor and with shirt torn and blade dragging the cobblestones beside his foot, stood with his head tilted back, eyes closed, lungs heaving.

Kristine wiped the ichor from her blade and toed the heavy base of the battle-ax. Her dress was torn, or possibly sometime during battle she'd turned the long gown into a mini. Her legs were streaked with black dust and glittering ichor and her cat ears were tilted to one side of her head. But her mascara was intact and so was her lipstick. Tired, and defeated, she still looked like a million euros.

Indi inspected her damage. Her wings hung heavily, and she sensed one of them was torn from when she'd dodged a collector but had swerved toward Kristine's sword. It hurt, yet she also sensed a strange tingling. Perhaps it was healing.

She'd kicked off her Louboutins. The dagged hem of her chiffon skirt was tattered and stained with black dust and ichor. She didn't want to know what a mess her makeup looked like. The long cut down her calf was from her sword, not a collector, so she didn't worry about having to face the jealous healer again. Her blood was pale pink and…it sparkled.

She touched the cut and rubbed what must be a mixture

of blood and ichor between her fingers. "This is me," she whispered. "And I'm ready for it."

To her side, huffing and taking things in as she did, stood a mighty werewolf. A tattered white dress shirt hung from one furred and muscled shoulder, while the black trousers barely clung and were still belted on. His body was shaped like a man, for the most part, covered in fur, and übermuscled. His chest was wide and heaving, and Indi had witnessed him howl more than a few times. It had been spectacular.

And...something had happened to Ry's werewolf amidst the calamity. In one moment, Indi had glanced over her shoulder to spy the wolf surrounded by a cloud of bright dust, its arms outstretched as it howled the deepest and wildest call to the night. His faery had joined the fight. She knew it as she now innately knew she had been born faery.

Ry glanced at her with his wolf's head, the long maw revealing rows of vicious yet white teeth. His wolf's eyes were gold and his ears twitched, perhaps to disperse the collector dust that had covered all of them, like soot. The faery sigil at his hip glowed brightly, a beacon to her confused and wanting heart.

Indi dropped the épée with a clank, wandered the few steps over to Ry, and reached out. She wouldn't touch him. And much as she wasn't afraid to touch him, she didn't know how he would react. She knew he was thinking with both a man and an animal mind right now. He was instinctual and reactive, also predatory.

However, as she stood there, the werewolf did something remarkable. He turned and held the sword horizontally before him, then bowed to his knee and laid it down before Indi's feet. Then he nudged her leg with the crown of his furred head, as if marking his territory. The wolf rose and stopped in a partial crouch when its eyes were level with hers.

"My werewolf prince who has, this night, owned his faery heart," she whispered. She glanced her fingertips over the glowing sigil on his hip. "I love you."

The werewolf stood tall and proud and thrust back its head as he let out a long and wild howl. Then Ry took off on a lope down the cobblestoned street.

Never walked up behind Indi. "He needs to run it off. The werewolf. He should be safe in FaeryTown."

"He let out his faery tonight," she said.

"I think so. I've never seen Ry so strong and focused before. And he does sparkle like never before. Good for him. How are you? Your leg is bleeding."

"That was me." She tugged aside the torn chiffon to reveal her bleeding leg. "Trying to get a handle on fighting in a freakin' dress. I'm good." She picked up the sword that Ry had said was enchanted to slay the sidhe. It hummed in her grip. And it didn't feel comfortable to hold it. "How about you?"

"I'll survive. There's some wicked energy coming off that thing. You'd better leave it for Ry to claim."

"I was going to take it back to the car, but yes, I feel the warning vibrations. It knows I'm faery."

"And that blade does not like faeries. Leave it here on the street. Seriously, Indi, that thing is screaming for Ry."

She quickly placed the sword back on the cobblestones. It gleamed and a single discordant note shivered in the air.

"Kristine!" Never wandered over to Kristine and bumped fists with her.

"It's not over." Indi felt compelled to say the words as she looked over the carnage. Because it didn't feel over.

They had defeated the hordes Malrick had sent this night. Dozens upon dozens, surely. Yet apparently the Unseelie king was sending them all over the world. Somewhere, in some part of the world, one or many of those vicious black creatures had gotten their hands on a human baby and whisked it away to Faery to be raised and bred as a slave to the Unseelie.

Was there no way to stop this horrible crime against the innocent?

"How can we stop this?" she whispered.

"It ends tonight," Ry called as he strode toward them. He'd shifted back to man form. His trousers hung at his waist and were shredded, but a few larger shreds covered the most important part. Otherwise, he was naked and gleamed with sweat and faery dust. His sigil no longer glowed.

Slowly, the curious inhabitants of FaeryTown, who had watched from behind windows, now slipped out onto the street, some flying cautiously at a distance, others still clinging to the shadows.

Ry picked up the sword that he'd laid on the street and thrust it above his head. "Malrick!"

Indi stepped over to stand beside Never and Kristine while Ry stood in the middle of the street, waiting. He filled the air with his presence, his utter masculine power and strength. Indi wanted to rush over and jump into his arms and kiss him. The elation of having participated in a battle—and survived—pulsed in her veins. But now was no time to interfere.

And in a glimmer of blinding silver and faery dust, Malrick stood before Ry. The faery king was dressed in silver finery that gleamed as if sewn with silver threading. His long black hair glinted and his eyes were wide and eerie. As the king surveyed his fallen minions, his expression took on a hint of mirth. And when he unfurled his wings, the crowd standing about gasped and stepped back into the shadows.

"My werewolf son calls?" Malrick asked casually. As if he had not a clue why the bother.

"Enough, Malrick." Ry spread his arms to encompass the piles of extinguished collectors that dirtied the cobblestones about them. "You've had your fun and games. I ask that you cease this insanity. You've taken more than enough human children for your own, and without reciprocation of a single changeling. You've changed the rules. I'm going to guess that won't go over well with those higher than you in Faery."

Malrick smirked. "Higher than me? You jest."

"I don't know much about Faery, but I'm guessing the Seelie king might have an interest in your untoward ways. But most important?"

Malrick crossed his arms and lifted his chin in defiance.

Ry glanced over his shoulder to Indi before turning back to his father. "You made a bargain with Indigo DuCharme. A bargain which you did not uphold."

"I did not specify I would cease sending collectors in areas beyond Paris," Malrick stated flatly. "And besides, she's also broken her half of the bargain. She was to stay away from you."

Ry approached his father with a growl. Any lingering observers scuffled behind doors. Ry lifted his hand to grip Malrick about the throat but at the last moment clenched his fingers and swung his arm out, away from the pompous faery king. "This ends right now. And if you cannot agree to that, I will come to Faery."

"You will? But that is all I want!"

Ry stepped to his father until he was but inches from his face. "I will come to Faery and sit the throne. Your throne. You won't need it. Because I will end you."

Malrick tilted his head with a sinister smirk. "You dare to threaten your own father?"

"That I do. And I don't care if traveling to Faery traps me there forever. It will give me great satisfaction to rip out your throat for all the pain you have caused others not even of your realm." Now he did grip Malrick's throat. "Take this as a warning and step back and cease. You've obtained great spoils for your wicked collection of human breeders."

He shoved Malrick away but did not relent his commanding pose.

"You'll not come after such spoils?" Malrick asked.

"Much as I would love to rescue all the human babies your minions have stolen, I don't see how it is possible. Not on my own. Nor with my resources."

Malrick lifted his chin, appearing to give it some thought. His glance swerved to Indi and she felt his disgust crawl over her limbs. But she didn't shiver this time. She had stood strong beside Ry and defeated Malrick's collectors. There was nothing she couldn't handle now.

"I suspect that changeling was not bred for such a fate," Malrick said quickly to Ry. "She may not be as pitiful as I first guessed. I suppose there are worse *things* for my son to associate with. And besides, it's probably a fling. You and your human ways tend to jump from affair to affair."

"Just like you?" Ry interjected. "You've no authority to pass judgment on relationships, Malrick. How many half brothers and sisters do I actually have?"

Malrick shrugged and flicked his beringed fingers before him as if shooing a bug. "Thousands?" He smiled, his silver eyes beaming. "I am quite a prolific lover."

"A fact best kept to yourself."

"The interesting fact is…" Malrick's gaze swerved to inspect the sigil at his son's hip. "You've welcomed your faery this night. I can feel my blood coursing through your veins now. You will become such a powerful ruler in due time."

"I don't wish to rule anyone. Ever. But the faery in me... I will no longer shun it."

Ry stretched out his hand in offering to his father. "Will you give me what I ask? In return I...well, I would like to visit you on occasion in Faery."

"You...would?" Malrick studied his son's hand while his face went through a remarkable series of emotions. And for a moment Indi thought his irises changed to violet. "You would come to visit me?"

"If I can be assured it would merely be a visit and that my return would be of my free will."

"Of course," Malrick agreed. He clamped his hand into his son's. "We have a bargain. That I will uphold. I swear it to you. I shall cease to send out collectors. Everywhere. You are right. We've collected quite a menagerie of bleating infants from across the world. That should give us a good start on repopulation. Will you visit soon?"

Ry squeezed his father's hand and then dropped it. "Maybe."

"Before your mortal winter?"

"Don't press your luck. But...it's possible."

Malrick nodded effusively and then it appeared to Indi as if his eyes watered. The man truly did love his son. She suspected it was deeper than surface and the need for someone to take the throne after he died. Despite being king, he must be very lonely. Perhaps he craved a connection to the vast and sordid family he had created.

Indi wondered about her faery family. Had they really had her only to then give her away? And then she dismissed the idea of learning about them. For now. She'd been raised by two amazing parents and would never consider anyone else family.

Unless his name was Ryland James.

Malrick looked over Ry's shoulder to Indi and he bowed his head to her. "Forgive me, Indigo Paisley DuCharme. I know you do not require it, but I grant you my blessing. And should you ever wish to learn about your sidhe family, you may come along when my werewolf prince son visits me."

She nodded but didn't know what to say. It wasn't necessary.

With that, Malrick stepped back and unfurled his wings. In a glint, the faery took to flight and passed through the fabric between worlds.

Indi rushed up to Ry and hugged him from behind. He reached back and slid a hand over her arm. He filled her arms with strong, hot muscle and smelled like those nasty collectors and sweat and wild and salt and air. And she never wanted to let him go.

"Well, that was better than a whole season of *Game of Thrones*!" Kristine announced. "And I'm bushed. I need to go home and burn this dress and soak these calloused fingers, sweeties. My manicurist is going to complain."

"I'll drive you home," Ry offered. He turned and Indi did not let him go, continuing to wrap her arms about his bare torso. "Just keep clinging, Princess. I might need the protection should what's left of my pants fall off."

"Oh, we want to see that," Kristine announced as she clicked by them in her heels and tossed her sword up against her shoulder.

Ry released Indi and shook hands with Never. "Thanks, brother."

"No problem. Are you serious about visiting Malrick?"

"Yes. I mean, I'm not overexcited, but...maybe the

guy deserves my unbiased and open mind for once. You know?"

"He's an asshole, but his place is a nice bit of real estate. And you are the prince."

"I'm not a prince. I'm just Ryland James. You need a ride anywhere?"

"Nope. I'm good. I've got a friend down the block where I can stop in to clean up and..." He winked and then bent to take Indi's hand and kissed it. "You and my brother make a great team. And you are handy with a sword. Watch your back," he called to Ry as he wandered off.

Ry collected the enchanted sword along with the épée Indi had been using.

And Indi jumped into Ry's arms, wrapping her legs about his hips and kissed him. "I wouldn't have you any other place," he said to her. "Wrapped tight about me with your lips on mine. Never is right. We're good together."

"We are."

He walked down the street to the rental car, where Kristine was sorting through the inventory in the trunk. Half an hour later they dropped her off and headed to Ry's place. They raced to the shower and shared a long hot soak.

Indi slicked her hands down Ry's wet abs and kissed his chest. "You don't need to shift to werewolf any more tonight?"

"I'm good. But there's tomorrow night. The nights before and after the full moon I'll have the desire to shift. I'm going to head out to the cabin."

"Kristine tells me your—" she made air quotes "—*cabin* is more like a castle."

Ry shrugged. "You want to come along and decide for yourself?"

"You know I do."

Chapter 28

Ry stood at the top of the castle tower, watching, as three stories below Indi practiced flying with her red and violet wings. She was a marvel. Every so often she looked up and waved to him. She couldn't get much higher than about three feet off the ground. He suspected her wings still had a bit of growth to go before they were complete. They were beautiful, soft and shimmery. Like her.

He swiped his fingers over some faery dust that he noticed on his wrist. Must be left over from sex this morning. His werewolf had no need to come out last night with Indi in his arms to sate that craving. And...he lifted his shirt to see the sigil that had only ever been a pale marking now did not glow, but it definitely had darkened.

He'd surrendered to his faery while in the midst of battle, and the burst of strength had been immense. From now on he would not deny that half of him, and looked forward to exploring exactly what this welcome part of him could offer.

Before coming outside, he'd called Kristine to tell her he intended to take a few days off, maybe the whole week. She had squealed and said all would be well at the office.

He knew that it would be.

When he turned to go down the spiraling stairs of the ancient castle, he was shocked to find Malrick sitting in one of the spaces of the stone crenellations, leg up and elbow resting casually on his knee.

"Do you have to do that?" Ry said sharply.

Malrick shrugged. "Do you wish to bell me like a cat?"

"Just because I agreed to the occasional visit doesn't mean we've suddenly become best friends or—"

"Or family? I understand. Believe me, I am honored at the concessions you've made and look forward to welcoming you to my home. Even if for a visit. But I did a little asking around after last night's adventure, and thought it would behoove me to fill you in with a few details on your not-so-graceful changeling below."

"She's still learning."

"She is terrible. Her wings are not ready to support her heavy mortal realm bones. I suspect she's changing both inside and out, and it'll be a while before she becomes completely sidhe."

"Is that what you came to tell me?" Ry shrugged. "Fine. I'll let her know to be patient."

"I was wrong about her being born a changeling. Indeed, she was taken from her crib to this realm and used as a changeling. But…"

Ry raised an eyebrow.

"She was never bred to be a changeling. She is…" Malrick sighed. "A princess."

"What?"

"I suspected something about her after noticing the distinct color of her wings, and so I asked around, sent out some assistants. She is Unseelie. And her mother is Touramire, queen of the Crystal Lands."

"I don't understand. Her mother is a faery queen? Why would she send away her daughter?"

"She did not." Malrick swung his legs around and jumped to stand before Ry, resting the heel of his palm against the tower wall. Simple black togs today made him slightly less imposing. "Seems Touramire had a vicious argument going on with a troll, who, in order to teach her a lesson, stole her child and sold it as a changeling to Riske. You do know Riske. I believe he takes a toll on all changelings brought to this realm. He used to buy and sell them in the days when the changeling practice was more common."

Ry tightened his jaw. The bastard had lied to him. In a manner. He had mentioned the toll part. And if he was doing brisk business, Indi might have been just another bleating infant to him.

"So Indi was born a faery princess?" Ry couldn't help a broad smile.

"Indeed. Tell her if you wish. But I'm sure she's fixed her life and memories to her human family. How will learning her truth change anything?"

"It's none of your concern."

"It is if my son should someday marry the missing Crystal Lands' princess. Until this winter, my son."

With that, Malrick winked, then jumped up to the crenellated wall and took a step backward. Ry could hear his wings whoosh out and he soared low, right over Indi's head, before disappearing through a tear in the fabric between realms.

"Hey!" Indi pointed to the sight.

Ry waved to her and called that he'd be right down.

"Was that Malrick?" Indi asked when Ry walked out into the grassy courtyard behind the castle. Yes, the man lived in a castle. And he was looking extra sexy today. No shirt, just some loose jeans hugging his hips, and all that glossy long hair blowing in the breeze.

"It was. You're looking good with the flying skills."

She shrugged, but dropped her wings so the tips treaded the lush emerald grass behind her. "I can't get very high. I don't know what's up with that."

"Malrick suggested you're still changing. Faery bones are light. I think they're like honeycomb. Your bones, which developed in this realm, are slowly changing back into what they were. Once that happens you'll be able to fly so high."

"And then will I be able to get small?"

"Maybe? I'm not sure, but I wouldn't doubt it. You want to go for a swim in the falls later?"

"There's a falls around here?"

"About a mile through the forest there's a clearing and a crystal-clear falls. My wolf always heads there when I'm out here."

"I could fly there?"

"We'll race."

She jumped into his arms, wrapped her legs about his hips and kissed him. "Why was Malrick here? Are you two buds now?"

"I don't think that'll ever happen. He, uh…" Ry set her down and clasped her hand. "Had some information for me that he thought I should know. And I think you have a right to know it."

"What do you mean?"

"Come inside. I'm hungry. We'll dive into the cheese and charcuterie we brought along and I'll tell you everything."

An hour later, they lazed before a fire crackling in the hearth. Ry had eaten all the meat and grapes, and Indi wished they'd picked up more wine. The man owned a castle, and yet he had no wine cellar? She would see to changing that.

And he had told her everything.

"I'm really a faery princess?" Indi rolled to her back. Her wings she furled up and out of the way, and she dragged her bare foot along Ry's bare chest.

He clasped her ankle and kissed each of her toes. "That you are, Princess Pussycat. What do you think about that?"

"I feel badly for my faery mother. But I'm not sure if I do want to meet her. I will always feel like Claire and Gerard are my real parents."

"They are. That doesn't have to change."

"It would be interesting to visit Faery and meet my mother. Queen of the Crystal Lands? How cool does that sound? Do you think she'd remember me?"

"I'm sure she would."

"A troll stole me. That's crazy. Thank you for telling me that. Malrick thought you'd keep it to yourself?"

Ry shrugged. "Malrick's an ass."

"But he is your father."

"Not my real father. Tomas LeDoux was the only man I've ever known as my real father."

She leaned in and kissed him. "Maybe someday the two of you can reunite."

"That would mean a lot to me. But I won't hold out hope."

"You should always have hope. But I'm thinking you and Malrick might hit it off."

"Don't get crazy."

"Okay, how about mutual respect?"

"I'll settle for mild interest."

"It's a good start." She crawled on top of him and he flipped to his back. "So you're a prince and I'm a princess. Kind of cool, huh?"

"You've certainly mastered the title. You in your faery finery and tiaras."

She touched the wolf's paw at her neck. "I'd trade it all for a simple life in this realm with my werewolf lover."

"I love you, Indi. I'm glad you stumbled drunkenly into my life."

"Never thought I'd be thankful for a drunk, but me, too. Now I want to get drunk on you. It would be a shame to let this fire and this warm wool blanket go to waste."

Ry shoved the food tray aside and pulled her down to kiss. He slipped her dress strap from her shoulder and kissed her there. "Here's to a normal life filled with not-so-normal experiences."

She tapped the sigil on his hip. "Like faery dust and wolf howls?"

"Just like that."

* * * * *

Thank you for reading
THE BILLIONAIRE WEREWOLF'S PRINCESS.
If you enjoyed this story, please know the majority of my paranormal romances are set in my world of Beautiful Creatures. You can find a list of my backlist titles at my website: www.MicheleHauf.com.

If you are interested in reading more about Never, he shows up in THE VAMPIRE HUNTER and THE WITCH'S QUEST.

Also, Malrick pops up in a few stories for a scene or two: MOONSPUN, MALAKIA, ENCHANTED BY THE WOLF and THE WITCH'S QUEST.

Follow me on social media at:
Facebook.com/MicheleHaufAuthor
Twitter.com/MicheleHauf
Instagram.com/MicheleHauf
Pinterest.com/toastfaery
Haufsbeautifulcreatures.tumblr.com